Riding West

To win the woman of his dreams, Parker takes matters into his own hands. And finds out the West is wilder than he ever imagined!

Just take her.

The advice seems radical, but Parker West is desperate. Try as he might, he cannot convince Celia Evans to marry him in the usual way, even after five years of courtship. Kidnapping her is drastic and rash, but he figures he has little left to lose.

Even though Celia is furious at being summarily tied up and carried off to the mountains, she finds she likes the sparks that fly when the normally cool Parker shows his more assertive side. At his secluded cabin, she finds out exactly what it means to be a woman, and that what she fought against all along is true: Under his normally reserved exterior, Parker is the lover of her dreams.

And when riled, he can give a girl a very wild, intensely pleasurable ride.

But there's a range war simmering, and the threat on the horizon takes the form of one very vindictive, crooked rancher. He wants Celia all to himself—and will stop at nothing to get her...

Warning, this title contains the following: explicit sex, graphic language, mild violence.

Lawless

An unlikely hero—until Fate steps in.

Cal Riker isn't just a wanted man. His skill with a gun makes his name synonymous with notoriety. Deserved or not, a deadly reputation can sometimes come in handy for things like saving a beautiful woman from a ruthless outlaw gang. They're all afraid of him—all except his enticing captive.

Laurel Daniels is furious at being abducted, even more so at the indignity of being purchased with ill-gotten money. Then she's terrified when she realizes the cool, silver-eyed stranger who bought her is none other than an infamous, legendary killer.

Is he truly as lawless as they say? As she discovers an interesting side to this renegade cowboy, Laurel starts to wonder...

Warning: Strong sexual content, lawless bad boys, language, some violence.

Look for these titles by *Emma Wildes*

Now Available:

Face of the Maiden

Untamed

Emma Wildes

A Samhain Publishing, Ltd. publication.

Samhain Publishing, Ltd.
577 Mulberry Street, Suite 1520
Macon, GA 31201
www.samhainpublishing.com

Untamed
Print ISBN: 978-1-60504-120-9
Riding West Copyright © 2008 by Emma Wildes
Lawless Copyright © 2008 by Emma Wildes

Editing by Jennifer Miller
Cover by Anne Cain

Riding West, 1-59998-846-1
First Samhain Publishing, Ltd. electronic publication: December 2007
Lawless, 1-59998-955-7
First Samhain Publishing, Ltd. electronic publication: April 2008
First Samhain Publishing, Ltd. print publication: April 2009

Contents

Riding West

Dedication

For my good friend, Olinda. May your own Parker West stroll through your door sometime soon.

Chapter One

Colorado, 1874

The sun cast lazy afternoon shadows, the heat rose from the earth like a palpable presence and a slight breeze carried the tang of sage and mesquite. The leaves in the cottonwoods rustled faintly in a hushed and subtle whisper of sound. Stepping out onto the wide front porch, Celia Evans shaded her eyes with one hand and saw the small plume of rising dust with a touch of curiosity.

The rider coming up the long lane toward the ranch had his horse at a full gallop, she saw that much, and suddenly she wished her father and brothers hadn't just left for town to purchase supplies. The ranch hands too, she realized with a small tremor of trepidation, were all out repairing fences or searching for missing cattle.

"Who is it?" Rose, her older sister, came outside to join her, gazing at the approaching horseman with interest. "He's moving right along."

"I can't tell from here." As she spoke, Celia registered the long-legged, signature gait of the black horse before she could recognize its rider. "I think it might be Parker. There can't be two horses like that in Colorado. Surely that's Diablo—look at him move."

Next to her, pretty in a simple gingham gown suitable for the hour and heat, Rose murmured, "He's coming fast, I'll grant that. Parker usually has a good reason for everything he does, so something must be going on."

"That's the truth," Celia said tartly. "He's practical to a fault."

"You're a little hard on him, aren't you? I realize he didn't quite propose to you in the romantic way a girl expects, but you lead that poor man a merry ride." Rose shook her head, her blond hair shining in the afternoon sun. "He's smart, good-looking and steady. He comes from a nice family that's well off, and he's been head over heels in love with you for years. When he finally gets up the nerve to ask you to marry him, you up and turn him down. I don't understand what you want."

Maybe a little excitement, Celia thought cynically. Parker West was the most practical, level-headed young man she'd ever met. His idea of courtship was damned boring because he was so infernally polite. In fact, all he'd ever done was steal one or two chaste kisses. It almost made matters worse that Rose was right. He was one of the best-looking men she had ever seen and Celia found him very attractive...physically, that is. She'd known him most of her life since they were neighbors and friends, but he seemed way too content with that platonic arrangement.

Or if he wasn't, he certainly kept that information to himself.

In short, he was just a little too *nice.*

The horse thundered forward and she could now see it was indeed Parker, his easy seat in the saddle recognizable. He was a fine horseman, whatever his other faults.

"What I'd like is a little sentiment, Rose." Celia lifted a brow in open derision. "When a man asks a woman to marry him, he shouldn't first list the logical reasons why it would be a suitable match. For heaven's sake, he shouldn't even say the word *logical* at all."

Rose gave a small hiccup of a laugh. "It was probably a poor choice, I agree. Parker should have known better since you aren't exactly strangers, but I expect he was nervous."

"He didn't seem nervous."

"Does he ever? He's been perfecting keeping his feelings under control around you for the past five years."

Was that true? Celia hadn't seen him since she'd turned him down nearly a week ago. He hadn't shown it, but she sensed her refusal had hurt him. She had the cowardly urge to go hide inside until he left, but she was also curious as to why he'd ride toward the house at such a breakneck pace.

He didn't slacken his speed until he thundered into the yard, pulling the horse up just a few feet from the porch where they stood. Diablo jerked restively at his reins as his rider slid off in one lithe movement. Parker controlled the stallion with a quick word and tightened grip, not even bothering to look at the animal.

Tall, wearing worn jeans that hugged his long legs, dusty boots, and a light blue shirt that spanned his wide shoulders, he doffed his hat, revealing slightly tousled dark wavy hair. His features were finely modeled and classically handsome; high cheekbones, dark arched brows, a straight nose and sensual mouth. "Good afternoon, Rose."

Celia saw her sister dimple in a smile. "Hello, Parker. I hope nothing is wrong. You certainly were coming right along."

"Nothing is wrong," he said coolly. "I'm just leaving on a little trip and anxious to get going."

"You sure must be." Rose obviously noticed he hadn't bothered to greet Celia, and the tone of her voice showed a shade of discomfort.

"I am." His eyes were a pale blue, like the sky at dawn, and when that light, intense gaze transferred to her, Celia felt a small quiver in her stomach. To her amazement, he said in the same unemotional tone, "You're going with me, sweetheart."

Rooted to the spot, all she could do was stare. Normally he was easygoing, with a quick, charming smile that she didn't see nearly often enough, and a reserved air. At this moment, however, as he took a long stride toward the steps to the porch, he looked downright...dangerous. His gaze glittered as it locked with hers and his mouth was a tight line.

Celia said incredulously, "I'm what?"

"Going with me." He looped his horse's reins around the post.

She took an involuntary step backwards as he bounded up the short stairs. "Are you out of your head?"

"Absolutely."

Strong hands caught her shoulders and spun her around. She heard Rose gasp and in moments, to her utter shock, her hands were bound behind her back. He did it so neatly and

15

deftly, she didn't even have time to struggle. Being a working cowboy, he certainly knew how to tie a good knot and do it fast, and must have carried the rope in his pocket. He turned her back to face him and bent, heaving her effortlessly over one hard shoulder like a sack of grain, his arm coming around the back of her knees as he turned to walk back down the steps to his horse.

"Tell your parents we'll be back when we work things all out, Rose. I'll keep her safe, they know that." His tone was even, and his arm tightened as Celia began to squirm in real protest, her undignified position uncomfortable with her bottom in the air and his shoulder in her diaphragm.

"Parker," she gasped as she spoke, "let me go. What on earth are you doing?"

"Stop struggling," he said curtly. "I promise you Diablo won't like it and will toss you on your sweet backside in the dirt."

In seconds she was perched in the saddle sideways, her bound hands making her seat precarious. Her outraged glare went from the man who put his booted foot in the stirrup and swung up behind her, to her sister watching from the porch with a look on her face that seemed a mixture of astonishment and laughter.

"You can't do this," Celia said between her teeth as his arms came securely around her to take the reins.

"The hell I can't, Miss Evans," he told her and touched the stallion with a heel so they jumped forward. "I believe I just did."

He'd expected her to be spitting mad, and he certainly wasn't disappointed.

After about twenty minutes of her furious protests, Parker finally decided to gag his beautiful prisoner, and if looks could kill, he would be stone cold in a grave somewhere.

Jesus, he certainly hoped he knew what he was doing.

Sitting in front of him, her back stiff with outrage, Celia's gorgeous dark blue eyes flashed pure fire. He'd seen her mad before—considering her somewhat tempestuous disposition, that wasn't new—but he was not sure she'd ever been *this* mad.

Damn, though, it might all be worth it—even if she ended up hating his guts—for the sensation of holding her in his arms. Her soft bottom bounced against his thighs as he urged Diablo into an easy canter, and he could smell the sweet scent from her hair. Her delicate features were flushed with anger, the smooth skin of her cheeks bright red, a bandana he'd brought for that purpose tied across her tempting mouth. She wore a light blue dress with tiny flowers patterned on the cotton material, and he could feel the voluptuous curves of her body through the thin cloth. Her hair was a lustrous gold touched with platinum glints in the light of the warm sun. It was tied back simply at her nape, and he couldn't wait to slip that piece of ribbon free and watch it spill over the sheets of his bed.

If his wild plan worked, in a few hours he'd find out if she was as spirited in bed as she was in every other way. His cock stiffened from his wayward thoughts and the slight sway of her breasts against his arm. Trying to ignore it before he got a full-blown erection with a long ride still ahead of them, he scanned the horizon periodically from habit.

In less than two hours, rangeland gave way to small hills. Ridges of timber rose in front of them, dwarfed by the majestic peaks in the background. Aspens fluttered leaves in the dying afternoon breeze as they began to climb in elevation, and it was considerably cooler under the shadows of pine and spruce. Parker knew the way well and judged they'd get there just before dark, which was exactly what he'd expected.

So far, so good.

The gag, once she'd tired of making muffled protests, seemed to have the effect of calming Celia a little and he felt slightly guilty about it in the first place. After they splashed through a small stream and he slid off to let Diablo have a short rest and a cool drink, he lifted her from the saddle. "If you promise to not screech at me like an angry bluejay, I'll take this off."

There was a moment of hesitation, her blue eyes defiant, but Celia finally nodded. He loosened the bandana and slipped it back into his pocket.

"You can untie my hands as well," she said in a voice that was only slightly uneven. "It's pretty uncomfortable, Parker."

Tying her hands had been both to make a point and to make sure she didn't scratch his eyes out or try to pull his gun and shoot him during the actual abduction. Celia was more than capable of doing both. Parker lifted a brow sardonically. "I value life and limb. I don't think so. We're getting close to our destination. I'll free you then."

The expression on her lovely face was a mixture of surprise and fury. He'd never denied her anything—few men would. "You don't care my arms are half-numb?"

"Nope." It was a lie, for his first inclination was to untie her at once and abjectly apologize, but being a perfect gentleman around the very tempting, very spoiled Miss Evans hadn't ever gotten him anywhere. She was almost twenty, and he'd been in love with her for years. Hell, he'd known her most of his life, he'd probably fallen for her when he was about five and he saw her right after she was born.

Lush lashes lowered slightly over the dark blue of her midnight eyes. She asked tightly, "What's gotten into you?"

Ignoring the question, he pointed at the bubbling stream. "Are you thirsty? I'll get you some water."

"No thanks," she replied in a scathing, bitter tone.

"Suit yourself." He shrugged and got out a flask from his pocket, uncorking it and taking a theatrical swig.

"You're drinking?" Celia's delicate features registered slight shock.

"Sure am." He stuffed the bottle back in his pocket and gave her a deliberately wicked grin. It wasn't that he didn't ever drink whiskey—he did in moderation—but never in front of her. With her father owning a big ranch, she saw plenty of drunken cowboys, and he'd never wanted her to think of him in that way.

"Maybe you'd better tell me just where we're going and what the purpose of this is. If you want to talk to me, we could do that at home. You don't have to drag me off like some barbarian."

"Talk? It doesn't work. I tried it. You were pretty lukewarm over talking about us. I have a better idea." Parker lifted a brow and deliberately ran his gaze over her slender form in a suggestive inspection, lingering on the full curve of her breasts.

"I think you can guess what I have in mind, Celia."

Her lips parted and a small flush crept up her neck and into her face. She half-whispered in outraged protest, "Parker."

Catching her by the waist, he lifted her back on to the horse and swung up behind her. "Don't worry, sweetheart, we'll talk afterwards if that's what you want."

The man had gone insane.

That's the only thing that could account for the transformation. Parker West was not a whiskey-drinking, high-handed wild cowboy. She'd met plenty of those in her life. He was a hard-working, sober young man who helped run a very prosperous cattle business, respected his parents, and was kind to children and little old ladies. Around Tijeras and the entire area, he was considered, in short, a paragon. A saint. A gentleman.

Thank goodness Rose had seen him grab her, tie her hands and ride off with her. Otherwise no one would believe it. Celia was pretty sure she still couldn't believe it herself.

The cabin stood in a small clearing, the location away from any semblance to a path. The small structure wasn't recently built by any means but seemed well kept even in the gloom of descending dusk, and there was a neat stack of firewood by the front door. The roof looked solid and next to it there was a small corral and a lean-to big enough for one horse. When they rode up, Parker dismounted and reached for her, lifting her in his arms instead of setting her on her feet. Cradled against his broad chest, Celia felt a small thrill in the pit of her stomach she wasn't sure was alarmed panic or furtive excitement. He was strong—she'd seen him work before and knew it, but he carried her as if she weighed nothing at all. Whatever his intentions might be, she needed to face the fact she was at a pretty severe disadvantage. Normally, Parker would do anything to please her, but in his current unprecedented mood, she just wasn't sure if he hadn't meant exactly what he'd insinuated earlier.

Her face heated as she remembered how he'd looked at her. There had been a dark sensual promise in his eyes she'd never seen before.

Shouldering his way through the door, he effortlessly carried her inside. The interior was dark, but she got an impression of simplicity in the plain small table with two chairs, stone fireplace and of course the bed that took up one corner of the room. That was where he put her, setting her down and saying curtly, "Stay put. After I see to Diablo, I'll come back and untie you." He pointed a finger at where she sat. "If you aren't right there, your hands stay tied, got it, Miss Evans?"

"I've got it," she said sarcastically, giving him a level stare. "And for God's sake, stop calling me Miss Evans. We've only known each other for about twenty years and you've never called me that before."

There was a flicker of something in his light eyes. One ebony brow edged up. "I can do whatever I want," he said pleasantly enough. "You might just keep it in mind."

Celia watched him stalk off in his loose-limbed graceful stride, not certain if she wanted to laugh or scream in outrage. However, though she fibbed earlier about her arms being numb, they had begun to ache in earnest now. Both curious and apprehensive to see what happened next, she sat in uncharacteristic meekness on the edge of the bed and waited.

The slow, melodic jingle of a spur signaled his return in what seemed like forever, but was probably only a few minutes. Coming inside, he carried a load of firewood, which he took to the hearth and deposited. It had been hot down in the valley, but once the sun went down, the air began to cool rapidly. Deftly, he stacked the logs and used a bit of tinder to ignite a small flame, fanning the kindling. Celia watched the way the flickering light played over the planes and hollows of his handsome face and felt the same betraying thrill twist inside her.

"I thought you were going to untie me."

He glanced up. "In a minute. Are you hungry?"

"No," she said truthfully. The odd sensation in the pit of her stomach was definitely not hunger.

"Good," he responded. He stood and came toward her, tall and seeming to fill the small space. When he was next to the bed, he bent and slipped a knife from his boot and with one quick movement, cut the bonds around her wrists.

"It's about time," she muttered irritably, rubbing her wrists. "For future reference, *Mr. West*, having a man tie me up doesn't particularly endear him to me."

"It's kind of hard to figure out just what does endear a man to you, so I guess I won't worry about it." The corner of his mouth quirked and he moved to drop into one of the chairs at the table, facing her. As she watched, he pulled out the flask again and took a drink, stretching out his long legs. "Now then, since your hands are free, you can put them to good use. Take your clothes off."

She stared, unable to believe he'd actually just issued that instruction. Frostily, she said, "I beg your pardon?"

"Take off your clothes." Sprawled in the chair, his booted feet crossed at the ankle, he gave her a lazy smile. He had taken off his hat, and his glossy dark hair was disheveled attractively, unfairly long lashes veiling his blue eyes. "It's a pretty simple order as far as I can tell, sweetheart. And by the way, it *is* an order. In case you haven't noticed, I hold all the cards here."

"If you think I'm going to strip naked in front of you, Parker West, you're insane." Celia took a trembling breath. It was hard to tell just how serious he was, but the way his gaze glittered, she was afraid he was dead serious.

"You *are* going to strip naked one way or the other, and if I'm insane, you've damn well made me that way. Now, are you going to do it yourself, or shall I help?" The question was spoken very softly, barely audible above the growing crackle of the fire.

The threat in his voice was real, even if the situation felt as if it were part of some bizarre dream. Her pulse beat rapidly, but she wasn't sure if it was fear or something else entirely. "I don't want your help, don't worry." Her voice was embarrassingly unsteady. "Maybe you could tell me the purpose of your request."

He laughed and it was a genuine sound of mirth. "Jesus, Celia, you must be joking. Surely you can't be that naïve. But if you'd like, I'll spell it right out for you. I want you to take off all of your clothes. Then I am going to take off all of mine. Then the convenient bed you are sitting on is going to be put to good use."

"What if I'm not willing?" She simply couldn't believe her ears. Had Parker—staid, steady Parker West—actually just said that to her?

"That doesn't matter much to me right now." The answer was swift and flat. He held the flask and gazed at her with no hint of remorse in his azure eyes as he lifted it to his lips.

Good God, had she done this to him? Celia knew she'd teased and flirted with him unmercifully the past few years, ever since she realized the depth of his interest in her. Parker was not the kind of man to compromise a woman's reputation, so he'd let her tantalize and string him along with his usual good-natured equanimity. Her family had scolded her over it often enough, and she had ignored their warnings that some day he might just get darned sick and tired of it.

Apparently that was exactly what had happened.

This was all her fault. She had two options. If he was serious, and he sure looked it, she could resist and make a decent, nice man into a rapist *and* a kidnapper.

Or she could give herself freely. Actually, she'd always assumed one day she would marry Parker, and if he hadn't waited so long to ask and bungled his proposal so badly, she would have said yes. When she turned him down, it wasn't like she didn't expect him to ask again. She'd counted on it, once he'd thought it all over in his practical way and realized she needed a declaration of his feelings, not a stupid list of why they suited each other.

For most of her life, she'd been more than a little bit in love with him. However, she had taken him for granted, that was for sure.

Maybe right now, she could make amends. In fact, the idea was intriguing down deep if she admitted it, because she'd always wondered what it would be like when they finally did make love.

Celia stood and began to unbutton her gown. "All right, Parker, you win."

Chapter Two

The flask hung suspended in his fingers.

Parker watched, fascinated and incredulous, as the woman in front of him calmly let her dress slip off her creamy shoulders.

It worked!

He wasn't good at bluffing, or at least he didn't think he was, but this outrageous gamble had actually paid off. The very idea Celia believed he'd force himself on her was a little insulting, but then again, he'd done his best to convince her he would. When her mother had come to visit his folks a few days ago and taken him aside, he'd been a bit humiliated when she'd brought up his ill-fated marriage proposal. Mrs. Evans had diplomatically discussed a more straightforward approach with her independent and headstrong daughter. He'd listened, too, frustration, both emotional and sexual, making him open to any suggestion.

Even this drastic one.

If Celia ever discovered her own mother was the one who told him to just take her off somewhere and be a little more persuasive in a physical way, she would be livid.

On the other hand, he was grateful as hell.

In a few moments shoes, stockings and petticoats were also in a heap on the floor. A telltale flush of embarrassed pink in her smooth cheeks, Celia stood in her thin cotton shift and lifted her chin. Her long-lashed eyes, so lovely and blue, showed her usual challenge. "I thought you were going to undress."

His mouth had gone entirely dry and Parker swallowed, remembering his role as forceful abductor with difficulty. When he spoke, his voice sounded hoarse. "You aren't finished. Take it all off."

Her upper teeth sank into the softness of her lower lip, but she didn't look away as she pulled free the ribbon at her bodice. The material gaped open, exposing the tantalizing swell of high, full breasts. Celia eased the garment down her arms and over the curve of her slim hips until it pooled at her feet and she was completely naked.

All he could think was that in his entirely male fantasies about this particular moment—and he'd had plenty—he hadn't done her justice. Her skin was flawless ivory, her limbs long and supple, and her firm breasts had a lush ripeness in comparison to the slender dip of her waist and length of her legs. He couldn't help but stare, his heated gaze examining the soft rose of perfectly shaped nipples and then slipping lower, to the small dark gold triangle at the juncture of her thighs. "Oh my God," he said involuntarily.

Her blush intensified, turning her cheeks scarlet. "I'll take that as a compliment," she said tartly.

"So you should, sweetheart." With effort, he lifted his gaze back to her face and repeated, "So you should. You are more than beautiful, Celia."

"Thank you." Her slim throat rippled as she swallowed. "But quite frankly, Parker, I've never stood in front of anyone in my life without a stitch on and it isn't exactly fair you're still fully dressed."

He was rock hard already, his cock so stiff it felt like he was going to burst out of his jeans. Considering her innocence, she was about to get an eyeful, but he was more than happy to oblige. Her easy acquiescence was a little unexpected, for he'd thought she would be more resistant, but who was he to argue. He stood and swiftly unfastened the gun belt around his waist, setting it on the table before he went to work on his shirt. "Let your hair loose."

There was a brief flare of irritation in her gaze over the autocratic tone of his voice, but she complied. When she lifted her arms to untie the ribbon, her lush breasts rose and quivered slightly in provocative invitation.

He tossed his shirt on the floor and fairly jerked off his boots. Stifling a groan when he opened his jeans, he pulled them down his hips and stepped free. Celia made a small noise—a swift inhale of breath—and she stared at the rampant length of his erection, swollen and high against his stomach.

"My enthusiasm over being here with you is darned obvious, isn't it?" He moved toward her in a long, slow step, not wanting to scare her to death. "I'm pretty much this way every time I'm around you and it isn't the least bit comfortable, I promise you."

She looked startled, her gaze traveling from his stiff penis up to his face. "You are? Why didn't you tell me?"

That question was so illogical, he had to laugh. "What exactly was I supposed to say?"

"You never even *tried* to do more than kiss me once or twice." She actually sounded a little miffed over it.

"Of course not. A decent man isn't supposed to take advantage of a woman who isn't his wife."

Her hair was a curtain of shimmering gold down her back, the tumbled curls reflecting the firelight and framing the delicate features of her face. Dark blond brows rose but she didn't step away when he reached for her. "Then perhaps you'd better put your pants back on, Parker West, for in case you've forgotten, we're not married."

"We will be."

He pulled her close and cut off her undoubtedly caustic reply by lowering his head and capturing her mouth. The sensation of her nude body pressed against his was more intoxicating than anything he'd ever experienced, her lips warm and soft. She was right, he hadn't done more than attempt a few chaste embraces, mostly because he wanted her so damned bad he didn't trust himself to stop when he should. When he exerted gentle pressure and she complied and parted her lips, his tongue slipped between and he felt the jerk of her surprise as he began to explore her mouth.

He was both relieved and pleased she'd obviously never been kissed so intimately, for he certainly wasn't the only man dangling after the gorgeous Miss Evans by a long shot. She was generally considered the most beautiful girl for hundreds of miles in this section of Colorado, and her three brothers and formidable father kept a pretty close eye on any man who came

25

sniffing around. Luckily, Parker was good friends with the whole family, otherwise he could count on them wanting his blood for what he was doing right at this very minute. When he'd talked to Celia's father before his doomed proposal, Gerald Evans had welcomed the idea of him as a future son-in-law.

Her tongue tentatively touched his as she responded, and the palms of her hands slid over his bare chest upward, so she could clasp her arms around his neck and press against him tighter.

Parker was pretty sure at that moment he had died and gone to heaven.

He broke the kiss, the throbbing in his cock and the ache in his testicles making him wonder just how long he would actually last once he was inside her. He kissed the fragile line of her jaw, the small hollow beneath her ear, and whispered, "Let's get into bed."

Not waiting for a reply, he lifted Celia in his arms and laid her down on the soft, patterned blanket. He followed at once, covering her body so his erect cock rubbed her thigh, his mouth taking hers in a kiss that this time was neither gentle nor in the least chaste. He invaded and probed with his tongue, rubbing hers suggestively. Celia opened for him willingly, and the light sensation of her fingers exploring the contours of his shoulders and back made him dizzy with need. His hand cupped her breast as they kissed, and he felt her tremble slightly.

"So beautiful," he murmured against her lips. "Do you have any idea how you feel to me?" He stroked the abundant fullness of pliant flesh in his hand, his thumb slowly circling the nipple.

"No," she whispered. "Tell me how I feel."

"Like a dream come true."

"Oh..."

She gasped when he lifted his mouth from hers and moved lower, to first lick one taut nipple, and then suck it slowly into his mouth. He massaged her other breast as he suckled, testing the fullness and weight. Her reaction was immediate as she arched with a small wild cry.

Parker had always wondered if she would be as audacious in bed as she was in everything else.

The answer was yes, he had a feeling. He was a damned

lucky man.

"That feels so good." Her fingers sifted through his hair and she pressed closer. "I never imagined."

The rhythm of her breathing already suggested arousal, as did the restless way she moved beneath him. Some women had very sensitive breasts, and apparently she was one of them, he realized with an inner smile. He transferred to the other breast, lavishing attention on not just her nipples, but the valley between, playing with the mounded flesh, nuzzling the undersides until she panted and moaned.

Perfect. He'd imagined having her hot, wet and willing beneath him a thousand times.

He shifted lower, skimming his mouth down her ribcage, licking her navel in a teasing stroke of his tongue, and then kissing the dainty blond curls between her legs. "Spread open," he urged, his fingers insistently easing her thighs apart.

"What are you going to do?" Surprisingly, she didn't resist but let him push her legs apart.

Parker grinned and positioned himself. "Something you'll like a lot. Just relax and enjoy yourself, sweetheart."

"I don't think—"

Her protest was cut off sharply at the first glide of his tongue between the moist folds of her labia. Her clitoris was already slightly engorged in arousal and he began to lick gently and circle the small bud. His hands slid beneath her to cup her luscious bottom and hold her in place. Celia reacted almost violently to the touch of his mouth between her legs, her slender body jerking. "Parker!"

Then she moaned.

She tasted sweetly female and it gratified him to know he gave her pleasure. More than anything, he wanted to feel her first climax with his mouth on her wet, warm sex. He teased and tasted, parting the folds to expose the pink satin flesh, savoring every secret place. Within moments she moaned in open abandon and spread her legs wider, her pelvis lifting in supplication. He could feel the rise of her approaching orgasm and certainly hear it in her obvious and vocal enjoyment.

Her low scream echoed in the quiet of the cabin when she went over the edge and her body twisted and shuddered in release. Parker waited until she was still and lax before he moved up between her open legs and kissed her lightly.

"Since I could tell you liked that, I'll share with you a little secret, sweetheart. We're just getting started," he told her with a dark smile.

That thing was just too big, she knew it as she watched from beneath the veil of her lashes. Surely all men weren't so large? Parker positioned himself between her legs, and with his hand guided his swollen penis so the dark crest touched her female entrance. Celia was too sated to be truly afraid of what came next, though normally she imagined she would be. Her body felt light, floating. That Parker would put his mouth *there* was an astounding concept. That it would feel so absolutely wonderful was just as shocking.

"That's it," he whispered, the pressure of his penetration beginning to stretch her vaginal passage. "Don't tense up. I don't want this to hurt you."

She wasn't at all tense—she felt marvelous. Her breasts tingled and were oddly tight, and between her legs there was still a small pleasurable throbbing. Perhaps she should be more intimidated over the act she knew little about but was certainly going to happen. She just wasn't, because after all, this was Parker about to take her virginity. If anyone could be trusted to take care with her—his audacious kidnapping aside—he certainly was the one.

Celia rested her hands on his wide shoulders, relishing the feel of his muscled, male body. He was lean but hard, and seeing him naked and aroused had awakened feelings she didn't even know she possessed. His bare chest was solid and sculpted, and when it brushed the erect tips of her breasts, she felt a thrill of pleasure.

Shamelessly, she opened her legs wider, wanting him inside her with an inexplicable combination of instinct and desire. His cock felt as big as it looked, stretching her very wide, and his jaw clenched as he braced himself above her. Dark hair curled against the strong, tanned column of his neck.

"Are you all right?" The question was asked in a rough tone

that sounded nothing like his usual voice. "Jesus, you're so tight."

"I'm fine," she replied, but as she spoke, she felt a stinging pressure. "Wait, stop...it hurts."

To her dismay, he completely ignored her request and instead, with a low murmured apology, thrust forward in an act of complete and full invasion.

It wasn't horrible, but the discomfort took the pleasure out of the moment. Celia cried out, more in surprise than pain. Now fully imbedded inside her, Parker looked into her eyes, his light blue gaze tender. "There's only one way to do this, sweetheart, and it always hurts the first time for a woman. Here, kiss me, and we'll wait until it feels better before I do anything else. Deal?"

"Deal," she responded in a whisper, not certain what else he was going to do exactly, but the way he looked at her made her heart beat faster. Their intimate position, too, was exciting, with his cock completely filling her and his lean hips resting between her open thighs. Celia ran her fingers through the dark silk of his hair and her lips clung to his when he lowered his head and took her mouth.

They stayed that way for a long time, softly kissing, his arms braced to keep his weight balanced. Until this moment, Celia wasn't sure she'd ever realized just how much bigger he was, his long body dwarfing her smaller, lighter frame. The frank masculine desire she saw in his eyes was exciting, also, and before long she shifted restively, lifting her hips a fraction.

He seemed to understand the signal instantly.

His cock slid backwards in a long withdrawal. When he moved forward again, a sound, unbidden, came from deep in her throat. She wasn't sure what was happening, pleasure or pain or a bewildering mixture of both, but whatever it was, it held her entirely captive.

"That's it," Parker told her thickly, "let me know you like it. I sure as hell have never felt anything so good in my whole life."

It wasn't like she wanted to make such unladylike sounds, but it seemed impossible to stay quiet. As he began to thrust in and out of her body, Celia got lost in the rising sensation of sexual enjoyment, the discomfort pushed to the background.

Her head tilted back, and her hands grasped the solid strength of his upper arms. She gave a small, soft cry with each measured stroke.

He felt so big, his hard cock stretched her wide, and the sensation was incredible.

It was building again, she realized. That marvelous blissful pinnacle of release edged upward, spiraling through her body, making her moan louder and louder. He moved faster, as if he knew exactly the right pace, and she moved with him in accord, her hips lifting in carnal need.

His lashes drifted shut and he said through his teeth, "I know you're close, but I can't hold on. I'm coming, sweetheart."

At that moment, she shattered into a thousand pieces.

The pleasure was so intense, she could feel the fierce inner clench of her muscles as the first spasm came. The second wave came just as quickly and she cried out, holding on for dear life, her nails frantically digging in.

Parker went very still, deep, deep inside her. His powerful body shuddered time and again, and he groaned her name in a way that penetrated her haze of incredible enjoyable release. To her amazement, she could feel his cock pulse with the contractions of her passage, and the warm flood as he spilled his seed against her womb.

The sound of ragged breathing drifted with the low call of an owl outside the cabin. Parker stayed inside her, not moving, and when she finally opened her eyes, his finely modeled mouth was lifted slightly at the corner in a satisfied half smile. "That was a good start."

It certainly had been. Her heart still pounded. Celia reached up and touched the clean line of his jaw, sliding her fingers to lightly trace his lower lip. "A good start to what?"

"I'm not planning on us going home for a few days at least."

The feel of him still inside her and the husky promise in his voice made her stomach tighten. "Is that so?"

"We need some time to talk, and maybe we'll find time for other things, too." His lashes, so dark and long, lowered a fraction.

He was too damned handsome for his own good, Celia thought. She arched a brow. "What kind of other things?"

"It'll be my pleasure to show you." His smile slid into a wicked grin.

Chapter Three

Gerald Evans tossed his dusty gloves on the table and scowled. "He did *what?*"

His oldest daughter, Rose, looked unhappy at having to repeat the story. "Well, he actually tied her up and tossed her over his shoulder. Then he just rode off."

"This was yesterday?"

Blond and pretty in a light green gown, the spitting image of her mother twenty years ago, Rose reluctantly nodded.

"They've been gone the whole night?"

"Yes."

"I'll kill him."

"No, you won't." His wife handed him a cup of coffee and smiled.

The day had dawned with beautiful clear skies and the kitchen was bright and sunny, fragrant with the homey smell of baking bread. Outside, his three sons unloaded the wagon of supplies, and he could hear Joshua and Jared having a good-natured argument over where to store the new fencing wire. Gerald had stayed overnight in town because he'd met with his banker to arrange a draft for some new stock he'd planned on buying, and so he'd been darned happy to be home.

Until he'd found out his youngest daughter had been kidnapped from his own front porch.

Holding the steaming cup, he registered his wife's serene expression with suspicion. In her fifties, she was still a lovely woman with blond hair showing just a hint of gray, unlined skin and refined features. Lila looked back innocently, but they'd been married a long time and he knew her well. He asked curtly, "Give me one good reason I shouldn't beat that boy to a pulp. Any man who ties up a woman and carries her off overnight has some pretty obvious intentions."

Pulling out one of the pine chairs from around the huge table, Lila sat down and calmly reached for her own coffee. "Yes, I'd say he does."

"They aren't married yet. Parker had better have kept it in his pants." Normally he never would have said such a thing in front of his daughter, and he felt his cheeks flush. "Sorry, Rose."

She laughed and gave him a slightly mischievous look. "With three brothers and a bunkhouse full of ranch hands, I've heard worse around here, Pa, believe me."

Lila said reasonably, "He *wants* to marry her, Gerald, so quit blustering. You know how he feels about Celia, just about everyone around here knows how he feels. If this is how he thought he could convince her, who cares if they marry before or after." One dark blond brow rose just a fraction.

Dammit, she still had the ability to leave him speechless after more than thirty years of marriage. They hadn't exactly waited until their vows had been legal and binding to consummate their passion for each other, but the gentle reminder didn't make him feel a whole lot better. Joshua had been born eight months after their wedding.

"She's my child, and I want her to be happy. If she turned him down flat the first time, what makes you think things will be different now?"

His wife and daughter exchanged a look that made him feel like an idiot. Rose said, "She's every bit as in love with Parker as he is with her, Pa. I know she's a flirt sometimes, but that's the exact point. Celia never pays attention to anyone else unless Parker is around to see it. Otherwise, she pretty much ignores other men, she always has. It's been Parker all along. She's just never let him see it."

The last thing he wanted to do was defend the man who'd essentially abducted his daughter against her will, but Gerald found himself saying, "Teasing him that way...it's plain mean."

"She does it—consciously or unconsciously—to rile him up

enough to declare himself." Lila looked a little too pleased with herself. "I guess it finally worked."

Women, he thought in disgust with a mental shake of his head. He had a pretty good idea his wife had a hand in all of this, because he just didn't see the very patient and responsible Parker West concocting such a harebrained scheme.

Yes, this was definitely Lila's meddling.

Gerald muttered to his wife, "I hope you know what you're doing."

ॐ

Her lashes fluttered and lifted, registering dappled sunlight at the same time she caught the tantalizing smell of frying bacon in the air.

Where was she?

Celia lifted to one elbow and blinked at the unfamiliar surroundings. The small space was neat and tidy, the plain rough table set with two plates and cups. There was already a pile of biscuits in a tin bowl. The sizzle of meat in a skillet made a soft, comforting sound.

She was entirely naked under the blankets, Celia realized with a jolt of memory. Her thighs, also, were slightly sticky. As the night before began to return in a small rush of erotic images, she blushed even though she was completely alone.

Parker West had done some fairly outrageous things to her body. Things she didn't imagine men and women ever did together. He'd had his mouth between her legs, for heaven's sake, and acted as if he *liked* doing it.

He'd put more than his mouth there. She remembered what it was like to be filled with his long, hard length, and a treacherous throb began in the very spot he'd invaded so carnally.

God help her, she'd liked it. Worse, he'd known it too, for she'd been vocal enough about her enjoyment.

It was a little humiliating.

But not enough to keep her from wanting to do it again.

The door swung open and he came inside, carrying the odor of pine and a breath of fresh mountain air. Dressed in his faded jeans, a patterned flannel shirt with the sleeves rolled up, and hatless, he looked boyishly handsome with his carelessly combed hair and a grazing of dark whiskers on his jaw.

She tried to ignore the treacherous reaction she had to his presence. "Good morning."

His smile always had the power to beguile and disarm, no more than a quick, almost shy curve of his well-shaped mouth. "Good morning. I hope you slept well."

It was a polite thing to say, but ridiculous, as he certainly knew just how she'd slept. Naked, curled against him, his arms loosely clasped around her waist as they shared the bed. "I slept just fine," she told him, unaccountably chagrined. She pulled up the blanket to cover her bare breasts.

"Are you hungry?"

She was famished actually. They had never eaten supper the night before as they'd been too busy doing other things. Celia nodded, watching him crouch to adjust the coffeepot on the coals in the fireplace.

"It's about ready," he told her with a nod toward the table.

Glancing around, she looked for her clothes but saw nothing but the swept floor and plain, sparse furniture. "I wouldn't mind getting dressed," she said pointedly. "Where are my clothes?"

"You don't need clothes." His expression was perfectly bland.

Speechless for a moment, she stared at him.

"I like you naked," he explained as if it were the most reasonable thing on earth he'd obviously taken her clothes and put them somewhere. "Shall we sit up and eat?"

Celia sputtered, "You expect me to sit at the table nude and calmly eat with you?"

He winked, an uncharacteristic wicked grin surfacing again. "It's a little fantasy of mine."

A part of her wanted to laugh, but a greater part of her wanted to strangle him. "Well, too bad. Parker, give me back my shift, at least."

He shook his dark head. "Not right now. I make the rules, sweetheart, in case you haven't noticed. It never did get me anywhere to let you lead me around by the nose, so while we're here anyway, things are going to be as I like them." His ebony brows lifted in open amusement. "And I like you naked. I like it a *lot.*"

He had to be the most infuriating, high-handed...outrageously handsome cowboy west of the Mississippi. Celia furiously watched him fill two plates with crisp bacon, steaming beans and biscuits, and had to admit the food smelled wonderful.

He looked wonderful, too. So tall and graceful in his quick, economic movements, the chiseled planes of his face and lean length of his body utterly masculine and entirely too attractive for her peace of mind.

Trying to eat with a blanket wrapped around her probably would be awkward and he'd end up getting an eyeful anyway.

Perhaps it was best to just comply, she decided with an inner glimmer of an idea. He might just be sorry he'd ever suggested this particular disgraceful notion.

When he set the plates on the table and gazed at her expectantly, an infuriatingly smug smile tugging at his mouth, Celia smiled right back. "I don't suppose there's much I can do about this...fantasy, is there?"

"Nope."

"I am hungry," she admitted, eyeing the steaming plates.

"It's not fancy but I'm a decent cook." Parker stood politely by the table, waiting for her.

"It smells good but I need to..." She wasn't sure exactly how to express what she needed, and that was to relieve herself and some water and a cloth would be welcome.

It was a little disconcerting to realize he understood perfectly. "I heated some water earlier," he said in an off-hand voice. "It's in a bucket on the porch."

"You don't expect me to go out there without anything on."

He just lifted his brows. "Who's going to see?"

Fine. If he wanted to be that way, she could give it right back.

She let her lashes drift down a fraction as she eased the blanket over her breasts, slowly exposing them. Sliding her legs over the side of the bed, she stood and stretched a little in a deliberately provocative way that thrust out her breasts as she shook back her long, tangled hair.

When she walked the few steps to the door, she saw his gaze had darkened slightly and he certainly wasn't looking at her face.

Good. If he was hoarding her clothes and making her walk outside naked, she was going to exact a little revenge.

True to his word, a bucket of warm water sat outside, and once she'd availed herself of the nearby bushes, she washed quickly, the morning air warming but still cool and crisp. He was still inside, standing by the table when she went back in. She shivered a little because she had no clothes but he pretended not to notice.

At least she was pretty sure he pretended. He seemed a bit distracted.

She sat down, waiting for him to sink into the opposite chair. The table was small, and they were close enough to touch. Picking up her fork, she asked pleasantly, "Any other fantasies I need to be aware of?"

His gaze was fastened on her bare breasts, but flickered up to meet hers briefly. "When it comes to you, I have quite a few."

The heat in his sky blue eyes made her feel that pleasurable pulse again between her legs. Celia took a small spoonful of beans and chewed and swallowed before she said dryly, "I'm almost afraid to ask."

"I think you'll find out soon enough." He seemed to have forgotten he had a fork. The utensil sat by his plate as he watched her eat.

"That sounds interesting since last night wasn't too bad," she said in a teasing tone, moving a little so her breasts swayed slightly. She might be fairly sheltered in some ways, but she did have three older brothers who occasionally made comments about women when they didn't know she could hear. Men seemed to have a fair fascination with a particular part of the female anatomy. Parker certainly seemed riveted on her chest at this moment.

"Aren't you going to eat?" she asked innocently before she took a bite of flaky biscuit. He hadn't lied about his cooking abilities. It was surprisingly light and delicious. "Or are you just going to sit there and let your food get cold while you stare at my tits?"

Looking startled, he growled, "Where did you hear that word?"

"Oh, come on, Parker. I have brothers and there are over a dozen hands on the ranch. I've probably about heard it all here and there."

"They should watch their mouths around you."

"This from the man who is forcing me to eat breakfast naked?" She couldn't help it, she laughed.

He was good-natured enough he also laughed, his mouth curving ruefully. "Maybe this was a damned poor idea after all," he muttered, and shifted a little in his chair.

"Are you...like *that* again?" Celia asked the question in mock sympathy.

What ever he was, Parker was not a fool. "I suppose you think it serves me right?"

"I sure do." She took another bite of her biscuit, looking at him in open challenge. "The question is, what are you going to do about it?"

She was a little witch, that was all there was to it.

It wasn't like Parker didn't know she could be a tease—she'd done it to him often enough before, but this time things were entirely different.

His gaze dropped involuntarily to the spectacular swell of her bare breasts. She truly had perfect tits—as she put it—beautifully shaped and full, with those delectable pink nipples that fit so well in his mouth. Parker didn't think he'd ever seen anything quite so arousing. When she moved, even just to take a dainty bite of her food, the luscious weight of her flesh swayed in a slight quiver.

There was no doubt about it, his prick was at full attention and even though he'd been darned hungry before, it paled beside the ravenous carnal hunger he felt right at this moment. All he wanted to do was to take her, and take her hard. He wanted to hear those small, sexy sounds she made as he plunged inside her warm, wet sex, and he wanted to feel her come all around him again.

For the past five years, he'd longed for her so badly he couldn't sleep at night. Though he didn't think it possible, having had her, he needed her even more.

"What do you think I should do about it?" he asked in a voice that didn't even remotely sound like his own.

"You could fuck me again," she said, her blond hair a glorious riot of disheveled curls around her bare, ivory shoulders, a glint of mischief in her dark blue eyes. "I'd guess it's the obvious way to relieve your discomfort."

Yeah, a wickedly gorgeous little witch who had definitely heard a few words not meant for her ears.

"Is that an invitation?" he asked.

"Do you need one?" Her mouth curved slightly. "You didn't seem to need one last night."

He didn't. Unless the open challenge in her gaze and obvious peaked state of her delicately pink nipples was an invitation. She looked like she wanted it, and he was more than willing to give it to her.

Parker stood and scooped her out of the chair. Taking her back to the rumpled bed, he deposited her without ceremony and unfastened his pants to free his straining erection. Celia watched him shove his jeans down his hips. She said breathlessly, "Hurry."

Oh God.

He couldn't get out of his clothes fast enough. He heard the rattle of a button as it hit the floor when he pulled his shirt off, and it seemed forever to get his boots off his feet. Celia watched him with languorous invitation in her beautiful eyes and her glorious body was posed seductively, slim thighs slightly parted so he could see the promise of heaven. As he finally tossed his jeans aside, she deliberately and slowly spread her legs open in an unmistakable carnal signal of exactly what she wanted.

God in heaven, he could tell she was already wet and ready.

He covered her and with one smooth thrust, sheathed himself to the hilt inside her luscious wet heat.

When she cried out, he had one split second of fear he'd hurt her, but then her legs wrapped around his waist and her nails lightly scored his back. She said breathlessly, "Oh, yes."

He should at least kiss her, he thought as he began to move, but from the urgent lift of her hips and the grasp of her hands, he guessed she was more interested in speed than finesse. The night before he'd taken care to make love to her as gently as he knew how and initiate her to sexual intercourse with a care for her innocence.

Right now, as she so saucily suggested, he simply fucked her.

His buttocks flexed as he thrust between her legs, his harsh breathing mingling with the soft sounds of her moans of enjoyment. The pleasure of being inside her was exquisite, and the soft friction of her tight nipples against his chest aroused him further. For someone who had been a virgin just the night before, Celia seemed to possess an innate sensuality. She knew just how far to lift her hips so he slid in as deep as possible, and the flush of enjoyment on her lovely face was unmistakable.

When it came to sex, she wasn't exactly quiet either, and he found it sexy as hell.

"Parker," she moaned, her inner muscles tightening with perfect, tantalizing pressure around his surging cock.

"Come for me," he urged, a faint sheen of sweat breaking out over his whole body. "I want to see you climax, sweetheart."

Her throat arched back, and her eyes drifted shut, the lashes dark against the elegant curve of her cheekbones. Celia panted, "Ooh...I...can't...take...it."

But she did take it. She took it hard for about another three deep strokes before she screamed and convulsed around his insistent penetration in open, abandoned release.

He climaxed in a violent rush of response, the pleasure so acute the entire world went blank. He ejaculated so hard his muscles shook as he emptied into her vagina. Parker buried his face in the fragrant silk of her tumbled hair and gasped, feeling small aftershocks of pulsing pleasure, only barely aware enough to keep his weight braced so he didn't crush the woman beneath him.

Tangled together in an intimate joining of damp skin and entwined limbs, they stayed that way without speaking for a few moments until Celia gave a small, soft laugh. It turned into genuine mirth, and Parker finally lifted his head and wryly raised his brows. "For your information, a man isn't flattered if a woman laughs at him after sex."

Her slender fingers lifted to stroke his cheek and she shook her head. "I'm not laughing at you, quite the contrary. I'm laughing at my mother."

"I'd appreciate it if when we're in bed together that we not mention our parents." Parker said it with a small grin, entranced with how beautiful she looked beneath him with her burnished gold hair and fragile features. Everything about her was feminine and alluring, and even though he'd kidnapped her and dragged her up to the secluded cabin, he had the distinct feeling he was the one who was a prisoner. "For instance, I'd take money on it your father would like to lynch me 'long about now."

Considering his cock was still buried deep inside her; that was undoubtedly true. In fact, if Gerald Evans saw them as they were in bed right now, Parker would be a dead man. Celia didn't deny it either. She said softly, "He likes you. My mother does, too. The reason I was laughing is because she took me aside a couple of days ago and gave me a pretty frank talk about what we just did. It was almost like she knew this was going to happen."

"Really?" Parker tried to seem bland. He gave her what he hoped was a questioning look, still braced on his elbows above her. "This I'm dying to hear. What did she say?"

"Actually, she told me the absolute truth in pretty accurate anatomical detail." Celia's dark blue eyes were amused. "I was horrified, if you want to know, and I really didn't believe her. I have to say when described, the whole process of sex sounds rather disgusting."

Considering she lived on a working ranch, she couldn't have been completely ignorant even before her mother's lecture. Parker gently slid free from between her legs and rolled over on his back, settling next to her. He really couldn't remember being more content in his life. "You've seen the stallions cover the mares. Not to mention the bulls with the cows."

"That's not a particularly gentle act and not at all the same thing."

"I wasn't exactly gentle a few minutes ago, either." He felt a little guilty, for she surely had to be sore from the night before. "I hope I didn't hurt you in any way."

"No, you didn't. Or if you did, I didn't care at the moment."

"You're sure?"

Celia, as usual, had the ability to unsettle him. She rose up on one elbow and brushed his mouth with a light kiss. Lush and gorgeous, with his sperm gleaming on her pale thighs in glistening rivulets, she whispered against his lips, "I liked it."

God help him, he was completely at her mercy.

"Me, too," he said in husky response and pulled her into his arms.

Chapter Four

The fence had been cut. This wasn't the first time, either.

John Evans swung off his horse and studied the tracks with a practiced eye. There had been about five of them as far as he could tell, and a good amount of cattle had been herded through the gap.

Parker West, when he got back from his little impulsive outing with Celia, was going to be livid. They were all losing stock, but their own operation and the West ranch had borne the brunt of the rustlers' attention.

True, the Wests ran more head than they did, but they were definitely both targets.

John wondered if he didn't know why, for he'd be damned if he didn't have a pretty solid suspicion of just who might be behind the recent upsurge in stolen cattle. He'd been thinking about it for some time but had been reluctant to say anything.

Joshua trotted up on his bay and swore softly, taking in the damage. "Fucking lowdown thieves. Parker is going to be pissed as hell."

Out looking for a stray mare that had escaped their pasture, they'd ridden all over the West ranch to see if she might have ended up there. This wasn't the only place that had been used to steal stock.

Taking out a paper and his bag of tobacco, John deftly rolled himself a cigarette with one hand, pouring the tobacco with the pouch between his teeth. He tucked the pouch back in his pocket. "I've got a theory about all this," he drawled.

"Oh yeah?" Josh slid off his horse, squinted at the tracks with an expression of disgust, and shook his head. "Enlighten me whenever you're ready, little brother."

"Colter's doin' this. Well, not him specifically, but he's backing them."

Josh was built like their father, heavy in the shoulders, and had a shock of brown hair, but they'd all inherited their mother's signature blue eyes. His eyes narrowed. "Rance Colter's rich. He doesn't need to rustle cattle."

John gave his brother a level glance. "Ever wonder how exactly he got so rich? I have. Besides, Rance Colter has been panting over Celia for the past year and she won't have anything to do with him. Has it never struck you as odd that we're losing cows right and left now that she snubbed him, and even more odd that Parker's getting it even worse? No one else seems to be having much trouble. Oh sure, here and there maybe, just for appearances, but we are definitely being singled out, Josh. Colter claims his cattle are being rustled too, but I don't trust that son of a bitch any farther than I can toss his sorry ass. I bet if we rode all around his property, we'd find his fences just as right as rain."

"Maybe." Josh looked thoughtful.

"If it is Colter, he's not goin' to be real happy when Parker and Celia come back married. Because believe me, Parker is smart enough to know when he brings her back, there had better be a ring on her finger."

"I'll kill him myself if there isn't." Josh said it with conviction.

The afternoon was warm and John gazed out over the grass to where the mountains rose above the valley. "I have a fair idea where he's taken her."

"Do you?"

He and Parker West were the same age, had been neighbors all their lives and they were solid friends. Parker had told him about the cabin a few years ago, but John wasn't sure exactly where it was located. West could be pretty private about some things and he liked his solitude now and again.

"I think I could find them. He's got a place he goes to hunt and fish and told me once where it was."

"So?" Josh scuffed the trampled soil with his boot. "What are you going to do, bust in on them?"

"No." John frowned. "Of course not. I'm just wondering if I'm the only one who knows where they might be."

His older brother's jaw tensed and his eyes flashed. "If you think for a minute Celia's in danger, you'd better say so right now."

They were all protective of their two younger sisters, but there was no question that while Rose was practical and demure, Celia was neither. Oh yes, she was a lady, their mother and three years at a private Eastern school had seen to it, but she had an underlying reckless streak that was not easy to rein in. Coupled with the fact she was so pretty, it made for a combustible combination.

Parker—if he had his way and actually got her to the altar and everything tied up right and tight—was going to have his hands full.

"He keeps the cabin pretty secret," John said after a moment of contemplation, uneasy, but not uneasy enough to ride up there. "I doubt anyone else knows about it."

"I wish the entire territory didn't know he up and took her," Josh muttered, staring at the mangled fence. "If you're right about Colter, it might set off something I have no desire to deal with. Colter has lots of friends. We could have ourselves a little range war damned easy."

"They aren't exactly his friends," John pointed out, gathering the reins in his hand and swinging into the saddle. "Let's keep in mind he has lots of money, which buys loyalty, but only so far. Shit, this could be a mess. I'd guess he owns every judge between here and Denver. Even if we could somehow prove he's behind this sudden increase in our stock being rustled, we can't fight this legal—it isn't going to work."

Josh grinned, vaulting on to the back of his big gelding. "Then we'll fight it the other way. Come on, let's follow those tracks."

80

The pool was cool and deep. Celia sank in, feeling the water rush over her thighs and then her breasts. Her first reaction was a shiver, but then she sighed with pleasure. The stream was a fast-moving rush of water, but this sheltered nook, bordered by a small drop-off and some large rocks, was a very nice place to bathe.

Rinsing her hair, she washed afterwards, the crystal water turning foamy from the soap before it ran clear again in seconds due to the current. When her soapy hands slid over the curves of her breasts—an act she'd done many times before as she bathed, but had never enjoyed—she felt a languid sense of pleasure and her nipples hardened.

What has Parker done to me? she wondered. Experimentally, she brushed her nipple again, rubbing lightly. It pebbled further under the light press of her fingers and between her legs she felt suddenly warm.

He could do that to her instantly. With a glance or the lightest touch. They'd been at the cabin for three days now and it seemed all they did was make love. Her body had become attuned to pleasure, and she was both sexually curious and eager to learn more about this sensual world she had no idea existed before this trip.

Not, she thought with a small smile, that Parker seemed to have any trouble obliging her. He looked at her with a pure male hunger in his eyes she found as arousing as the actual feel of him inside her.

However, he still hadn't told her he loved her. Neither had he officially proposed again.

Leaning back against a flat rock, she semi-floated in dreamy contentment, letting the stream run over her skin.

"Now that's any man's dream come true."

Her lashes lifted at the familiar timbre of the deep voice. She knew he was nearby, because despite their seclusion, he refused to leave her unguarded at any time. Parker stayed fairly close to the cabin even when he was doing necessary chores like gathering kindling or hunting. Celia smiled lazily, a deliberately provocative curve of her mouth. "I was just thinking about you."

He stood on the bank, his blue eyes slightly narrowed as he examined her nude body through the running water. He'd been out earlier looking for game, and his rifle was still in his hand. "Were you?"

"Yes." She moved upright so her breasts bobbed in the water, drawing his gaze.

"Care to tell me more?" There was a slight husky edge to his voice she now recognized. The dappled sunlight gleamed off his dark hair.

"I was thinking about how much I like it when you fuck me." It wasn't a thing any lady would say and her mother would faint if she heard, but Celia gave him a provoking grin and said it anyway.

His brows shot up. He said dryly, "That might just make me the luckiest man on this earth, but we are going to have to do something about your language, sweetheart."

"I thought all the rules were suspended here. You're sure acting like they are. Besides, at home, I have to be the perfect proper young lady my parents think they raised. As far as I can tell, nothing proper has happened between us since you tossed me on your horse." She was only half-teasing, for she did feel a certain lovely sense of liberation, and not just sexually. On the ranch, someone pretty much kept track of her all the time, and a lot of it was simply her older brothers were so protective of her. She appreciated their concern, but it was stifling at times. Lately they wouldn't even let her take an afternoon horseback ride on her own.

She wouldn't mind a ride of an entirely different sort now.

"We're going to have to go back soon, you know," he told her.

She did know, but at this moment, she simply felt needy in a way that was as old as man and woman. "Well, if I'm not mistaken, right now we're here, and we're alone. If you want to *truly* feel lucky, come on in." She stood up, giving him a full view of her naked torso, droplets running off the curves of her breasts and pearling against her skin. Cool water swirled around her waist.

"There's an invitation I'm not likely to turn down." Parker set his rifle aside carefully in the soft springy grass by the side of the stream, and his gaze suddenly glittered.

Celia watched him undress, anticipation weighing her limbs with a delicious potent languor. He stripped with efficient swiftness, and she saw that he was hard already, his erection stark against the flat taut plane of his stomach, lifting the full sacs of his testicles. When Parker waded into the water, he stopped and swore briefly, giving her an accusing look. "I forgot how cold this water is."

"You get used to it." Celia moved toward him. Where he stood, the water was only about thigh deep and she could feel the sandy bottom under her feet. Unmoving, he let her come closer, the ripple of the current gushing around the well-muscled contours of his legs.

Reaching out, she slipped her fingers around his blatantly aroused cock, registering his slight gasp. "Is my hand cold?"

"Yes, but I don't care." His voice sounded strangled.

She had already learned he liked it when she touched and stroked his testicles and cock. In fact, it gave her a certain sense of power whenever she caressed him so intimately, for it was clear how vulnerable he was to just her touch. Running her fingers up and down, she explored the velvet-tight skin of his stiff erection, felt the distended veins and the smooth hardness. The engorged tip seeped a clear sticky droplet and on impulse, she bent and licked it off.

His whole body jerked. "Jesus!"

It didn't taste bad, she decided, and his reaction was definitely worth it. "Don't women do this?" she asked curiously, giving another small swipe of her tongue over the swollen crest. "You do it to me."

"Some women do." His powerful body was tense as a bowstring. "But I would never ask *you* to do it."

"Why not?" She glanced up from under the veil of her lashes, her mouth still just an inch or so away from the crest of his erection. "Doesn't it feel good?"

His broad shoulders lifted a fraction and his response was ragged. "It feels...I can't find the adequate word to describe it, so yeah, I guess I'll say it feels good. Too damned good, but..."

"But what? Tell me what to do, Parker."

"Celia, you can't ask me that." It wasn't more than a whisper but his eyes were half-closed and she could feel the surge of his penis in her hand in response to her question. He definitely wanted her to do it, she decided, but as usual was too polite about the whole thing.

She said tartly, "I guess I'll have to give it a try and see how it turns out."

It felt wickedly naughty to drop to her knees in the streambed and let the cool water caress her back and shoulders as she took the tip of his cock in her mouth. Parker's hands wove into her wet hair and he groaned. It was pretty easy to guess he wouldn't ask her to do it because proper young ladies didn't put their mouths on a man's erect sex. No matter all that had happened between them the past few days, he apparently still thought of her that way.

She liked to unsettle him, and old habits were hard to break. Besides, maybe in the past her flirtatious teasing had left him frustrated, but he certainly wasn't going be left unsatisfied this time.

Celia took as much of his length to the back of her throat as possible, licking, tasting, gently sucking. He mumbled another incoherent protest, but she ignored it, her hands grasping his thighs for balance. It wasn't long before he gasped out, "Stop."

She would have continued but he tugged her head up forcefully enough that she obeyed, and this time she was the one who gasped as he lifted her out of the water. Wading deeper in the pool, Parker had a taut, almost fierce, expression on his face. Celia felt the coolness of the flat slanted rock at her back as he braced her against it. He parted her legs almost roughly underneath the water and thrust inside her throbbing cleft.

Perfect.

The contrast of the cool water and his hot cock pushing into her was arousing, and so was how he held her hips in place and moved with a wildness that was unlike Parker's normal reserve. She liked making him lose control, and her arms wound around his neck as she spread her legs wider and clung to him. It wasn't long before she felt the escalating rise of orgasmic pleasure, the tempestuous rhythm of his lovemaking a perfect match for her own raw need.

When she climaxed, her cry rose above the sound of rushing water, and her thighs tightened around his lean hips. Parker pushed into her contracting passage until he exploded, pouring into her in a hot rush of liquid release.

He held her there, pressed against the rock. His uneven

breathing was warm against her cheek and his arms felt strong and secure.

That was perfectly fine with her, Celia thought, gazing at her lover. She wouldn't mind if they stayed that way forever.

It was certainly the best bath she'd ever had.

§

Parker crouched down and stirred the pot, glad he'd taken the time to bring supplies up to the cabin a few days before he'd gone after Celia. The stew smelled darned good, if he did say so himself. He'd killed and skinned a rabbit earlier, and with carrots and potatoes from his mother's carefully tended garden, it promised to be delicious.

"I hope you know I can't cook."

He glanced up and smiled wryly. "I know."

Celia sat at the table, her arms folded as she watched him with a slightly rueful look on her lovely face. "I really can't sew much either. Both my mother and Rose say I'm pretty hopeless when it comes to domestic skills."

"Luckily, those aren't the skills that interest me." Still crouched by the hearth, Parker gave her a sinful wink. "You're damned good at what pleases me most and you're still just a beginner, sweetheart."

She blushed, her cheeks tinting a delightful, enchanting pink. "I suppose you're an expert judge, is that it? I have to say it has occurred to me the other night sure didn't seem to be your first experience with sex, Parker."

Whoa, he didn't want to travel through this particular territory, though it did please him Celia seemed a little jealous. Her blue eyes held a hint of unhidden resentment.

He said cautiously, "I'm twenty-five."

"What has your age got to do with anything?"

"Men are a little different than women." He straightened and leaned a shoulder against the mantel, hoping he didn't sound defensive. "We kind of regard virginity as something to dispose of as quickly as we're able to do so."

That response apparently wasn't the one she wanted. Her chin lifted a little and she gave him a level accusing look. "I see. Just how old were you when you were *able* to dispose of it?"

He'd been fifteen, and his first time had been with a beautiful Spanish girl a few years older. Conchita had eventually married one of his father's cowboys and moved to New Mexico, but he still thought of her from time to time. Since then he hadn't been exactly celibate, but once he realized exactly how he felt about Celia Evans, his cock had more than a passing acquaintance with his hand. Parker said coolly, "Pretty young. But I've never regarded sex as a casual thing, Celia. I wouldn't ever pay for it like a lot of men do—and I haven't really even looked at any other woman since I fell in love with you a good five years ago."

Her expression changed then, softening from defiant accusation to something entirely different. "You've never said it to me."

Parker blinked. "Said what?"

"That you're in love with me."

He shoved his fingers through his hair in exasperation. "The whole world knows I'm in love with you. There isn't a question *you've* known it for a long time."

She shook her blond head, soft golden curls brushing her slender shoulders. "You can be so dense, Parker."

Maybe he was, because he sure as hell had no idea what exactly she wanted from him. "I proposed," he pointed out.

"You told me you thought we should get married because we'd been neighbors all our lives and you thought not only would we suit each other, but it'd be nice that I would live so close to my family."

Put that way, he supposed it didn't sound particularly romantic. Parker crossed his arms over his chest and flushed slightly. "All of that is true."

"This is big country but we have other neighbors. I suppose I should consider marrying one of them."

Her flippant tone irritated the hell out of him, not mention the fact he intensely disliked the idea of any other man touching her, even if she was being sarcastic. "You're marrying me tomorrow in Tijeras, sweetheart, so you can get over that notion. The judge comes into town every Thursday."

Celia shook her head and stood up, looking luscious in her simple blue dress, her eyes flashing. "You can't *tell* me to marry you, Parker."

"I think I just did, *Miss Evans*."

"Go to hell."

"That sassy mouth of yours has got to be reined in."

"I dare you to try." She looked more beautiful than ever with high color in her cheeks and fire in her gaze.

"We *have* to get married, sweetheart. I've fucked you, remember?" The minute he said it, he regretted it. He wasn't handling this right, but she had the ability to get under his skin the way no one else could. She used the crude word now and then in playful banter because he disapproved, but he knew she didn't really think of what happened between them in bed—and a few other places—that way.

He didn't think of it that way either.

Her soft mouth tightened. "You sure have. Just like you fucked all those other women, however many there have been. I notice you didn't marry them, so it makes that particular argument invalid, I'm afraid. Excuse me, I think I'm going outside for a short walk. I don't think much of the company in here."

Lord, this is not going well.

She turned and stalked toward the door and at first Parker figured he'd just let her go cool off outside. When Celia thought about it, she'd know they were obligated to get married, and more than that, he was convinced she felt the same way about him as he did her. Then he'd ask her politely again to be his wife, and leave out all mention of the points of his first proposal she apparently didn't appreciate.

She furiously swung open the door, and Parker changed his mind.

No, she wasn't walking out on this argument. Whenever he played the passive suitor, he lost ground. It was an old pattern, and it had gotten him nowhere. On the other hand, she seemed to like it when he was a bit more assertive. Letting her flounce out would be a mistake.

He lunged away from the mantel and caught her in three long strides, just as she stepped out on the tiny front porch of the cabin. Celia made a choked incensed sound of surprise as his hands grasped her waist, and he barely avoided a wild swing of her fist he suspected would have hurt if it connected. Parker dragged her back inside and kicked the door shut, ignoring her struggles.

"Get your hands off me," she said icily, doing her best to kick him in the knee. "I do not want to talk to you right now."

"Too bad. I *do* want to talk. Right now." Crossing the small space, he fairly tossed her on the bed.

She tried to sit up but he wouldn't let her, catching her arms over her head and pinning her to the thin mattress with his longer, much larger, body. She always felt wonderful beneath him, and he could feel the generous swell of her breasts through her dress and his shirt, not to mention the perfect cradle of her hips against his crotch.

With a lethal glare, she called him a very, very bad name.

In answer, he kissed her.

It was his intention to be forceful, but instead he found he molded his mouth to hers with gentle persuasion that said more than any words he could find. At first she was stiff and unyielding, but it lasted all of two seconds. Her lips parted and let him inside the sweet recesses of her mouth, welcoming the gentle glide of his tongue.

His bride-to-be loved sex, he'd already discovered that. With her tempestuous personality he wasn't precisely surprised, but her uninhibited reaction to the physical act was more than what he expected. In the past three days, she had initiated sex as often as he had, and he simply could not believe how incredibly she responded to him.

That was a weapon he wasn't too proud to use.

He kissed her long and slow, until he could feel her lift her hips in supplication and need. Trailing small nips along the elegant line of her jaw, he nuzzled the hollow beneath her ear. "You make me crazy, Celia."

"Do I?" He'd released her arms and she slid them around his neck.

"I think you have a pretty clear idea you do," he said, not

able to help a small note of cynicism in his voice. "In fact, I'm sure you do it on purpose, damn your sweet hide." He kissed the slim column of her throat, finding the place where her pulse beat quickly under the delicate skin.

"But you fell in love with me anyway?" There was an underlying note to her voice he recognized as arousal, coupled with a question she apparently needed answered.

"I sure did." It was perfectly true.

Her pelvis lifted again, pressing his growing erection. "Show me, Parker."

"If you agree to marry me, I'll be more than happy to oblige, ma'am."

For a moment, the dreamy look in her eyes clouded. "That's not fair."

"Is there anything about what's between us that is fair?" The raw note in his speech was as honest as anything he'd ever expressed in his life. "Let's talk about fair for a moment, sweetheart. If you knew how many hours of my life I've spent thinking about you, wanting you, and not just this way," he lightly thrust against her with the bulge in his jeans, "you'd realize just how much I want to spend the rest of my life with you."

For a moment, she said nothing. Then she lifted her mouth to his in a passionate, searing kiss. When they broke apart, she said huskily, "That isn't precisely what I was looking for, but it's good enough. Fine, I'll marry you."

He wasn't about to let her refuse, but still Parker felt a thrill of elation at her capitulation.

Her lashes lowered and her gaze was pure feminine allure. Her soft lips moved in a slow, enticing curve. "Now, if I'm not mistaken, you're in good form to hold up your end of the bargain." She wiggled suggestively against him, making his cock swell even more. "Prove to me you love me."

He had absolutely no problem with that request. Parker grinned. "If you insist."

Her blue eyes held the heavy look of sensual need. "Believe me, I insist."

Chapter Five

John Evans lounged in the doorway of the shop, one shoulder propped on the doorjamb. His seemingly casual pose was at odds with his heightened attention.

As he predicted, Colter was in town, and he could smell the stink of real trouble.

Shit.

Sometimes he just plain hated being right.

His gaze narrowed on the small, dusty little building that served as both jail and courthouse, John waited. Across the street, his brother Jared stood by the entrance of the general store, his stance just as deceptively relaxed. Joshua was outside the saloon, watching for the small group of men Rance Colter had brought with him to town to leave.

If Colter had a notion of self-preservation, he wouldn't try anything. Yeah, he had more guns if it came down to a count, but Parker was no slouch shot, and Jared was generally considered to be one of the best in Colorado. John knew he and Josh could handle themselves just fine as well, but they were there more for prevention than anything.

It couldn't be coincidence that on the day the circuit judge came through, Colter suddenly decided to make an appearance. Any fool could figure out if Parker wanted to marry Celia, this was the day he'd bring her into town.

Which is exactly what had happened. A few minutes ago they'd ridden up and gone inside to see the judge. John had a glimpse of a small boy, who had been loitering by the courthouse steps, running off toward the saloon where Colter and his men had been drinking most of the afternoon.

Not a good sign.

Intent on the façade of the building, he almost didn't realize a woman walked by until he caught the movement out of the corner of his eye. He glanced up and straightened immediately, politely touching the brim of his hat, his expression neutral. "Good afternoon, ma'am."

"Good afternoon, Mr. Evans." She smiled faintly, holding an infant in her arms, two small children crowding her skirts. Dressed in a blue gown, Mrs. Reed looked young and pretty, with her dark hair neatly in a bun and her eyes showing a hint of curiosity over his vigilant post outside the dressmaker's shop.

He glanced at the wide blue eyes of the baby she held for a long moment, and then back at the doorway of the saloon. Very quietly, he said, "You might want to take the children inside and off the street."

Maybe it was the tone of his voice, but the young woman complied at once, hustling the children through a nearby doorway.

Sure enough, a few minutes later, six men came out of the Lucky Lady.

Fuck.

The stickiest part of this was to make sure Celia stayed safe. That was why John had insisted they all come to town today. He'd heard rumors Colter had made a few drunken public comments to the effect that if he'd known all he had to do was tie Celia Evans up and ride off with her, he'd have made his move a long time ago.

John just had a bad feeling in his gut. The rancher was a ruthless bastard. He knew it, and most of the area knew it. He'd completely approved of Celia's lack of enthusiasm for his attempted courtship. Unfortunately, Rance Colter was also used to getting his own way, especially in this section of Colorado.

As he watched the tall, lanky form of his adversary walk purposefully down the street, John loosened his gun a little in the holster at his hip. That son of a bitch was going for six-to-one odds. Well, he was in for an unpleasant little surprise because the Evans boys were in town to even things up a little.

Jared made his move exactly on time. "Hey, Colter," he shouted, tipping back his hat a little.

The slow way he strolled out into the dusty street in front of them didn't look threatening, but the way he held his body spoke volumes. Jared might be the youngest of the three of them, but he was by far the wildest. On cue, John walked out from the opposite direction to stand by his brother between the group and the courthouse.

He said pleasantly, "Good afternoon, Rance. By the way, just so you know, Josh is behind you all, watching your backs, so to speak."

All six men had come to a halt at their sudden appearance, and John saw several of them glance back to make sure what he'd just said was perfectly true. Josh stood a ways back in the middle of the street and it was easy enough to see he was armed and didn't look all that friendly.

"Hello, Evans," Colter said coolly, but his face suddenly looked a little flushed. He was older, in his mid-thirties, with handsome, almost sharp, features and eyes so dark they looked black. He dressed with dandified care, and today he'd played it up more than usual. His frock coat, brightly embroidered vest and trousers were well-cut and expensive, and a gold watch chain glittered beneath his coat. Even his hat looked new, and his boots were polished to a high sheen.

He looked like a man planning to get married.

Hell.

Without taking his gaze from the group, John said conversationally to his younger brother, "Our friend Rance here sure is dressed up. I'm wondering now if Parker is unexpectedly having trouble getting the judge to cooperate. I'm also wondering if that same judge is expecting our well-dressed friend to appear and maybe substitute in as Celia's new husband, and Parker might wind up dead in the bargain."

Only a year older than Celia, Jared had a good dose of the same hot-tempered disposition. He spat out, "Jesus, I think you might be right, John."

Colter attempted a pleasant smile but it came off as a sickly smirk. "Look, boys—"

"If John is right, that's the dumbest plan I've ever heard of, Colter." Jared slightly shook his blond head in derision, but his gaze stayed watchful. "Even if you managed to pull it off and coerce Celia into marrying you, your life would be a living hell, man. Not that you'd suffer for too long, because I'd kill you, *if* she didn't do the job first."

They must have hit close to home, because Colter's mouth tightened and his eyes glittered. "Last I knew, your sister was kidnapped. That's against the law, even here. Let's just say my affection for her compels me to make sure she isn't made to do anything against her will. West should be strung up for taking an innocent woman by force up into the mountains for the better part of a week. The judge happens to agree."

John gave a small, hard laugh. "I'm sure he agreed after he saw your money. And for your information, it's damned hard to make Celia do anything she doesn't want to do. If she's marrying Parker West, it's because she wants to marry him. If I didn't think that, Josh, Jared, or myself would take care of the matter, believe me. This isn't your affair."

"I can't see as how you all have taken care of anything. You let him ride off with her." Jealousy, open and undisguised, twisted Colter's face. "She's soiled goods now, but I'm still willing to make her an honest woman."

"What'd you call my sister?" Jared's face had gone livid, but his voice was icy and his hand hovered close to his hip.

Colter wasn't a complete fool. He could hear the very real menace in the question and his expression changed from fury to fear as his swarthy complexion went pale. Several of his men moved uneasily, showing their discomfort with the situation. One of them muttered something under his breath about not signing on for a big fight over a woman.

The last thing John wanted was for things to get out of hand. Since they stood in the middle of the street, here and there people had begun to notice the confrontation. John said tersely, "Look Rance, there's more of you, but all three of us are damn good shots and I'm pretty sure your men here don't get paid enough to die. Besides, with Josh back there, we kinda got you surrounded. If we start firing, who knows what direction you need to look, and believe me, you go first. Here's what's going to happen. Your men are going to step aside. Then we are going into the courthouse, and you're going to tell the judge it's just fine to marry my sister and Parker West. In exchange for your cooperation, I'll do my best to keep him from killing you when he finds out what you've been up to. Right now, I'd guess he's already pretty mad. It takes a lot to get him going, but he can be dangerous if you push him too far."

For a moment Colter looked like he might argue. Jared said in a brittle, sarcastic voice, "You got a second choice, of course. I could call you out for what you just said about Celia. You see, I'm sure you know I'm not nearly as reasonable as John here, and you just thoroughly pissed me off."

Looking a little green, Colter visibly swallowed, obviously backing away from the challenge. "I meant no offense. I've got some influence in these parts and I'll be happy to talk to the judge if that's what you all want."

Every man with him looked a little disgusted, John was glad to see.

Jared said scathingly, "Yeah, that's kind of what I thought you'd say, but I have to tell you, I'm damned disappointed I don't get to kill you."

ॐ

Parker stared at the man sitting behind the small desk and actually looked a bit dangerous for a change, his usual easygoing demeanor replaced by a visible lethal anger. He said in an ice-cold voice, "Do you mind repeating that?"

Judge Ramsey, portly and ruddy-faced, looked unfazed. "I said my authority permits me to refuse your request on the basis that this young woman is apparently here under duress."

Celia laid a restraining hand on her bridegroom-to-be's arm, feeling the tension in his muscles. "I assure you, Judge, I'm here of my own free will."

Ramsey transferred his attention to her, his gaze brushing her probably somewhat disheveled appearance after their long ride down from the mountains. "Did Mr. West here abduct you, Miss Evans?"

She'd been raised to respect the law—such as it was at times in this part of Colorado—but she had a distinct feeling that no matter what she said, for some reason this man had it in for Parker. She lifted her chin. "Where did you hear that?"

"I'd appreciate it if you'd answer my question, young lady."

"I can't see if it matters how Parker chose to convince me to marry him, as long as he did convince me. I want to marry him and that's why I'm standing here."

"I'm not going to reward a crime by making a mockery of the sanctity of marriage." That pompous statement was made with a smug smile.

"Crime?" Parker's voice held a menacing note and Celia tightened her fingers in an unspoken message. She'd only seen Parker truly angry once or twice in her life and when he did finally get to that point, he was as volatile as a sweeping summer storm. "I've been courting Celia for the past five years. When I asked her father for his permission to marry her, he gave me his blessing. I made a mess of my first proposal and just wanted a chance to talk to her alone. It worked, I might say, and all we want is to make this legal and be on our way."

"Well, too bad, Mr. West, I—"

The door into the small building—used to house extra prisoners when the jail was full or to conduct legal proceedings—flew open and Ramsey stopped midsentence as a man stumbled as he was pushed inside. Celia recognized Rance Colter with a lurch of her stomach, compounded by astonishment when she saw her brothers—all three of them. Jared had his gun drawn and the forbidding look on his face would give anyone pause.

"What's this?" Judge Ramsey demanded, but the superior look on his face had vanished. In fact, he'd lost some of his ruddy color.

"Howdy, Your Honor." Jared indicated Colter with his pistol. "This here gentleman has something to say to you. I suggest for his health you listen."

"You cannot come in here waving weapons at innocent citizens." The bluster was unconvincing as the judge refused to even look at Rance Colter.

Celia wasn't too fond of looking at him either. He made her skin crawl and had from the first moment she'd met him, but at the moment, she couldn't help but stare, wondering what was going on.

The tall rancher shot Parker, who looked more furious by

the moment, a baleful glance, but cleared his throat. "I might have been mistaken. Rumor had it Miss Evans was taken against her will. Apparently she had no problem riding off with West..."

He trailed off in a squeak as Parker swung furiously around. Celia quickly stepped in front of the man she wanted to marry and blocked him from doing something damned foolish, like murdering someone in front of a judge. She said softly, "Don't. He isn't worth it."

The plea registered but still his expression was deadly.

John stepped forward and stood next to her, on the opposite side from Parker. "I'll stand in as witness and best man, Your Honor. Do it."

The judge seemed to realize that just Colter's health wasn't in question and fumbled to pick up a small book. As he hastily recited the words she barely registered, she made what must have been the appropriate responses because a few minutes later, Parker turned to her, hauled her into his arms and kissed her.

Hard. Long. Until she heard someone—it sounded like Josh—chuckle.

ॐ

Her wedding had been a circus, and now her wedding night seemed to consist of a long, grueling ride to the West ranch and an armed escort in the form of her three brothers.

It was probably not an auspicious way to start a marriage.

She was half asleep when they rode up to the ranch house, and it was full dark. For a moment she blinked, not sure where she was, still comfortably resting against her husband's broad chest.

Her husband. That seemed extraordinary. She and Parker were finally married.

"You got it from here?" John said it with a slight amused tone to his voice, reining in his restive mount. "If so, we'll be off home."

Parker gave a grim little laugh. "Yeah, I got it. She'll be safe.

Thanks for being there today. I guess I didn't realize how far Colter had gone around the bend. I knew he tried to court her, but Celia didn't tell me he was so intent he'd try something like what he did with the judge."

"I doubt she suspected. I just took a guess myself. I've got a few other guesses you might be interested in. My father and I will ride over tomorrow and I think we need to have a talk." John's face looked tight in the thin light of a few stars visible through a haze of high streaming clouds.

At the mention of her father, Celia stirred with a small, sleepy yawn. Her other two brothers sat on their horses in the shadows. "Will you all tell him I'm fine? I don't want him to try and kill Parker or anything."

Jared grinned at her, a flash of white teeth in the dark. "Hey, sis, if we haven't killed him, Pa's not likely to do it. We've all been waitin' for you to come around and marry him. I guess Parker finally lost patience and took matters into his own hands."

His hands, yes, certainly, Celia remembered very well those hands...everywhere. There wasn't a part of her body he hadn't touched and done a thorough job of it. However, it was irritating that everyone seemed to be on Parker's side all the time.

Her husband slid off Diablo in a graceful movement and nodded at her brothers. "I guess I'll see you all tomorrow, then."

They rode off in a small thud of hoof beats that retreated into the distance and died. She felt a small qualm as Parker's hands closed around her waist and lifted her from the saddle. "I guess I live here now." She didn't mean for her voice to sound so subdued, but as her brothers left without her and headed toward the only home she'd ever known, it struck her deeply just how much her life had suddenly changed.

"Hey." Long fingers touched her chin and tilted her face up. He peered down at her. "*We* live here. Together."

"That just feels so...different."

"Yeah, I know, sweetheart." His fingers trailed down her throat and along her collarbone in a light caress. "But do you know how long I've wanted to bring you here as my bride?"

She shook her head.

"Let's just say it's been a very long time. Come on, let's go inside. I'll tend to Diablo in a few minutes."

The house was low and rambling, and Celia knew it almost as well as she knew her own home. It was a clear evening and the windows were open, the aroma of fresh baked bread mingling with the cool, sweet air. Inside, the big house was furnished in a curiously charming mixture of antiques that Parker's mother had brought with her from her childhood home in Connecticut and practical, plain handmade pieces. A huge stone fireplace dominated the living room, and there was a brightly patterned Indian blanket on the wall along with a few framed portraits. A beautiful cut glass lamp from France sat on a rough-hewn pine table in a corner, and on the floor there were several luxurious oriental rugs.

It was a lovely place and she wasn't certain why she felt so unsure of herself. It certainly couldn't be wedding night jitters, for she'd practiced *that* part of marriage often enough in the past few days.

"My mother's bound to be in the kitchen," Parker said, giving her hand a slight squeeze. "I can smell something wonderful. I told her to expect us sometime this evening, so she's probably gone all out."

Celia stared at him. "You told her to expect us this evening?"

"Do you think I'd just ride off and not tell my family when to expect me back?" His ebony brows lifted a fraction, and Parker looked genuinely puzzled.

Of course he wouldn't. He was Parker West and that would be irresponsible. Even when he planned on outrageously kidnapping someone, he'd let his mother know just when he'd be back home.

She resisted his tug on her hand. "Forgive me if your arrogance irritates me," she snapped out. "If you told your mother to expect the both of us, that certainly seems to mean you didn't ever intend to particularly give me a choice in whether I wanted to marry you or not."

"Oh Lord, are we going to have an argument *now*? We just walked through the door, sweetheart, and quite frankly, I'm tired and hungry."

Thin-skinned and more than a little tired herself, she asked sharply, "Did your mother approve of you riding off to abduct me?"

Parker looked at her, his blue eyes direct. "Yes, she did. Since it was her idea, *your* mother approved of it too. I was a little skeptical because I was pretty sure you'd be mad as hell at me if I tried it, but I must say it all worked out just fine. Now, please, aren't you interested in some hot water, hot food and then afterwards a soft bed? I know I am."

"My mother?" She felt her mouth fall open, shut it, and then was more furious than ever. "She told you to tie me up and ride off with me?"

"Not precisely. Let's just say she suggested I needed a different approach."

It was hard to believe but since she knew Parker was not a liar, it must be true. She sputtered, "Well...well...for your information, I was mad as hell."

"But you got over it." His fingers raked through his hair in evident exasperation. "Look, I know this afternoon was probably not how you imagined getting married—it wasn't exactly my ideal wedding either—but let's not fight over it."

Parker had a vision of an ideal wedding?

There was probably nothing he could have said that would have dissolved her anger more quickly.

He was right, she was being unreasonable and argumentative for no reason.

Well, maybe not for *no* reason, for it had been a pretty stressful day. If her brothers hadn't been there this afternoon, who knows what might have happened. She utterly despised Rance Colter.

Something could have happened to Parker. In fact, it was more than likely he would not have survived a confrontation with Colter, for she knew full well he would die to protect her and he'd have been completely outnumbered without her brothers.

Celia burst into tears.

She had absolutely no control over the sudden emotional reaction and it embarrassed her, but it happened just the same. Obviously it wasn't quite what her new husband expected either, for he stood in unconcealed dismay for a moment or two before she felt the comforting strength of his arms come around her shaking shoulders and draw her close.

Her face buried against his chest, she sobbed. He said nothing at first and she felt his mouth graze her temple. Eventually he whispered uncertainly, "Sweetheart?"

She loved the inflection in his voice when he said the endearment. "I'm sorry," she mumbled against his shirt, trying to stem the tide of tears. He smelled wonderful, like the forest in summer, clean, with a hint of spice, and entirely male.

"What's wrong?" His fingers sifted gently through her hair. After a small hesitation, he asked quietly, "Are you sorry you married me?"

It was so far from what she was actually feeling that Celia gave a muffled laugh. "No."

His lean body relaxed a fraction. "Then what is it?"

"I love you."

Pressed against him, she could feel him go very still. His long fingers tightened around her nape. "What did you just say?"

"You heard me." It was a little humiliating to realize she'd said it before him. Even though he'd confessed he'd been in love with her a long time, he had never said it flat out. Celia pulled away and wiped her damp cheeks, giving him a defiant look. "Not that you aren't completely irritating in about one thousand ways."

She expected him to at least smile, but he simply stood there staring at her.

"Parker?"

The sound of his mother's voice calling out in question broke through his apparent trance, and he glanced down the hall toward the kitchen. He said in a somewhat uneven tone, "They must have heard us ride up. Come on, sweetheart, we'd better go on in. I know my family is anxious to welcome you."

ℰℭ

The glow of a pipe and the scent of tobacco mingled with

the night air. Soft sounds of the insects in the long line of cottonwoods bordering the lane to the house made a backdrop for the distant bark of a coyote. Sitting in a chair next to his father on the long porch as was their habit each evening, Parker said neutrally, "I didn't want to discuss it in front of the women, but there could have been real trouble this afternoon."

Puffing on his pipe, his father, Russ, exhaled and said succinctly, "So I understand. I never did trust Colter, but that was one hell of a high-handed plan, even for him. Did he think the Evans boys wouldn't come after him for ambushing your wedding, or for that matter, I wouldn't get my men together and track him down?"

Somberly, Parker stared over the corrals and neat fences, shadowed in the thin light of a rising moon. "Think about it. His ranch is built like a fortress and would be damned easy to defend. Once he got holed up, especially with Celia inside, anyone would be hard pressed to do much. Unfortunately, if he had managed to forcibly marry her and get her back to his place, he could do whatever he wanted with her—and we both know exactly what that is—and her brothers would have damned little recourse. Legally wedded and bedded, even if it is akin to rape, would brand her as his for the rest of her life, even if she managed to get out of there. He'd own her, and around here, possession means a lot."

His father raised a brow and said dryly, "Luckily, you beat him to it, though I have a feeling that wasn't the exact order of things."

"It worked, that's all I care about. I've finally figured out a very direct, firm approach works best with the former Miss Evans." Parker grinned.

"I'm happy for you, son. Your mother and I both are. She is a fine young woman, though I suspect you aren't going to have a calm, uneventful life." Chuckling and shaking his head, the older man murmured, "She may look like an angel, but she has a lot of fire."

Yes, she certainly did. Parker couldn't help but think of her wild, flaming passion in bed. Or for that matter, the turbulent look in her blue eyes after she told him she loved him. "She's a handful," he said in rueful agreement, "but I always knew it. I guess I just can't help how I feel. There have been times, believe me, when I would have preferred to be head over heels for someone else. Hell, for that matter, Rose is sweet and pretty and utterly docile and we probably would suit each other better, but I've always just regarded her with brotherly affection, whereas Celia..."

"I understand. There's nothing platonic about the way you look at your new bride, Parker, but that's how it should be."

"Yes, sir." Parker stood and smiled. "Speaking of which, this is officially my wedding night and as much as I enjoy talking with you—"

"She'll be waiting, I expect." Even in the gloom, his father's eyes twinkled. "I'm counting on grandchildren, so I wouldn't dream of keeping you. Try and get *some* rest, son. Tomorrow we need to repair the cut fences and get an idea of how much stock we lost. I think it would be prudent to hire more hands, to stock up on ammunition and make sure they are all well armed, and take charge of what is starting to be a real problem around here."

Parker agreed completely, but his attention was not particularly on missing cattle and damaged fences. With a nod, he went into the house. His mother sat by the fireplace in the living room, her sewing in her lap, and he bent and gave her a kiss on the cheek before heading toward his room. The bedrooms were at the back of the ranch house, down a long hallway, and his was the first on the left. The door was shut, and he paused for a moment, the concept of knocking on his own door novel and a symbol of the change in his life.

He had married Celia Evans. She was his wife, and every single night she would sleep in his bed, in his arms. His heart tightened in pure joy and even as he lifted his hand to knock, he decided against it and simply opened the door.

She was in bed already, her shining hair spread over the pillows, sleeping soundly. Stifling a small oath, he felt a small wellspring of amused chagrin as he began to undress in the unreliable moonlit illumination let in by the thin curtains at the window. It had been a trying afternoon, and he really couldn't blame her for being tired. She'd even wept, and he had never seen that before from his gorgeous, but obstinate and willful, bride. He sensed her sudden trepidation over her new wifely role, especially since she had lived her entire life in the same house with her protective family constantly around her. Though his father and mother welcomed her without reservation, finding her place in a new household was going to be a drastic change.

Slipping under the blankets, he moved closer, doing his best not to disturb her slumber. Inhaling her sweet scent, Parker closed his eyes.

Chapter Six

The house looked dark except for one lone lamp burning in an upstairs window. John dismounted and quietly led his horse around to the back, where a small, weathered barn sat behind the house. The lone occupant was a raw-boned draft horse and it nickered softly in the shrouded gloom, the smell of hay and manure in the air. John put Mercury, his sorrel gelding, in one of the empty stalls, tossed in some hay, and made his way soundlessly toward the porch. He knocked, two very soft raps of his knuckles, and waited.

The woman who opened the door wore her dressing gown, and she stepped back without a greeting. He slipped inside and closed the door, dropping the latch into place. The place smelled good as it always did, like cinnamon and fresh baked bread, and he said quietly, "We saw Parker and Celia safely home. I rode straight back."

"You haven't eaten, then. I've got stew, pie and coffee."

He nodded, following her toward the kitchen. Alice Reed motioned him to the table, but didn't light a lamp, so he watched her in the semi-darkness as she moved to set the pan of stew back on the cookstove and pour the coffee. Dark hair, thick and curly, hung down her back, and her profile was clean and calm as she worked.

As usual, they didn't talk, but sat companionably while he ate, the faint howl of the rising wind outside the only noise. When he finished his coffee and the last bite of pie, he nodded his thanks and she smiled slightly. He helped her clear the table, and when her hand slipped into his, followed her into the bedroom.

Emma Wildes

With her three children sleeping in the next room, quiet was a necessity. The first time they'd been together, he had been disconcerted by the situation, but he was used to it now.

He undressed quickly, unbuckling his gun belt and making sure it was within reach. Alice took off her robe and prim nightdress and lay down on the narrow bed, her nude body gleaming in unspoken offering.

Just the sight of her, compliant and waiting, made him harden painfully, and he unfastened his pants with a suppressed groan and eased them down over his erect, pulsing cock.

She made love like a lady always, all soft, quiet sighs and light touches, but there was nothing ladylike about her opulent body. Her breasts were generous, the translucent skin showing a faint veining of blue, larger than ever since she was still nursing the baby she'd had last fall. He took the soft, heavy weight of one in his hand, lightly stroking. Her expression, shrouded in the dark room, went from almost wistful to dreamy as he gently touched and fondled her to readiness, knowing it was time by the way her breathing grew erratic and the urgent glide of her fingertips down his spine. When he moved over her, she opened her legs and grasped his hips, her eyes drifting shut in the darkness. John was hard as hell, throbbing, and he pushed inside the wet, warm heat of her welcoming vaginal passage with a low growl of pleasure locked in his throat.

Perhaps it was her fragile vulnerability that always made him so gentle, maybe it was because her bastard of a husband was abusive, but he moved slowly, almost reverently loving her with his body. Sexual intercourse was a matter of soft, wet sounds as he slid his cock deep inside with slow penetration, and withdrew in a delicious slide of carnal friction.

It was heaven to be inside the woman he loved. It hurt like the very devil to know he couldn't claim her because she belonged to someone else.

Her inner muscles began to contract around his possession, he could feel the tiny, subtle ripples around his rigid penis, and Alice made a small noise, no more than a low whimper as she started to climax. She clung to him, shuddering, and his heart began to pound as he felt his own orgasm rise in response.

70

At the last moment, he withdrew and held his rigid body above her as the force of his ejaculation spilled hot sperm over her stomach and ribcage. It was too soon for her to have another baby and it was the last complication she needed right now, anyway.

The entire time, they didn't say a word. But then again, there was nothing to say. She was married, and though her husband had disappeared about six months ago, Harold Reed had done that before and turned up again like the no good drifter he was. John knew she struggled during the times her husband was gone, but any offers of money had been met with quiet, dignified refusal.

He worried like hell about her, and about the children, especially because he was damned sure her last baby was his. Alice hadn't confirmed or denied it, but he'd done some figuring and if Reed wasn't such a self-absorbed, selfish drunk, he might have come to the same conclusion.

She'd named the child John, which might easily have been a small act of defiance her husband would never appreciate.

"I was worried today," she whispered so low he almost couldn't catch it. "They're saying in town Colter was trying to strong-arm your sister into marrying him and he'd paid off the judge."

He reached for his kerchief and carefully wiped his discharge from her smooth skin. "Yep, I think that's pretty damn close to the truth."

"Be careful. The man's a snake."

"Parker is the one who needs to be careful." He spoke in the same almost inaudible tones.

One slim hand lifted, very briefly, to touch his cheek. "When I saw you there, my heart froze. It's harder than ever in public, John. Maybe we should stop this."

He knew exactly what she meant, but he had no intention of stopping, not as long as he still breathed. He drew her close, his lips against her ear. "Maybe he won't come back this time."

Dark hair moved against her back as she shook her head. He could feel her despair. "Maybe he will."

"If he lifts his hand to you ever again, I swear I'll kill him. You can't ask less of me."

"Shhh." She lifted a finger and pressed it to his lips. "The only thing I have in this life is the fact I am at least a respectable woman. If you kill him, people will know. Besides, he is the father of my children. I can't wish him dead."

John stared at her and she looked away. With one finger, he tilted her face back up so she was forced to meet his steady gaze. "What am I, then?"

Her eyes glittered with tears. "The only man I have ever loved. That has to be enough."

By God, it wasn't, he thought as he slipped his arms around her and cradled her close.

It wasn't nearly enough.

℘

She woke alone, which was a definite disappointment, but then again she wasn't surprised. The sun was fairly high and Parker undoubtedly rose early—a prosperous ranch didn't run itself.

It felt odd to look around and realize this room, so starkly masculine in its plain wooden walls and simple dresser, the only decoration a patterned Indian blanket on one wall, was now the private space she shared with her new husband.

Celia rolled over and sighed, pressing her face into the linens that still held the impression and scent from his rangy body. A curious feeling washed over her and in direct reaction to the familiar masculine smell, her breasts tightened. His absence caused a twinge of regret, for she could feel the weight of the blankets on her bare skin, the softness of the downy mattress, and a sudden acute desire to be near him.

It was startling to realize after resisting the notion of being in love with calm, practical, *boring* Parker West for so long, how deeply her emotions truly ran.

He was anything *but* boring, actually. No, he hadn't courted her with flowery words, nor was he audacious and bold in his pursuit, but what she had seen as being unassertive and a little dull was simply his normal quiet and easygoing personality.

She had been exhausted, both mentally and physically, the

evening before and it was typical of Parker to let her sleep even if it was their wedding night. She hadn't intended for it to be that way. In fact, it was a little disappointing he hadn't wakened her.

What did he think, she pondered in exasperated chagrin over his consideration, that she went to bed stark naked every night? She had intended to be waiting for him, ready—and eager if she admitted the truth—to make love for the first time as husband and wife.

Now she would have to wait all day and after the sexual freedom of the privacy of the cabin, that was a frustration. After nearly a week of his constant companionship and ardent attention, she was a little spoiled.

She stretched and shook back her long hair, and finally slid out of the warm bed. The floor was cool and she quickly padded over to the basin on a small stand. The water in it was still slightly warm, which meant Parker must have brought hot water while she slept, and there was a clean towel. A trunk containing some of her clothes sat in the corner of the room. Apparently once her new husband had performed his outrageous abduction, her family had sent it over, the outcome of his wild plan not in question.

A quick wash felt marvelous, and she dressed in a plain rose-colored gown. Combing her hair and tying it back simply with a matching ribbon, she left the room and headed for the kitchen. Her mother-in-law was there stirring a pot on the cookstove, and she greeted her with the same beaming smile of welcome as the night before. "Good morning."

"Good morning." For no reason whatsoever, Celia blushed. Or perhaps there was a reason, for she had slept naked next to Rita West's son last night. Her new status as a married woman meant everyone now knew she and Parker had sexual relations. It was perfectly natural and acceptable, but still, it was a little embarrassing.

No wonder brides blushed, Celia thought as she accepted a cup of hot coffee and sank down into a chair at the wide plank table.

Mrs. West was a slender woman with dark hair just beginning to show streaks of gray and the same sky blue eyes as her tall son. The older woman wiped her hands on her apron and, with a knowing smile at the pink color of Celia's cheeks, asked in open amusement, "I take it you slept well enough, dear."

"Yes," she admitted, taking a quick sip of the steaming beverage in her cup.

"Parker was up at dawn." Rita put a biscuit on a plate with quick efficiency and ladled milk gravy over the top. "I must say he was in a right good mood for having to ride out to look at the damage the rustlers did to our fences while he was gone."

Not certain how to reply to that comment, Celia hastily drank more coffee.

"It's good to see him smiling again. After you turned him down that first time, he was pretty subdued, let me tell you." A slice of fried ham went on the plate and Parker's mother came over to slide it in front of her. "I worried a little you wouldn't come around and instead marry one of those wild cowboys always dangling after you. No matter he's a grown man, no mother wants to see her son's heart broken. He never said much, but there was simply no hiding the way he has always looked at you, my dear, so I am glad things have turned out as they have."

"I'm glad too," Celia admitted. She said with just a shade of defensiveness, "I would have said yes the first time he proposed, but you should have heard it."

Her mother-in-law sat down opposite and smiled ruefully. "That bad, was it? I'm afraid men don't understand much about being romantic, and Parker has always been so practical and steady."

"I've noticed," Celia muttered. "His new approach was entirely different."

"But effective, apparently." Rita gave her a shrewd look. "You accepted him this time."

She certain had *accepted* him in a very earthy, carnal way, but that had nothing to do with his marriage proposal. Heat filled her cheeks again and she mumbled, "Yes." Quickly she added, "Breakfast looks wonderful, thank you very much."

"Go ahead and eat, child. I'll not put you on the spot any longer."

The food did smell delicious and dismay filled her as she

picked up her fork. On a working ranch, everyone contributed and she didn't have a lot to offer as a new daughter-in-law. At home, she had helped with the various odd jobs her mother gave her, but a lot of her time had been spent out of doors. She loved to ride, and her family had indulged her. As the youngest of five, with three overprotective brothers and Rose, who was a whiz at everything domestic, she hadn't had much responsibility. Celia cleared her throat and said apologetically, "I am not much of a cook, I'm afraid."

"Oh honey, I already know that. Your mother told me. Nor a seamstress either, I hear." Rita looked serenely unperturbed. "That's perfectly fine, for if you make my son as happy as he was this morning, that's a wonderful contribution to the household. Of course," her light blue eyes held a small twinkle, "I wouldn't mind grandchildren as soon as possible. If you wouldn't balk at working on it, I would appreciate it."

She wouldn't balk at all, but it didn't seem ladylike to say so. For the third time, Celia blushed vividly.

ॐ

Parker urged Diablo along, anger seeping through his veins, making his formerly buoyant mood slowly dissolve. The big stallion stepped daintily around the ripped-out posts and bits of curled wire. The day was fine, with blue skies and wispy high clouds. The smell of sage mingled with the tang of autumn.

Next to him, his father, John Evans and Gerald Evans rode in the same angry silence. The sheer audacity of the thieves was evident, as was the fact the substantial herd that grazed in the north pasture was severely depleted. What cattle hadn't been stolen had probably wandered off, for the section of missing fence was almost a quarter-mile long.

"This is worse than I thought," he finally admitted, reining in. "What the hell? Don't they think we'll react to something this blatant? It's one thing to steal a calf here and there and brand it before we can get to it, but it's another entirely to drive so many of our stock any distance. For that you need a lot of hands. We have a lot of land to cover, but I'll hire more men to guard the fences before I lose another cow."

"Where you goin' to get them?" John asked, his hat pulled low, shading his fine features. "Colter is behind this, Parker. Both Dad and I are convinced of it, and he owns a lot of men around here. You hire someone, and they could easily already be working for him. So they take your pay and help him steal our stock. The bigger he gets, the worse this thing will fester."

"John thinks this recent upsurge in activity has a lot to do with Celia." Astride a big rawboned roan, his father looked at Parker, his eyes a little shadowed. "After what Colter tried to pull yesterday, maybe it's true. He thinks he's above the law, that he owns it and can do as he pleases. Maybe *that's* even true. You need to watch your back, son, for you have the woman he's decided he wants."

Parker felt a sort of helpless fury at the notion of having to guard his life—and his new wife—against the machinations of a man who was both a bully and coward. "I'll watch it," he said curtly. "And I'll watch her."

Gerald Evans looked at him. "You do that," he said coolly. "While I am not sure I approve of your methods in persuading her to do so, you are now married to my daughter and I have to trust you to keep her safe."

"When you try to bridle her, she'll not take the bit easy." John gave him a quick grin that lightened the grim expression on his face. "Celia is hard to curb, but then I expect you know that. She likes to ride every afternoon, and to be able to do as she damned well pleases in general. Making her stick to the house is the best way to keep her from trouble, but she isn't likely to look kindly on it."

Unfortunately, Parker was pretty sure he was right. "I'll reason with her."

Both Gerald and John burst out laughing. Even his own father looked faintly amused.

"Well, hell," Parker muttered. "I'm glad this is so funny."

"You're the one who was so hell-bent on marrying her," John pointed out, relaxed and graceful in the saddle, his mouth curving. "Don't say I didn't warn you. And it isn't funny at all, except the way the two of you deal with each other. Sorry, Parker."

Celia's older brother, had, upon occasion, pointed out her

headstrong streak. Parker agreed slowly, "You warned me, all right. How we deal with each other is my problem, I'll own it, but that aside, let's face it—Colter is unbalanced. That makes him both ruthless and dangerous. I can't tell what he might try."

Gerald Evans said gruffly, "If we stand together, we have a much better chance of catching his men at work, and maybe even get someone to talk and admit Colter is paying them and pocketing the proceeds from the stolen cattle. I think Russ and I should talk to some of the other folks who are losing stock, see if we can figure out how to stop this wholesale thieving and let us all get back to the business of honest ranching in this valley."

Parker's father nodded in tacit agreement. "I'm game."

As he gazed at the wide area of ruin and saw the few grazing animals where there had once been a sizable herd, Parker also inclined his head in agreement.

He wasn't really concerned over the missing livestock, though he supposed he should be. His concern was more for his beautiful, passionate wife.

Celia had been hard won. There wasn't much doubt about it.

Hopefully she wouldn't be even harder to keep.

Chapter Seven

The slight crackle of the fire lent a subdued noise to the background, but Celia barely noticed. Up and down she moved, her hands braced on her husband's wide chest, his hard cock sliding in and out, going so deep inside her she could not believe the sheer joy of it.

It felt too good. Despite her resolve to not make a sound, a moan escaped. A loud one.

Beneath her on his back, Parker said in terse urging as his hands clasped her waist, "God, yes, Celia, don't hold back."

"I don't want anyone to hear us." She gasped, and her body continued the urgent motion, straddling his lean hips, her need so fierce that she couldn't have stopped if her life depended on it. The bedroom door was shut, of course, but she couldn't help but wonder if the slight rhythmic creaking of the bed was audible to anyone passing in the hallway.

"No one will hear us," he promised, his good-looking face flushed with arousal and pleasure. "Ride me hard, sweetheart."

She did, not able to stop her compliance to that gentle but insistent demand. Her movements grew faster, and her heart pounded as she felt the approach of her climax. "I'm coming," she said raggedly. "Oh, Parker."

At the exact crucial moment, he thrust up hard, giving her what she wanted, the forceful penetration pushing her off the edge. She could feel her vaginal passage squeeze tight around his stiff shaft as acute pleasure washed through her, and suddenly all inhibitions were lost as she gave a low keening scream.

Parker's hands tightened on her hips and his eyes closed.

The eruption of his orgasm was an unmistakable hot flood, his cock flexing erotically as he spilled deep inside her. Dazed a little, Celia slid forward on his damp chest and sprawled in abandon on top of him. He felt so good, she thought, drifting in complete physical contentment. So hard, so male, so utterly attractive. Since he'd taught her the incredible pleasure men and women could give each other, she just couldn't keep her hands off him.

It was a little irritating because for so long, he'd been the one trailing around after her. When had the tables turned? She had practically dragged him off to bed after helping clean up after the evening meal, barely able to wait for nightfall and his return from a last trip to the corrals. Hopefully her eagerness hadn't been apparent, but she had the embarrassing notion it had been.

"That certainly made my uncomfortable state when I tried to go to sleep last night worth it," he murmured, breaking the silence of their post-coital afterglow. "It was bad enough when I would get a raging erection from just thinking about you miles away, but lying in my bed with your very tempting naked body next to mine took discomfort to a whole new level, believe me, sweetheart."

He still felt fairly hard and big between her open legs despite his recent climax. Celia lifted her head and smiled playfully at her husband, arching her brows. "You have yourself to blame for that one, Mr. West. Next time, wake me up."

One long-fingered hand caressed her back. She could feel the calloused hardness from all the work he did handling ropes and other tools, but the touch was gentle and almost reverent. Against the clean white pillowslip, his hair looked very dark and was rumpled from where she had run her hands through it. He explained in his typical logical tone, "Yesterday was a long one. You were exhausted, Celia. I'm not such a selfish brute as to not allow you a decent night's sleep."

"You think I would have minded?" She shook her head and laughed lightly at the sincere expression on his handsome face. "Good heavens, Parker, it was our wedding night and you didn't even make love to me."

His brow furrowed a little. "Like I said, you were tired."

"You are the most unromantic man sometimes."

Defensively, he said, "I was trying to be thoughtful."

As usual, she simply was unable to resist teasing him. He made it so easy with his serious nature. Celia rubbed her hand seductively across one muscled shoulder and traced the impressive bulge of his biceps. "Hmm, well maybe you were, but that doesn't change the fact that we didn't celebrate our marriage like most newlyweds. Tell me, if you weren't so darned considerate, Parker, how many times do think we would have done it?"

There was a slight wariness in his light blue eyes. The dancing light from the fire played over the clean planes of his face. "Made love?"

"Yes." She gave him an audaciously wicked look from under her lashes. "So think about it. If you had to estimate, how many times would you have fucked me?"

"Celia." His voice held exasperated reproof over her shocking language.

She ignored the censure, their bodies still intimately joined and the feel of him beneath her, and *in* her, arousing despite their recent satisfying activity. She shook back her long hair and gazed into his eyes, letting her lips tilt into a teasing, provocative curve. Her breasts were against his chest and she moved so her taut nipples rubbed his skin. "At the cabin it was often three or four times each night, not counting what we did during the day. So, I'm afraid, you see, I know that you are capable of making it up to me as I was utterly neglected last night. The way I see it, you owe me at least five."

"Five?" His eyebrows shot up. "How's that figure come to mind, Mrs. West?"

She loved the husky timbre of his voice when he was aroused and could feel evidence of it also in the slight swell of his cock within her. "Well," she whispered and leaned forward to lick his lower lip. "At least three from last night—that's a low figure, by the way—and then three for tonight. Now, we just took care of one...so that leaves five."

"I take it you are trying to kill me," he said dryly, but his azure eyes glittered suddenly with pure male anticipation. "However, I would be the last person to want our marriage to get off on the wrong foot and it would be one hell of a way to go. I'll do my best to make up for my lack of sentimental impracticality."

"That sounds fair enough," she purred, and then gasped as she suddenly found herself flat on her back, his movement so swift as he rolled over, she was unprepared.

"How do you want it this time?" he asked, rocking against her open thighs. "Slow? Or hard and fast? In case you haven't noticed, I'm nearly ready for our second go."

"I've noticed," she responded, lifting her hips and relishing the way his swiftly returning erection stretched her wide, the tip against her womb. "Believe me, I've noticed. And as for how I want it...you know how I like it."

"Hold on." He kissed her hard, with open salacious intent, his tongue suggestively twining with hers as he began to move in long strokes between her legs.

Celia sighed with pleasure into his mouth, opening wider, lifting her legs to wrap them around his lean waist, taking and giving in the same erotic measure. The palms of her hands rested on his hard buttocks and with a small thrill she felt the powerful flex as he pumped into her.

It was a little wild, it was a bit forceful, and not anything like Parker's usual unruffled calm.

It was *exactly* how she liked it.

She reveled in the fact she could make him lose control, but even more in the fact he wanted her so fiercely.

But most of all, she reveled in the fact she loved him.

శు

It was damned late and the fire had died completely away, but that didn't matter because he was so warm, the cooling air felt wonderful.

There wasn't much doubt his new wife was one wicked little temptress. Both of them panting, they lay in the wrecked bed in a tangle of arms and legs, a sheen of perspiration on their bodies. Parker wasn't sure just where he was in terms of making up his supposed neglect from the evening before, but they had to be close to their goal.

Right now, he needed a moment.

Not just physically, because he was sure Celia could get him hard again in an amazing short span of time, but he needed to talk to her and maybe this was a good opportunity. Carefully, he eased out from between her legs and propped himself on one elbow.

His wife looked more than delectable with her glorious pale hair in disarray around her slender, flushed body. Those spectacular bare breasts he so admired were a little swollen from his attentions, the nipples still erect from her recent orgasm. It wasn't surprising he could see small runnels of sperm on her creamy inner thighs and he felt a sense of pure possession and satisfaction he had branded her his so thoroughly. On her side in a languid repose, she looked a little sleepy, and maybe that would make her more cooperative.

Maybe, he thought with an inner grimace. At the best of times she was disturbingly independent.

He never had been good with the careful way he approached her, and she certainly never had any trouble letting him know it. So a direct statement seemed best. "I want you to stay close to the house for a while, Celia. No rides, no visits to town, no excursions of any kind unless I say so and send a guard."

The look of sated contentment vanished and her dark blond brows snapped together. "What?"

"I don't want Colter carrying you off."

She rose up and stared at him. "Don't be absurd, Parker. Not even he would kidnap another man's wife."

"I'm not so sure, and until I am, you need to stay right here." He'd never been so sincere, especially when gazing at her perfect, alluring beauty. Naked, her voluptuous body tinted pink in orgasmic afterglow, she was enough to take any man's breath away.

Her lovely mouth tightened mutinously. "Like hell I will. I am not going to skulk inside because of that cur. I think you're crazy, anyway. He didn't try it before, why would he now?"

"No, I beat him to it, didn't I? Besides, I know for a fact your brothers kept a very close eye on you, sweetheart."

"If he tried anything like that, Colter knows you'd kill him,

Parker."

"I would, or die trying, that's for sure," he admitted stoically, knowing he'd made his point when she blanched, some of the rosy glow fading from her smooth cheeks. "But he has a lot of men bought and paid for, not to mention the law around here. You saw what happened with the judge. That was a bit of a crazy plan, which is exactly what he is—crazy. The man is plain loco to try something so blatant. Unfortunately, he also has a lot of money and a lot of influence and he wants you bad, apparently. Let's face it, if it wasn't for John's instincts, he probably would have gotten away with it. We've never cared for each other, but I expect now he hates my guts knowing I've had you."

Uncharacteristically silent for a long moment, Celia simply looked at him, her lovely eyes showing consternation and defiance.

He played his trump card by adding softly, "You say you love me, sweetheart, well prove it and do as I've asked. Hopefully he'll be run out of these parts or hung from a tall tree for rustling before long, because John is sure he's the force behind our recent big losses and is determined to prove it. Not even a bought judge could save his neck if we have good enough evidence. It's a pretty serious crime."

"I know that," she said crossly. "I'm not a child and I've lived out here my whole life. Damn you, Parker, I hate being cooped up inside."

A flicker of triumph went through him, for the sulky tone of her voice told him he'd won. "No, you aren't a child in any way," he agreed softly, shifting so he loomed over her, their mouths inches apart. "You are a damned sexy, gorgeous woman."

Lush lashes lowered a fraction. "Am I?"

"It's been proven beyond a doubt I think so, but let me demonstrate one more time."

With leisurely thoroughness he kissed her, their mouths melding together, lips clinging, tongues brushing in small erotic strokes. He moved to her breasts, gently licking her sensitive nipples, taking the rosy peaks into his mouth, stroking the mounded flesh with his hands as he listened to the telltale sounds of enjoyment she couldn't seem to stifle. When she reached for his cock and circled him with her slim fingers, he felt a surge of sensation as he stiffened in response. As he lavished attention on her beautiful breasts, she brought him to readiness with light, sliding caresses, fondling his testicles until he groaned against her soft, satiny skin and moved between her parted thighs.

She was wet and well-lubricated from repeated intercourse and his cock slid in easily, sheathed by exquisite tight heat. Never docile during intercourse—or out of it either—Celia moaned and opened wider, her hands urgent as they pressed the small of his back. "Yes, just like that...I want every bit of you inside."

Enraptured enjoyment flooded through him as he glided backwards. Through his teeth, he said, "Believe me, I want to give you every hard inch, sweetheart."

"Then do it," she ordered, her throat arching back as he drove in deep, not shy in bed, not since that first time when he'd taken her virginity at the cabin.

Hell, even untutored and innocent, she hadn't been particularly shy in the act of sex.

Marveling at the depth of his need even after so much sexual excess, his lower body thrusting with increasing speed, Parker heard his harsh breathing in staccato gasps as his orgasm rose. Celia clung to him, matching every possessive thrust with the acceptance of her body, her eyes darkened with passion.

Her vaginal walls began to contract, gripping his surging cock. He knew so well the signs of her impending climax by now that it was easy to gauge exactly how to move and when he could let himself go. She began to shudder and moan his name and he put his arms under knees and lifted her legs, pushing in as deeply as possible.

She climaxed in spectacular abandon, and his own release was ferocious and left him numb and shaken. When he collapsed to his side, he could barely speak, but managed to say between gasps, "Am...I...still...unromantic?"

His wife laughed, a small musical sound that was entirely feminine. "Sex isn't romance, Parker."

"It is for men," he argued with a small, teasing grin, pleasantly exhausted, his senses replete. "And tonight I think

I've been very romantic, Mrs. West. Besides, I think I just finished making up for your lost wedding night."

She snuggled up to his side. "Don't be so smug. I suppose we're even, though our notions of romance aren't quite the same."

The light, curvaceous feel of her body next to his felt as wonderful as making love to her. Knowing she was almost asleep already, he tenderly brushed a stray tendril of blond hair from her cheek and kissed her forehead. "I love you, Celia. I think I was born to fall in love with you, to be your lover, to take care of you and hopefully raise our children. I would sacrifice anything to keep you safe and give my life gladly in exchange for yours."

Her eyes, which had been half-shut, flew open. After a moment, she whispered, "Heaven help me, though I believed it was hopeless, I think you were just romantic, Parker West."

With a low laugh, he gathered her closer and drifted into a contented sleep.

℥

Rose gave her a mischievous smile as they walked along the path to where the barns sat by a small grove of cottonwood trees. "John brought me over. I haven't seen you since Parker stalked up onto the porch, tied you up, and rode off. He and John were supposed to ride out early but somehow your husband overslept."

Celia murmured, "We were up late...uhm...talking."

Her sister snorted in an unladylike sound. "Yeah, talking, I bet that's what you were doing, all right."

"Maybe not *just* talking." Celia laughed.

"I'd say very little talking and more other things. Good heavens, why did you wait so long to marry him?"

In retrospect, she had no idea. Defensively, she protested, "He didn't even ask me until right before he had his wild idea— no, Ma's wild idea—to just carry me off."

Rose looked startled. "Ma told him to do that?"

A rueful smile curved Celia's lips. "So he claims and we all know Parker is as honest as the day is long."

"That's true enough. And apparently it was good advice." Rose gave her a sidelong glance.

Since she was just too contented to argue or even be embarrassed, Celia merely asked, "Speaking of such things, how is Robert?"

Robert Campbell was her sister's beau and though he was just a ranch hand, he seemed to be steadier than most of the cowboys in their father's employ, and there was little question they were smitten with each other. Rose sighed. "He wants to ask Father if we can get married but we're both afraid he'll say no. I know Josh, John and Jared like him well enough."

The morning was clear and a little cool, and the air smelled like early autumn with a delicious tinge of Indian summer. "Marry him," Celia advised, still bemused from the night before, the slight soreness between her legs the evidence it hadn't been some sort of erotic, sensual, blissful dream. "Make Pa agree. I promise you it is worth it."

"Is it?" Rose, dressed in demure dove gray, looked at her curiously. "The way Ma described it...well, it didn't sound so appealing." She added somewhat shyly, "But I do like it when he kisses me."

"Just wait until he actually takes you to bed." She and Rose had always been very close, and though she wouldn't talk about something so personal with anyone else, it seemed natural to discuss it with her sister. Celia felt an inner, secret shiver of memory. "It is indescribable. I had no idea it would be so wonderful."

Rose looked dubious, but intrigued. "It sounds...messy."

She couldn't help it, recalling the stickiness of her thighs that morning, and the absolute chaos of the bed, she laughed out loud. "It is, I'm afraid. But you won't mind a bit."

"*You* don't, that's obvious."

"How is it obvious?"

"You are glowing, Celia."

Was she? Well, she didn't doubt that. "I'm happy."

"I take it you are. Parker looks a little on the happy side

himself, even if he did seem a mite tired." Rose's smile faded. "But let me tell you who isn't happy."

It wasn't hard to guess. Celia frowned and said quietly, "John."

Her sister nodded. "I have no idea what's wrong, and it isn't just this rustling problem, Celia. He's restless and rides out often, sometimes gone the whole night. I don't know exactly how to describe it—"

"You don't have to, I've sensed it too. But you know John, he isn't likely to talk about it."

It was true, their middle brother was the most private of all of them. Celia added slowly, "I think maybe that's why he's so focused on catching whoever is stealing our stock. He wants to forget something else."

Her blond hair shining in the sun, Rose nodded. "That makes sense, I guess."

"A woman?"

"He isn't courting anyone that I know of." Her sister shrugged.

That in itself was curious when she thought about it, Celia realized. He was good-looking, steadier than most of the wild young men she knew, and yet he didn't pursue every available female in sight like other cowboys. Jared and Josh were a little legendary for their interest in the opposite sex and John used to be the same way, but over the past couple of years, he had changed.

"I'm worried about him," Celia confessed uneasily. "He's edgy and has been for some time."

"That's my feeling too," Rose agreed somberly.

The corrals were nearly deserted, but as they strolled up to look at the new colts born the night before, two men came into view. One was mounted, his horse poised on a small rise in the distance where there was a clear view of both the ranch itself and a good deal of the valley. He appeared to be just sitting there, but every once in a while he'd lift something to his eyes and scan the horizon. The other was a young cowboy, dressed for the range in chaps and boots, who leaned against the rails of the main corral. Celia didn't know him personally, but she smiled automatically. She couldn't help but wonder why he seemed to simply be loitering about when everyone else was out working, either on repairing the fences or trying to round up lost stock.

"Ma'am, miss." He tipped his hat and smiled, acting nonchalant, but there was a watchful expression on his lean, sunburned face. He was also more heavily armed than an average cowboy, even carrying a rifle for no apparent reason on a pleasant late summer morning. From his vantage point, he would have the drop on anyone riding up the main drive to the house.

It wasn't too hard to figure out, Celia mused with some irritation, that Parker really was having the ranch guarded.

No, he was having *her* guarded, and it made her feel like a bird with clipped wings.

Chapter Eight

The bastard was back.

John heard the news first from his mother, who mentioned it in passing, not having the slightest notion of his feelings for Alice.

Apparently Harold Reed had ridden into town two days before, half-drunk as usual, and the general consensus seemed to be pity for his poor wife.

He really couldn't bear to think about it and now was not the time anyway.

The night was almost pitch, with low clouds that obscured the moon and a heavy wind picking up from the north. They were in for some weather, he could smell it in the air as he crouched behind a small group of trees, most of them dead, and listened to the unmistakable sound of hoof beats grow and swell in the darkness.

Maybe this hadn't been such a long shot gamble after all.

He and Parker had ridden over what felt like half of Colorado earlier that day, and both had come to the conclusion that if they wanted to steal cattle and easily herd them south, this would be the place to do it.

Parker hadn't agreed it was a good idea to sit in the dark and wait to see if it happened, most probably because he wanted to get back to Celia. John, on the other hand, didn't have a beautiful woman who waited for him at home in a warm bed with open arms.

He had nothing but a hopeless passion for another man's wife, a child he couldn't know or acknowledge, and a helpless fury that translated to restless nights and a sick feeling churning in his gut.

Was he with her now?

John shook it off, narrowing his eyes against the shadows. He was one man against what was undoubtedly an outfit of dishonest cowpunchers who didn't mind taking the risk of hanging for money.

It sounded like perfectly good odds to him and suited his mood.

Carefully, he lifted his rifle and waited until he could see the shadowy forms loom up, a single-file line that followed the fence. One, two, three...five altogether, that wasn't so bad. With the advantage of surprise, he could handle five of them, but his real purpose was to keep one of them alive. Stealthily, he followed on foot, staying a good distance back. He had one of his usually accurate hunches about where they were headed and it wasn't far.

Sure enough, in less than half a mile, he could hear their voices, and proceeded slowly, edging along the fence line. The occasional low of a cow came from the small herd grazing still in the inadequate light, their forms indistinct.

There was not much cover, and it was a disadvantage, but he really wanted to catch them in the act. Not just trespassing, which they certainly were, but actually showing their dishonest intentions. When he did, well, they were going to get a little warning on how slinking midnight thieves were welcomed on the West ranch. He wasn't a patch on Jared on the draw, but he was one hell of a good shot with a rifle.

Suddenly the clouds tore open for a moment, giving him a clear glimpse of exactly what they were doing. Two were still on their horses, but the other three were hard at work on the fence. He could hear the snap of the wire and felt a cold fury that made his hands rock steady as he aimed his weapon. He narrowed in on the man closest, not more than a hundred yards away. The shot rang out, startling in the quiet of night, and there was a small cry as his target staggered backwards, tripped over one of his companions who was cutting the bottom wire, and fell.

Chaos broke out as the startled thieves scrambled for horses and guns, the two mounted men whirling their mounts, trying to find him in the dark. Crouched next to a thick fence post where he was probably hard to spot, John smiled grimly and fired again. One of the mounted men pitched forward and his horse cantered off, the slumped figure sliding off its back.

Two.

With the second shot, the men were able to figure out the direction of their danger. However, they had no more cover than he did, and were vulnerable because a man on a horse was a sight more visible than one on the ground. Wisely, all three seemed to decide it was better to cut and run than try a gunfight in the darkness. He got off two more shots that as far as he could tell didn't find their mark, before they vanished off in a flurry of pounding hooves in the opposite direction.

"Fucking bastards," he muttered in satisfaction, standing up. Still cautious, gun in hand, he walked over to the closest rustler, the man's prone form unmoving. In the dark, it had been a little tricky to know exactly where he'd hit him, but he hadn't aimed to kill, just to wound. Unfortunately, when he nudged the body over with his booted foot, he saw the sightless stare with resignation. The rustler had hard features with a grizzled dark beard and John did not recognize him.

It was a different story with the second man. Not only was he still breathing, he was conscious, a low moan echoing out when John knelt next to him and pulled open his vest. It looked like the bullet had caught him low in the shoulder. It was hard to see properly, but from the liquid gurgle in his labored breathing, it had nicked a lung.

"Goner?" The wounded man asked with effort, his face waxy in the gloom. He was young and fair-haired, with the reddish complexion of a range hand.

"I'd guess so," John confirmed with a curt nod, feeling a pang, because even if he had meted out justice in his mind, it was a shame someone so young had gone wrong. "You fell in with bad company, cowboy."

"It feels like...like a hoss is sitting on my chest. Gawd Almighty, I told 'em we should lay...low...for a while after the past few weeks. Ranchers were going to get riled after such...big raids."

"Told who?" John asked urgently, seeing the sudden flutter of the man's lids. "Look, it's pretty low down, stealing another man's cattle, trespassing on his property. Make it up to me by telling me who you work for. You haven't much to lose at this point."

"Nothing...to gain either, mister." The young man gave a ghastly smile. "Who are you—West?"

"No, John Evans. I'm his brother-in-law, but you haven't exactly been ignoring our stock, either. Is Colter behind you?"

A small bubble of frothy blood stained the man's lips. He stared upward, and then blinked and seemed to refocus. "Aw...what the hell. I hate Colter's guts anyway, but the money was good...yeah, I'll tell you if you give me your word you won't leave me until I'm gone. I don't fancy dyin' all alone. Don't ask me what the difference is."

"I'll stay. You have my word on it." John felt another shimmer of regret.

"Okay, it's this way... Colter hired the band in Abilene months ago. Half of us rustle the cattle, the other half drives it east. Our cut is..." A coughing fit made more blood bubble forth, flowing over his chin, but he went on. "Our cut is big, we couldn't...turn it down...man. Easy money, he promised. Hole up in the mountains, ride down for a raid now and then... Gawd, I'm so cold."

"How many of you?" Still kneeling at his side, John could see the young cowboy was fading fast.

"Must be...twenty. Most of us are wanted somewhere or other. We stay out of town." A low gasp whistled out. "Out of sight...he has more men at his ranch. His regular hands are as crooked as we are."

Shit.

"Can any of his men be bought?"

The boy nodded weakly. "Hell yes, we can all be bought. You think any of us have any loyalty to a man the likes of Rance Colter? Nah...it's...about the money."

Well, that was interesting information. "Give me a name. Anybody hate Colter and the deal he's giving us as much as you do?"

"A couple...let me think...leave a note at the saloon for Uvalde. He's decent down deep...we were pards. He's Texan...but he likes redeye a mite too much. Killed a man in a fight he doesn't even remember and now he has a price on his head."

"Will do."

"One more thing...Colter's plain loco to ruin...West. It's personal...something about a girl. Offered a bonus to anyone who can kill him. I think...thet's all...I know."

"Much obliged." John asked quietly, "What's your name, cowboy?"

Silence.

The wind whispered past, low and eerie, but the sound of labored breathing had ceased. Stiffly, John got to his feet and felt more than a little weary, though he at least had confirmation of his suspicions.

Goddamned Colter. That greedy bastard had killed this boy as certain as if he had pulled the trigger himself.

ဢ

Parker was having a fantastic dream. In it something warm and soft and infinitely smooth rested in his hand, the luscious weight stirring a light sigh of male appreciation from his chest. Silken strands of tangled hair tickled his nose, and there was a tantalizing fragrance to it, familiar and arousing. What's more, he could feel the warmth of a satiny bare bottom nestled perfectly against his groin...but unfortunately a sharp staccato of insistent sound rang in his ears and ruined the whole thing.

He opened his eyes and in that exact moment, Celia mumbled sleepily, "I think someone is knocking."

The weight in his hand was her all too-enticing breast, the curve of her body fitted closely to his, and considering he had a good start on a sizeable erection, the interruption was not particularly welcome. Hell, it was still dark outside.

"I'm coming," he grumbled, reluctantly rolled away from his lovely wife, and slid out of bed to reach for his pants. Jerking them on, he stalked to the door and yanked it open.

To his surprise, John stood there outside, looking gaunt and strained. Parker swept his gaze over haggard features, a bloodstained shirt, and registered the tense set of his brother-in-law's shoulders.

"Sorry," John said tersely. "Your father heard me ride up and let me in. He's making coffee."

That was enough. "Go to the kitchen and wait for me," Parker said with a small nod of acknowledgement, his voice low. "I'll be right there."

He found a clean shirt, ran his fingers through his hair, and smiled reassuringly as his bride sat up in a flurry of gleaming pale hair and ivory skin, an alarmed expression on her face. "Who was that?"

"Go back to sleep," he suggested evasively.

"What's so important so early?"

"I'll let you know when I find out, sweetheart."

"Maybe I should—"

"No, you shouldn't," he said firmly, knowing that if she saw how her brother looked at the moment, she would be more than just a little alarmed. "Get some rest, because with any luck, I'll wear you out later."

"Parker—"

"Stay in bed." He said it curtly, with as much authority as he could summon, and her mouth parted in surprise at his vehemence.

After a moment, she sank back down and gave him the utterly female seductive smile that made him have those arousing dreams in the first place. The blanket had fallen down around her slim waist, exposing the luscious curves of her bare breasts. Her nipples were high and pointed. "All right, if you promise to come back soon. I was half asleep, but it seems to me we were just about to start something interesting."

If he wanted anything on earth, it was to crawl right back into bed, settle on top of her lissome and desirable body, and oblige her. He managed to say in a reasonable tone, "I'll be back just as soon as I can."

Even with John bloodied and obviously bringing urgent news, it was damned hard to close the door and walk away. Parker shook his head in resignation as he went toward the kitchen. The powerful effect she had on him in the past was nothing compared to what he felt now that they were lovers. Bewitched, enthralled, captivated—he wasn't sure how to classify it, but it was a powerful combination of physical attraction and emotional commitment.

He simply couldn't imagine his life without her.

Both his father and John sat at the big table in the kitchen, the sky outside just beginning to show a touch of indigo, but he judged dawn was still an hour away. The comforting sound of the coffee just starting to boil filled the room.

Parker dropped into a chair and leveled a look at his brother-in-law. "I take it you couldn't get the idea of waiting by the north pasture out of your head. Looks like the hunch paid off. Is that your blood? Celia would have my head if we didn't patch you up right off."

"Not mine. I don't have a scratch." John had removed his hat and his blond hair was disheveled, a light dusting of a gold beard showing on his lean jaw. There were lines by his mouth that weren't usually there. "There were five of them, bold as hell. Rode right past me and started to cut the fence. I killed two of them, but one of them lived long enough to hang Colter out to dry."

The ranch was just so big, there was no way he could possibly guard every inch of it, so Parker had concentrated on placing men around the best grazing land where he had most of the stock. For whatever reason, John had been certain they would strike at a much smaller herd to the north, and apparently he had been right.

"Too bad he didn't live, if he was willing to turn over. Maybe he would have testified in court."

Parker's father said forcefully, "Little good that would have done. The word of one thief against Colter's? Not in any court around here."

"Your father's right." John leaned back a little in his chair, his blue eyes holding an icy resolve. "We're going to settle this ourselves. It's the only way. After tonight, they'll know we're fighting back. Colter has an outfit hired to do the dirty work. They stay out of town and out of sight." He paused, and then added coolly, "It seems you've got a price on your head, Parker. Besides that, the rustler swore Colter was out to ruin you."

"That lowdown slinking skunk," his father said through his teeth.

The news wasn't much of a surprise, but it still wasn't all

that wonderful to hear. "Don't tell Celia," he said quietly. "She'll think it's her fault, and indirectly it probably is. The day we were married I realized just how crazy jealous he is. He looked at her like a hungry wolf looks at a doe."

"Don't I know it." John's mouth tightened into a thin, dangerous line. "He was trailing her like a hound until she finally made it clear she wasn't interested. I'm not sure exactly what she said, but to say he didn't take to the rejection kindly is an understatement. We started to lose stock right away in significant numbers. The correlation of those two events sure stuck in my mind, and it was the first time I started to suspect he might be behind the outbreak in thieving."

"It didn't occur to me," Parker admitted, anger and apprehension clear in his voice. "But I've never liked Rance Colter, and the reaction was strictly from my gut. Maybe I did know deep down he was a sidewinder, but now it is way too personal. I don't care so much about him offering money to get someone to kill me, but he wants my wife." He looked deliberately at his father, and then John. "Let me tell you, he isn't getting her, not on God's green earth."

John nodded coolly. "You up for a fight then? Because I'm going to tell you, this is going to get worse before it gets better, Parker. Luckily, I have an idea."

He looked at his brother-in-law. "I'm all ears."

"Colter buys his loyalty. For a price, let's see if we can turn one of his men. It'll cost, but it might be worth it if things get more out of hand than they already have."

Never in his life would it have come to mind to pay a dishonest cowpoke for information, but maybe John was right. He nodded reluctantly. "You know how to go about doing this?"

John said, "Yes, indeed, I do."

๛

Celia settled onto the wagon seat and adjusted her skirts, giving her brother a curious look. "Not that I'm objecting because I'm tired of being stuck inside, but why did Parker agree to let you take me to town?"

"Most of the men are out," John informed her curtly, his blue eyes distant as he climbed up on the seat. "We need supplies and you'll be safe enough with Jared, Josh and me, I reckon. Better than at the ranch with only two or three men posted."

"I certainly should be," she retorted. "You all are packing enough hardware for a small army. Mind telling me exactly what's going on? Parker has been a little tense these past few days, though with him it's hard to tell sometimes. His father, too, is suddenly carrying a gun, even inside the house."

John slapped the reins and they rolled forward. "You know we got trouble with Colter, Celia."

"I know Parker thinks there could be. I take it you agree."

"'Fraid I do." His hat was pulled low and his profile was unnaturally stern.

It was a lovely day, one of those clear Colorado mornings when the air smelled as sweet and intoxicating as wine, and every brilliant detail of the landscape stood out in jeweled colors. The breeze was spicy with sagebrush, and the touch of it was cool and clean. Celia turned her face into it as they rumbled along, a small trail of dust in their wake.

She would be enjoying herself if it wasn't for John's grim expression and the fact her two other brothers each rode just ahead, one on either side of the buckboard. "Has something happened I don't know about?" She spoke slowly, assessing his reaction. "I mean it, John, you'd be better off not keeping secrets."

"Parker doesn't want you all upset."

"I don't give a damn what Parker wants." Celia felt a flicker of annoyance over being treated like some fragile bit of china.

John gave her a level look. "No? Well, if that's true, and I suspect it isn't, you *should* give a damn. He's your husband, and as far as I can tell, loves you enough that he'd die for you, little sister. Make sure it doesn't come to that by taking a few orders now and then. You aren't good at it, I know it full well, but you aren't stupid, either. This thing is going to get settled one way or the other. Blood is going to be spilled, mark my word. Do as he says, and the chances of it being his go way down. He's a levelheaded man in every way except when it comes to you."

It was a fairly long-winded speech for her middle brother and Celia was taken aback by his vehemence. For a few moments she stared out over the landscape, seeing the brilliant blue of the sky only abstractly. Then she said in a subdued tone, "I'd die for him, too, John."

"I bet you would, Celia, but it would be best if it didn't come to that." John had a welcome note of humor in his voice. "I've wondered more than once if Colter realizes just what he'd be getting if he did manage to make off with you. I don't do a lot of gambling, but my money might be on him trying to give you back as fast as possible."

"Very funny," she said, but couldn't help but give a small laugh.

Her brother sobered. "Actually, I wasn't trying to joke about it. I'm glad you know how to shoot straight, and even more glad you can ride like an angel."

"Do you seriously think he'd try something? I mean, I'm *married* to Parker. He must know he can't kidnap me and get away with it." She still felt disbelief over even the notion of it.

John said with chilling conviction, "All I'm sure about is that I want to be around when that lowdown coyote is strung up."

Chapter Nine

He sat on Diablo and surveyed the swale with a jaundiced eye, seeing the hoofprints where horses had trampled the ground not more than a day or so before. Instead of rage, Parker felt a calculated need for both revenge and justice.

Next to him, his foreman scratched his balding head. "Drove 'em off toward the east, boss."

"Yes." Parker gazed over in the direction his cattle had disappeared. "Okay, Leighton, let's bring the rest of the herd down. Even if we have to bring in feed, I want all the West cattle concentrated in as small an area as possible where we can at least attempt to guard them."

The older man nodded in approval and spit a stream of tobacco juice on the ground. "That'll be a mighty big undertaking for the next few days. We're talking about thirty thousand head at least."

"Not as big as it would have been last week. We're losing stock right and left."

"Same amount of land to cover, though."

"I know it." He had thousands of acres and animals scattered all over it. "We're just going to do our best. If we can get them together, at least we can keep them. As it is, this ranch is easy pickings for those rustlers. They just pick a pasture and take when they want."

"You got it. I'll spread the men out."

"Make sure they're all armed. John Evans is going to town today to stock up on ammunition. That'll send a message to Colter sure enough."

Lean and wizened, with a face weathered to the texture of soft leather, Leighton gave him a steady look. "I'm glad yer fightin' this thing. Me and the hands talked it over and if he's really behind this, Colter's dealing you a bad hand."

This wasn't exactly news, and Parker felt his lips curve in the parody of a smile. "I agree."

"He ain't going to stop easy. I've lived out here most of my life and seen his kind come and go. Crooked as a rail fence and mean as a snake isn't a good combination. On the other hand, he's pretty lily-livered, if you ask me, hidin' behind hired guns and keepin' that big ole spread of his like an armed camp."

"I know he isn't interested in an open fight."

"His kind never is." Leighton stared out across the vista and tipped back his hat. "I've seen range wars before. This ain't gonna turn out that way, take my word."

No westerner got to be Cap Leighton's age without acquiring some wisdom, so Parker raised his brows, tightening Diablo's rein just barely to keep the restive animal still. "No?"

"Nope. Range war takes two sides, and usually neither one of them is entirely wrong or entirely right. This is just really between you and Colter, boss. He's thievin', lyin' and generally fighting dirty because you took the woman he wanted. That ain't a range war, that's a personal brawl."

"Maybe so," Parker agreed grimly, "but in the meantime I have to try and protect my stock, and more importantly, my wife."

"He won't come out in the open." Leighton spat again, as if in emphasis. "If he goes after her, it's gonna be underhanded and sneaky, like a fox creepin' into a henhouse. No matter how many guns he has, he isn't up to a real battle."

"I pretty much think he's a coward myself, but until he does something—"

"Oh, he'll do something." Leighton nudged his horse with his heel and said over his shoulder, "I'm just predicting it ain't gonna be what you expect."

જી

Her mother-in-law had given her a small list and Celia dutifully picked up thread and two bolts of calico, a bag of salt, and she was in the act of reaching for the sugar when a raised voice drew her attention. She glanced up to see a tall man lurch toward the dry goods, his face drawn into a formidable scowl. He was lanky, and his clothes hung on his bony frame, while a scruffy grazing of whiskers made him look even more unkempt. A dark-haired woman with two children at her skirts and a baby in her arms watched him approach with a completely impassive expression on her face.

It wasn't her business, Celia reminded herself, but though Alice Reed might not show any emotion at the approach of her drunken husband, she had gone pale. Celia's mother had mentioned Reed had turned up again, like a persistent toothache, and it sure looked like he was hitting the liquor just as hard as ever.

"You don't need that, woman." He snatched a small package of buttons out of Alice's hand and tossed it randomly so it fell into a bin of dried beans.

"Your shirts...the children's clothes need mended, Harry—"

"I said you don't need it. Come on, let's go home. I'm hungry."

She fumbled in her pocket and produced a crumpled piece of paper. "My list...I haven't finished shopping yet...we need coffee, and—"

He cuffed her on the side of the head. It wasn't a hard blow, but it wasn't gentle either, and she staggered back a little. "Shut up. We're goin'."

One of the children, a little boy with wide eyes and a headful of curly dark hair, began to cry. Immediately the other one began to sob too, but it was clear from how quiet they kept the sound, they'd learned the hard way not to make too much noise. Mrs. Reed clutched the baby in her arms closer to her breast and looked over to where the proprietor, Tom Delarney, stood behind the counter. Celia had always liked jolly Mr. Delarney, and his plump face wore the same disgusted expression she imagined she had herself. Tom said kindly, "You just leave the list with me, Alice, and I'll get the stuff together for whenever you want to pick it up."

"Thank you." Alice held out the paper, but before Tom

101

could move to take it, Harold Reed snatched it from her fingers and ripped it into tiny pieces, letting them litter the floor. "We ain't made of money. Now move."

This time he slapped her. Maybe it was harder than he intended and in his inebriated state he couldn't judge correctly, or maybe he intended to snap her head back and send her stumbling into the counter.

Either way, Celia didn't care. There were a few other customers in the store, some of them men who might have intervened, but she was standing fairly close to the fracas. Without thinking, she moved, suddenly finding herself positioned between Harold and his now bleeding wife. "Touch her again," she said with lethal sincerity, "and I'll see to it you never have any other children, Mr. Reed, for you'll certainly be lacking the right equipment."

For a moment the loutish Reed looked surprised and taken aback by her defiant protective stance and the less-than-ladylike threat, but then his eyes narrowed into glittering slits. "This ain't your business, young lady."

"No?" Celia was so furious she could barely speak. "The moment you struck a woman holding a baby, you made it my business. You are a coward and a lowdown drunk. I can smell you from here, and it isn't at all pleasant. I suggest you leave right this minute before one of my brothers comes in. Go home, take a bath and sober up."

"The Evans boys don't scare me none, but sure, I'm goin'. With my wife." He jerked his head sideways. "Alice, move it."

"No, she's staying," Celia countered. "She hasn't finished her shopping."

"Listen, Miss Evans, you are starting to rile me."

"It's Mrs. West," she said coolly, tilting her chin and looking him squarely in the eye. "And quite frankly, I don't care about you in any way."

He raised his fist, his face contorting. Celia braced for the blow, knowing he was more than capable of doing it, though if he were sober he hopefully wouldn't ever be so foolish.

A voice rang out, cold as ice. "I wouldn't. Do it and you're a dead man, Reed."

John. *Well, it was about time*, Celia thought with relief as the man in front of her lowered his hand and went rigid.

Her brother walked slowly toward them, tall and wide-shouldered, the low jingle of his spurs audible in the sudden silence. His gaze swept over the tableau, assessing Celia's strategic position between Alice Reed and her husband, and something settled into his expression that made Celia take a deep breath. Her brother was slow to anger, but when he truly lost his temper, it was an impressive display.

"You strike your wife?" John asked between his teeth. His eyes looked like two blue chips of ice.

Behind her, Alice made a small sound, like a moan of despair. Reed blustered, "What if I did? This ain't yer interfering sister's affair, and it ain't yours, Evans."

"Like hell it isn't." John didn't take his eyes from the man, who now looked a little green under his untidy beard. "Celia, take Mrs. Reed and the children outside. Have Jared escort you to the buckboard. They'll be coming home with us. I'll be there in a few minutes."

Glad enough to obey, because she had a feeling what happened next was not going to be pleasant, she nodded. Quickly, she took the infant from Alice's shaking arms. "Come on," she said reassuringly as they started for the door, cradling the child who stared up at her with wide blue eyes. "Everything will be fine."

The corner of her mouth bleeding, Alice glanced back, trembling. "John is going to kill him. He isn't armed, I don't want—"

Celia interrupted tersely. "How can you worry over him when he treats you so terribly?"

Alice Reed looked at her with tearful dark eyes and her expression momentarily tightened. "I meant that I don't want John to be charged with murder because Harold doesn't have a weapon. Believe me, Mrs. West, it isn't my husband I'm worried over. I've been concerned all along it would come to this."

That seemed to be a strange statement. Celia looked at the child she held and took in a quick breath, seeing the shock of thick fair hair and having a sudden glimmer of what the pretty Mrs. Reed might mean.

Jared waited for them outside, an unmistakable look of

astonishment on his lean face as she emerged from the store without any purchases, but instead a bleeding woman and three children. "Mind telling me what's going on? John went in to fetch you. Where is he?"

Celia shook her head, seeing with relief the dusty street was fairly empty. "Ask him later, will you? In the meantime, go inside and make sure he doesn't kill anyone. We'll wait at the wagon."

Jared flashed his reckless smile and shook his blond head. He muttered, "I told John and Josh bringing you along was just asking for trouble."

℘

The fight had been short but satisfying.

He stood over the prone body of the man he despised more than any on this earth, and felt fury seep from his veins like a drug. Reed was no longer moving, collapsed in a tumble of fallen boxes, blood running freely from his mouth and nose. John glanced up and saw Jared a few feet away, looking nonchalant and laconic, a slight grin on his mouth. His younger brother said, "I thought you said it would be a nice, peaceful trip to town. Celia sent me in to make sure you didn't kill anyone. Is he dead? 'Cause I sure as hell don't want her mad at me."

"He's not dead," John muttered in disgust. "The drunken fool didn't even throw a punch." He glanced up and said, "I'll pay for any damages, Tom, you know that. Just add it to my tab."

Delarney ambled out from behind the counter, his sizable bulk precluding any fast movement. "Don't worry about it, son. It needed doing and if I was about twenty years younger, I'd have done it myself. You boys carry this piece of refuse out and dump him in the street, will you? I don't need him trashing up my place and bleeding all over. You get him out of my store and we're even."

"That's decent of you." John bent and grabbed Reed's shoulders and Jared took his feet. None too gently, they dragged him outside and tumbled him into the dusty street.

John looked at his younger brother and saw the open curiosity there with resignation. "Alice is going home with me. Where she belongs."

"I gathered that, somehow, from the way Celia herded them all toward the buckboard." Jared looked noncommittal, but added quietly, "I guess I'm not surprised. I knew there was someone—both Josh and I did. We talked about it, but hell, it's your private business."

"Did you see the baby?" John asked, now that the first wave of anger had passed, feeling both relieved and released now that things had come to a head. "He's mine, Jared."

"I saw him." Jared tipped his hat back. "So I'm an uncle, huh? That'll take some getting used to but I figure it's a fine thing."

"Yeah, well, the way Parker and Celia stay in bed half the day, you'd better get adjusted to it. Come on, I bought all the ammunition they had in stock. Let's get it and the women back to the ranch."

As they walked down the street, John glanced around, wondering if Colter had any other men in town. He'd guess there would be at least a few, and Celia's interference in the Reeds' quarrel would not go unnoticed.

A small smile curved his mouth. His sister was a lot of things, among them headstrong, independent and stubborn, but she had spirit and a fierce sense of right and wrong. When he had walked into that store and realized what was going on, he'd felt both furious and grateful. The way she stood there, just daring Reed to hit her, well, it might not be the bravest thing he'd ever seen, but it was damned close.

Alice sat on the seat of the vehicle, her dark eyes haunted as she watched him and Jared approach. He met her gaze head-on, and noted the small crust of blood and her swollen lower lip with as much detachment as possible. Celia sat in back with the children, still holding his son. He saw from her speculative look that she just might have figured a few things out.

Good. It saved him an explanation. He'd have enough of those when he arrived home and told his parents what was going on. He didn't have any doubts that his mother and father would welcome Alice and the children, but he'd been keeping secrets a long time.

That was all over.

Without a word, he climbed up next to Alice as Jared and Josh swung onto their horses. Then he gently slapped the reins and they moved forward.

Between getting to beat the hell out of Harold Reed and his brief meeting with the young outlaw who worked for Colter, it had been a satisfying afternoon.

๏

Parker rubbed his forehead in frustration. "I'm not precisely angry, Celia."

"You act angry." His beautiful wife unbuttoned her gown as she spoke, her slim fingers slipping each fastening free. "Or as angry as I've ever seen you save for at our wedding, though I can't figure out why. Since you rode in, you've barely spoken to me."

He watched her slip her dress off her shoulders as she readied for bed. "I'm bone tired from herding cattle all day. Then I come in to hear you were involved in some confrontation in town in which you actually could have been hurt. I agreed you could go because your brothers would be with you, looking out for things. I guess I thought you'd have the sense to stay out of trouble. Obviously giving my permission was a bad idea."

Clad only in her lace-trimmed shift, Celia tossed back her loose hair and gave him a furious look. "Don't act like I'm some sort of child you have to be responsible for, Parker West. And for your information, Harold Reed was slapping his wife around in front of me while she was holding a baby. Her children were crying, and he'd hit her so hard her mouth was bleeding. I hate to disappoint you, but I was not going to just stand there."

"He could have done the same to you, Celia. He's a mean drunk, and he's a hell of a lot bigger than you are. If he hurt you, I'd have to go after him, and I've got to tell you, I have a feeling there's going to be plenty of killing without throwing in another feud on top of it."

"I can fight my own battles, don't worry. If he *had* hit me, it probably would have been the mistake of a lifetime. As it is, I suspect John more than took care of the problem."

As usual, riding herd on a bunch of ornery cows was nothing to managing his lovely spitfire of a wife. When he heard what happened, he couldn't help but admire her nerve, but most certainly was unhappy over the fact she'd stepped straight into the path of an abusive bully. Every time he thought about it he got angry again because her impulsiveness frightened him to death.

He loved her too much to let anyone harm a hair on her head, and worrying over Colter was bad enough.

"Until further notice, that's your last trip to town," he said with imprudent authority. "Don't even bother to ask me."

Half-undressed, with the glory of her unbound hair in a golden mass around her face and bared shoulders, Celia gave him a glare that rivaled a cornered mountain lion. "Go to hell, Parker. I'm your wife, not your prisoner."

He was glad their bedroom door was firmly shut, and hopefully his parents were already asleep down the hall and couldn't hear the argument. "If I have to keep warning you about your language, sweetheart, you're going to regret it." He sat down in a chair to take off his boots.

"If you think you're sleeping here, think again," Celia informed him, her cheeks pink with affront. "I'm not interested in bedding down with a narrow-minded ogre who treats me as if I haven't a lick of sense."

Unperturbed, he neatly set aside his boots and proceeded to unfasten his shirt. "I'm sleeping right here with you."

"I'm sure they'd welcome you in the bunkhouse." Her tone was saccharine with sarcasm.

"I'm sure you'll welcome me just fine, my sweet wife."

"I'm not going to fuck you, if that's what you're thinking. Right now, I don't even *like* you." She stood on the other side of the bed, her chin tilted upward and her blue eyes flashing fire.

God, she was beautiful and desirable as hell.

God, she had quite a sassy mouth.

"You really love to push me, don't you?" Parker jerked his shirt off over his head, leaving it half buttoned. "And for your information," he dropped his tone to a husky, suggestive whisper, "you don't have to like me for it to feel good."

He had really thought he was too damn tired to make love to her, but his cock had decided otherwise the minute she had started to undress. He was hard, pulsing, and when he deliberately shoved his pants down his hips, it jutted upward in an obvious declaration of his intentions.

"Will you force me?" She eyed his rampant erection. "Because I'm not interested, Parker."

Like hell she wasn't, and he didn't miss the flicker of excitement that crossed her face, no matter how much she tried to hide it. From past experience at the cabin, he knew she liked it if he acted like he was going to give her no choice, though he was sure she knew down deep he wouldn't make her do anything she didn't want to in bed. "I might," he lied, moving around the bed in slow steps. "Are you going to fight me?"

"I'll scream," Celia informed him, backing up as he advanced.

He grinned. "I know. You always do."

"I mean it. Your parents will hear."

"That's fine with me. What? Do you think they'll come running? I doubt it, not if our bedroom door is closed." He crowded her into the corner on the other side of the bed and placed an arm on either side of her shoulders. "You see, sweetheart, as your husband, I've got certain rights."

That infuriated her, but he had known it would. Celia shoved at his bare chest and looked adorably irritated. "You can be an arrogant ass, Parker West, though most people don't see it."

In response, he captured her hands and pushed them up above her head, his body pressing hers against the wall. He rubbed his stiff cock against the warmth and softness of her body through her chemise and inhaled her fragrance. Lowering his head, he whispered suggestively in her ear. "I bet you're already wet, Celia."

She kicked him in the shin, and he winced, but didn't let her go. Instead he transferred her slim wrists to one hand and with the other delved beneath the short hem of her shift. She squirmed in resistance and made a small sound as his fingers slid between her legs.

Sure enough, she was wet, hot and ready. He slipped two fingers all the way in, exploring her vaginal passage with leisurely thoroughness, amused and aroused as she parted her thighs even as defiance sparked in her gaze. "Go fuck yourself, Parker, and leave me alone."

Okay, well if the lady wanted outrageous language and the pretense of resistance, he'd give it to her.

"No thanks, I'd rather fuck you," he said calmly, and in one swift movement picked her up and deposited her on the bed. She tried to roll away but he caught her easily and settled on top of her, using his weight to keep her pinned to the bed while being careful not to crush her in any way. Celia gave him a mutinous look, but her cheeks were flushed becomingly, and he could feel the tight points of her nipples against his chest through the thin cloth of her chemise.

He kissed her lightly, and then nuzzled the side of her neck as he bunched the material of her shift around her waist. "You want it, sweetheart, let's face it. Hard and fast in that tight, wet pussy of yours, my cock pushing in as deep as possible, and you taking it like you always do, to the hilt. We both know you're going to come for me over and over, and I am more than happy to give you what you like so much."

Finally, he'd shocked her a little, for her eyes widened.

Parker smiled with dark purpose. "Spread your legs. Why make us both wait?"

"No," she said faintly, but it was the merest protest and her lashes drifted downward as he easily pushed her thighs apart with his knees and positioned himself.

At the first plunge, she gasped and arched. His cock found heat and heaven, and he felt the wash of pleasure like a warm, enchanting tide. He began to move, at first slowly, but there was something about the frantic lift of her hips that spoke volumes about what she needed and he was just the man to oblige her.

The only man, he reminded himself as he drowned in sensation.

Heated, urgent and captivatingly passionate, Celia moaned with each thrust. For someone who had supposedly felt resistance to the idea of lovemaking, she certainly seemed to be enjoying it. Parker hadn't any doubt in the first place of her capitulation. It was a decided bonus in marrying someone with her fiery personality.

If every argument ended this way, he wouldn't mind a little spat now and then at all, he decided as he felt the riveting rise of his orgasm. Beneath him, his beautiful wife responded to his penetration with complete surrender and her usual uninhibited recklessness.

"Parker," she breathed as the first tremor of her climax began.

The exquisite contractions of her inner muscles as she began to quiver and arch took him the last step, a searing burst of pleasure assaulting his senses as he emptied into her in a forceful, red-hot rush. Gasping and spent, he rested his forehead against the silken skin of her shoulder and felt the thrumming of his heart finally begin to slow.

Celia's fingers slid through his hair in light strokes. "That was a dirty, rotten thing to do, Parker."

A faint smile tugged at his mouth and he lifted his head. "How so?"

Her blue eyes were full of reproach, but she continued to toy with his hair, sifting through the wavy strands. "You can't use sex to win an argument."

"All right." He kissed her, slow and sweet, his lips moving softly against hers. "We can pick up right where we left off, if you'd like. Or, better yet, we could take off the rest of your clothes and make love again."

"I thought you were tired."

"I thought so, too."

Celia squirmed a little against his hips, his half-rigid cock still inside her. "I suppose we could discuss your despotic ways in the morning." Her smile was pure teasing coquetry.

He licked her upper lip with a seductive glide of his tongue. "You like it when I'm despotic."

"Sometimes." Her lashes fluttered a little. "I know I like it when you fuck me like you just did."

"Sweetheart, what will it take to rein in your language?"

She laughed, sliding her hands luxuriously up his back. "I don't think it's possible, Parker."

"Is that a challenge?" As always, her striking beauty mesmerized him, and her sensuous nature made him feel humbled by his good luck. "You definitely need a firm hand. I might just plant mine on your tempting backside the next time you choose to cuss like a grub-line-riding cowboy."

"That," his lovely wife said with a mischievous grin, "sounds like it could be fun."

Chapter Ten

The acrid smell was the first sign of disaster on an otherwise calm summer morning.

Running from the kitchen, Parker's mother gestured frantically toward the corrals. "Fire! Celia, quick, grab a bucket. The barn is on fire!"

It had been dry lately, and something like that didn't bode well. Celia dug out two buckets they used for carrying water for washing dishes and hurried outside. What she saw made her heart freeze, for not only did smoke billow from the big barn, but it looked like the bunkhouse was also engulfed in flames. The two little buckets she held seemed ridiculous compared to what was happening, but she dashed to the well, just the same.

The horses trapped in the burning building were screaming, she realized, the shrill sounds rising above the distant roar of the flames.

Oh God.

"I'm going to free the horses," she shouted, and shoved a bucket toward Parker's mother. The older woman said something back, but she didn't hear it as she ran toward the blazing building.

The haze of smoke made it impossible to see what exactly was happening, but she needed to reach the frightened animals. Running, eyes streaming as she got closer, she wondered where the men Parker had left on guard duty were.

In a moment she had her answer.

She tripped over one of them and went sprawling, the bucket in her hand going flying. For a moment she was stunned, and then Celia scrambled to her feet and stared at the prone body of the man lying in front of the barn doors. He was young, his face turned away, and she saw the glassy reflection of his open eyes.

Dead. Her mind registered the word even as she emotionally rejected it.

A great gust of smoke whirled around her and the crackle of the flames brought her out of her stupor. Whatever was happening, she suddenly knew the two buildings were not on fire by accident. She stooped and gently eased free the knife still strapped to the young cowboy's lean waist, touching him with reluctance. His gun was nowhere in sight, so probably whoever killed him took it.

Maybe Parker had been right all along. This certainly seemed a bold frontal attack.

Armed with the knife, she eased toward the barn doors, only to find a second man there, half-propped against the building, his head hanging on his chest. She could see the crimson dribble of blood soaking his shirt and a small sob caught in her throat.

With effort, she stepped past and frantically tugged at the bar holding the doors closed. Inside, it was chaos, with the animals kicking at their stalls and whinnying. She could barely see, but moved to open the doors, trying to stay out of the way as they thundered out toward freedom. Luckily, Parker pastured most of his horseflesh, and there were less than a dozen animals to free, but Diablo was among them and she knew he would be heartbroken if anything happened to the stallion. The big black was in one of the last stalls and he bolted the minute the door was opened, clattering outside in a wild flurry of flying hooves.

Her lungs felt as if they would burst, and Celia staggered back outside in the wake of the last escaping horse.

It was surreal to emerge into fresher air, and she coughed, stumbled and tried to blink away the burning in her eyes.

A shout drew her attention. There were riders, she realized, at first with a stab of relief, and then with a jolt of fear. She swiped at the smoke-induced tears on her cheeks and registered these were men she'd never seen before. They rode dark horses, and as they spotted her, they spurred their mounts her way.

In a haze of panic, she turned to run. She made it past the corral before she heard the thunder of her pursuers right behind her. There was no place to go, she realized in despair, for the long lane was open and made her easy prey.

In minutes, she was surrounded.

Chest heaving, she stood in the crowding circle of the riders and counted at least six men. "What do you want?" She managed to ask it in a thin, breathless voice.

One of them, burly and bearded, with flat dark eyes and a red bandana around his thick neck, spoke up. "Jest for you to come on a little ride with us, ma'am."

"No, thank you." Celia gave him a level stare, trying to catch her breath. "Go back to whatever hole you inhabit and tell Rance Colter to go to hell."

"You can tell him yerself, if you'd like, Mrs. West." He slowly dismounted. "Come on, now, I'd jest as soon make this easy on you."

Well aware of the amused gazes of the other men, most of which gave the impression of seedy dishonesty, Celia felt the weight of the knife in her hand with a little comfort, though not much. At the moment, her hand hung at her side, the weapon concealed in the folds of her skirts.

"What are you," she asked contemptuously, "procurers for a man without the guts to do anything himself? You stack the deck, don't you? Six men to capture one woman?"

The big man narrowed his eyes a little. "We git paid well, that's all we care about."

"To murder innocent men, burn down buildings like cowards and condone rape?"

His face reddened a little and he reached out to take her arm roughly. "What happens to you after we take you to Colter ain't our concern."

"Isn't it?" Stalling for time, Celia tried to shake off his grip. "Unless you sprang out of a pile of horse dung, which is possible, you had a mother once, maybe even a sister. Would you take one of them to him and leave her there?"

One of the men was younger than the rest, not so hard looking, and glanced away as she deliberately raked the group with her scathing gaze. His discomfort showed at least a modicum of decency, but he was in the minority.

The stocky outlaw pushed her toward his horse, none too gently. "Mebbe it would be best if you kept yer pretty mouth shut."

The push, which sent her almost staggering into his horse, made her furious. She was past being frightened. Even now she could hear the roar of the fires as they consumed the two outbuildings. The abduction seemed a continuation of the nightmare.

She needed to do something to stop this.

Parker loved her. It wasn't simply desire, it wasn't merely their undeniably electric physical bond, it was emotional and deep and as essential as breathing.

If it was in her power, she would not allow him to suffer knowing she had been kidnapped. For he *would* suffer, horribly, and as sure as the sun came up in the morning, he'd ride straight to Colter's ranch, probably getting himself killed in the process.

The bearded man grasped her waist and hefted her onto his horse.

At the same moment he grasped the saddle horn to mount up, Celia leaned over and sank the blade of her weapon deep into his brawny shoulder.

He screamed and cursed, the sound giving her a small thrill of primal satisfaction. In a flash, she grabbed the reins and dug in her heels, scrambling to get a better seat as the animal took off in startled reaction. She was nearly thrown out of the saddle, but managed somehow to hang on, the stirrups dangling wildly as the horse plunged away.

If there was one thing she could do, it was ride. In moments, she found the stirrups and leaned over the neck of the outlaw's horse in encouragement as she guided it at a full run away from her captors. At least some of them came after her, for she could hear the sounds of pursuit, but she had two advantages. She was light, and the burly outlaw had a big brute of a horse, rawboned but muscular. The second was she had ridden over to the Wests' so often before her marriage, she knew the land like the back of her hand.

In fact, it felt good to feel the lash of the wind, the wild flick of the horse's mane against her neck and cheeks, and see the ground flashing by beneath them. Without hesitation, she rode west toward the nearby river and its concealing line of cottonwoods and oaks. There was only one decent place to cross it, and if she could get out of sight long enough, they might get delayed looking for a way over.

Anything, she thought grimly, to escape Colter.

Daring a swift backward glance over her shoulder, she saw with a glimmer of hope that the closest of her pursuers was a fair way back. Still uncomfortably close, but not breathing down her neck either.

Yes, she could definitely lose them.

Exhilarated, Celia sent the horse recklessly down a small ravine and up the opposite side in a full gallop. Behind her someone shouted and she urged her mount to veer toward the left, avoiding uneven ground.

Disaster happened in the form of an unseen hole. The big horse hit it with his right front leg and went to his knees in full stride. Celia barely realized what happened before she was pitched from the saddle, the world turning crazily as she flew through the air. She hit the ground hard enough that the breath left her lungs in a gasp, and for a moment everything went black.

Hell, she thought hazily as she fought the horrible sensation of not being able to breathe.

ဆ

Tightlipped and grim, Parker stared at the smoldering remains of the bunkhouse, but his mind was elsewhere. His heart felt like it was squeezed in a vise. "Jesus, I thought I was being careful. Four men are dead and my wife is missing."

His mother looked at him, her face still streaked with soot, her red-rimmed eyes brimming with tears. "When I realized what was happening, I went inside for the shotgun. When I came out, I saw her riding away." She added in a whisper, "They went after her."

Not violent by nature, he fought the urge to plunge his fist through the one wall still standing, the wood charred and smoking. "I'm going to kill him."

His father slipped his arm around his mother's trembling shoulders in an unspoken gesture of comfort. "Maybe she got away, son."

"If she did, where is she? This happened hours ago." There was no way Parker could keep the bleakness from his voice—it just wasn't humanly possible.

"Boss, jest stay calm. We can track 'em if we hurry." Cap Leighton rubbed his grizzled jaw. His pale eyes reflected outrage. "Still plenty of light left."

He had to do something, make good steady decisions, and in his whole life that had never been a problem. Now, when he needed a clear mind, all he could do was feel a terrible despairing panic. He dragged his hand across his face and took a deep breath as he looked at his father. "You and Cap take half the hands and try to track her and the men who went after her. I'm going to where she's likely to be."

"If you ride straight on over to Colter's place, he'll be more than happy to make your wife a widow." His father had deep lines around his mouth, making him look a decade older. "You can't go there and face him head-on. You know you won't make it anywhere close to the house. He'll be expecting you, Parker, and he'll be ready with an ambush. That won't help Celia, just the opposite."

"What the hell else you expect me to do?" Usually he watched his language very carefully in front of his mother but at this particular moment, he didn't even bother to apologize. "I can't wait around trying to figure something else out. I don't have the luxury of time, and we all know it. If Colter is crazy enough to set fires and have another man's wife kidnapped, he's capable of anything."

Dear God, he couldn't bear to think of Celia being brutalized. It made him physically ill, and he couldn't afford to feel that way at this moment.

"That girl has a lot of spunk," his mother said softly. "Don't sell her short, Parker. Whatever Colter has in mind, she isn't going to make it easy for him. Endangering your life needlessly won't make her happy."

"Maybe not," he acquiesced painfully, "but we all know she is one woman in what is virtually an armed camp, Mother, and I love her. I have to go after her. It isn't a choice."

His gut clenched again and he turned to Cap. "You get your men and go. Tell the rest of the hands we're riding out immediately and to bring as much ammunition as they can carry."

"You got it, boss."

"Send word to the Evans ranch. You know they'll stand beside you." His father gave him a sympathetic but steady look. "The delay will chafe, son, but take as many men as you can."

He'd done so already, having dispatched one of his hands the minute he saw the smoke rising as they rode in back from the range.

"I won't wait long," Parker said curtly. He added with despairing sincerity, "I just can't."

℘

Celia sat on the edge of the chair and tried to stifle a wince. Her hands were bound, her feet were tied, and she was locked away in what looked like an unused storage room. Other than the chair she sat in, it was bare except for a dusty floor. The walls were adobe and looked thick, and the ceiling low.

Not a very heartening prison, but better than Rance Colter's bedroom. It wasn't promising just the same.

Luckily, the damage to her person from her precipitous fall seemed to be mostly superficial. Her dress was torn and dirty, and she had a significant scrape across one shoulder, but she had hit a patch of scrub grass and at least not broken any limbs, or worse, her neck.

What she wanted to do was cry or scream. Neither seemed productive. The ache in her injured shoulder throbbed in time with her heart.

The rattle of the key in the door made her look up. The creak of the hinges sounded like a shriek in the otherwise complete quiet.

Colter.

He stepped into the room and she fought a shudder of revulsion. Since his men had dragged her off, she hadn't yet seen him, and his presence filled her with an intense loathing. The glitter in his dark eyes as his gaze swept over her didn't bode well for what came next. "Hello, Miss Evans."

Her chin came up in a gesture of obvious disdain. "That's Mrs. West."

"Not for long." As usual, the rancher wore the latest style in trousers and waistcoat, his step into the room a slight swagger. Even his boots held a high shine. He wore his hair a little long, like a fancy gambler, and his olive skin held a flush, as if the success of his scheme excited him.

Why wouldn't he look triumphant and self-satisfied, she thought bitterly. Here she was, tied up like a prize steer and at his mercy.

If he even had any.

"You rash little fool," he remarked, looking at where her shoulder was bared by her torn dress, "you could have been hurt trying to get away."

"I *was* hurt," she responded pointedly. "Notice the blood? Maybe you could summon the decency to untie me and send someone with water so I could at least wash it off."

"Once a few things are settled," he said with a meaningful, unmistakably salacious look. He openly studied her breasts beneath the thin material of her gown. "I'll make sure you are taken care of in every way. Right now, it's best if you stay put here, out of the line of fire."

"Parker's going to kill you."

"There's no way he can get past my men."

Celia let her lip curl in a small, scornful smile. "No? We'll see."

"Yes, we will. I'll win. Money always does, make no mistake." He sauntered closer, and she felt ill from the way he stared at the skin exposed by her torn dress. Even his hired lawless thugs hadn't ogled her the way he did. "When Parker West is dead, you'll be free and clear."

She laughed, even though a chill ran up her spine at his statement. "My husband won't be that easy to kill, Colter."

"Really? I figure you'll learn how wrong you are here in a little bit. I'm expecting him to arrive any time."

"Maybe," she responded, looking him in the eye. "This is an uncertain part of the country. Sometimes things don't go according to the way men expect."

He leaned in close, so close she could smell the whiskey on his breath. She recoiled, but he grabbed her chin and forced her to look at him. "Let me tell you what to expect, you haughty little bitch. Tonight you're going to lose some of that uppity air, believe me. I'm going to use you like a half-breed whore and no one is going to stop me. Remember when you told me you would never consider marrying me? Well, I'll just take what I want from you anyway. It isn't like you aren't a soiled little dove. You've been spreading those pretty legs for West, so I'm sure he's got you well broke in. I'd rather have been first, but I'm looking forward to this just the same."

It wasn't like she had any illusions over the purpose of the abduction, but that flat declaration made her feel sick. The nausea became acute when Colter let go of her chin and instead cupped her breast through her gown. He squeezed, watching her expression, and she returned the look with stony hatred.

"I'll be back," he vowed and stalked out.

The sound of the door closing brought relief he was gone and an acute dread for what might happen next. She wasn't even all that worried about the disgusting threats her captor had just made, for in truth, if something happened to Parker, she wasn't sure she wanted to live.

Please be careful, she prayed, shutting her eyes tightly, fighting the hot sting of tears.

Please.

I love you so much.

∞

John squinted at the sunset, oblivious to the glorious rosy hue spreading across the horizon except that it signaled the coming dusk.

Perfect.

The lone horseman trotted up and slid off. He didn't offer his hand, but his nod was brief and said it all. "She's tied up and stuck in one of the ranchero's old rooms. It's at the back, on the left side. The door is locked, but it's old. He isn't worried about her escaping."

A muscle twitched in John's jaw. "Has Colter touched her?"

The cowboy, young, sandy-haired and obviously Texan from his accent, shook his head. He had a hungry look in his eyes, but hadn't quite acquired that ruthless air that characterized so many outlaws. "Not in the way you mean. He went in there for about five minutes." His mouth curved in a humorless smile. "Surely even a dog like him would take longer than that. Besides, I was outside the door the whole time. They just talked."

"I bet that wasn't a pleasant conversation." John relaxed a fraction. "I know my sister. When she's mad, she's like a West Kansas tornado. Anyone with smarts will get out of her way."

The young man, who had only given the name Uvalde in their previous dealings, laughed shortly. "Yeah, I noticed that. You should have seen her face us all down. Then she stabbed Moze, who's three times her size, and if her horse hadn't fallen, would've gotten clean away."

"Is she hurt?"

"Scraped up a little." Uvalde glanced at the scarlet sky, his profile melancholy. "Tonight ain't going to be pleasant for her if you don't get her out. I admire her pluck, but Colter's gone to a lot of trouble to make sure this all happens his way."

It was something John already knew. "Explain to me exactly where she is."

Uvalde nodded and dropped down, finding a small stick and sketching a diagram in the dirt. In the fading light it was a little difficult to see, but John memorized it.

He glanced up. "Do I need to know anything else?"

"There's a sharpshooter on the roof. Name's Henderson. He's good. If you take him out, it's gonna make things a lot easier for West and his boys. He's right here." He pointed out the location.

Considering Jared and Josh were both riding with Parker, not to mention their father, it was good information to have. Of course, once John started shooting, it would be pretty obvious he was on the opposite side. It was risky, but then again, he'd known it would be. "Much obliged."

The young man gazed at him with somber eyes. "This ain't my kind of deal, and most of the hands—good men or bad—feel the same way. Stealin' stock is one thing, but I was raised to respect women. Your sister's only fault is to be too pretty for her own good. Most of the men think Colter's a coward. They ain't going to hold over this."

"Both Parker West and I are banking you're right."

"I can see where you might not trust me easy. I'm wanted in two states." Uvalde swallowed convulsively and looked away. "I'm not proud of it. Who would be? But deep down, I'm still decent. I hope you get her out. I also hope Colter hangs. If anyone deserves it, he does."

John hoped to hell the young man was sincere. "We'll handle the money as agreed, when she's back in our hands safe and sound."

"Nope." The young outlaw shook his head decisively. "I've thought about it. I'm doin' this on my own hook. Double-crossing Colter feels right to me. Taking money for it doesn't. Tell West I'd like a job. A good, decent job riding cattle. If he's willing to forget what's happened, that'll be enough for me."

"To get his wife back unharmed, I'm banking he'd give you almost anything you asked for."

"They say he's a fair sort."

"Sure is," John confirmed, taking off his hat and handing it to the other man. "He really loves her."

Uvalde gave him an undecipherable look. "Maybe something like that will come my way someday if I can make a fresh start." He took off his own hat and put on John's.

"Maybe, cowboy. At any rate, as long as we live through this, I think you can count on a job and that second chance." John pulled out his rifle and checked both his revolvers. Then he mounted the other man's horse. As a disguise, it wasn't much, but he figured they were about the same height, both wore dark shirts, and the hat shaded his features. Riding the outlaw's horse, he might just pass for Uvalde and get inside unnoticed. "West and his men are waiting about a half a mile away, behind that ridge." John pointed in the right direction. "Tell him to give me a small head start before they ride up and start shooting."

Uvalde nodded.

John thought about Alice, waiting for his return, and his sister, tied up somewhere and despite her usual spirit, probably deeply frightened. He added somberly, "Also tell him not to get himself killed."

"Will do."

℘

The knife slid cleanly between her wrists and the rope miraculously fell away. Celia rubbed her chafed wrists with relief and felt like sobbing with joy. "John."

He'd never been particularly demonstrative, but his arms slid around her briefly in a tight hug. "You hurt?"

"No." For a moment she let her head rest on his shoulder. It felt solid and safe.

"Good. Come on, now, steady up. We've got to move because all hell is about to break loose."

Even as he spoke, the first report of gunfire rang out. Her brother grabbed her hand and shoved his revolver in it. "You know how to use this, Celia. I may need you."

She nodded, hearing more shots, her stomach clenching in both fear and worry. Silently, she followed her brother through the door, grateful to be out of the dank little room. It was almost dark, she saw, and as they edged along the side of the building, most of the commotion seemed to be to their left. Rifle in hand, John led her to the edge of the wall.

In front of them was the courtyard, the ranch house built on three sides around it in a Spanish hacienda style. Once there had been a fountain and a small pool, but the pool was dry and the tiles crumbling. There was no actual gate any longer, but an opening that was still easily defended, because anyone trying to come through it was fair game. On either side of the entrance, several men crouched on the thick walls, just waiting for a clean shot at the approaching rescue effort. They had their backs to Celia and John, and it would be simple to kill a few before the others realized what was going on, but once they did, they would be vulnerable as hell.

"Hold on," John said so quietly she almost couldn't hear it. "They haven't rushed it yet. That's good. Parker's keeping his nerve. Don't move. I'll be back."

"John—"

"I'll be back, Celia, I swear it. Just stay put."

In the fading light, she could see a faint sheen of sweat on his face. He boldly stepped around the side of the building. If any of the men guarding the wall had turned around, they would have seen him, but they were riveted on whoever was firing at them from the other side of the courtyard wall. John walked about ten yards, and then he threw his rifle up, steadied it at his shoulder, and shot.

She saw a man pitch from the roof of the structure across the courtyard to go sprawling on the ground.

John was right, at that moment, all hell broke loose.

Several of the men turned, startled at hearing gunfire so close behind them. Her brother dove for the broken fountain, found cover, and began to shoot. Exposed and susceptible from an inside assault, men scrambled to get out of the way, and suddenly Colter's front wall defense was no more.

The riders came through fast, the thunder of dozens of animals clattering through the entrance filling the air. Parker was in front—Celia would recognize the gleam of his dark, wavy hair anywhere, even in the semi-darkness, and Diablo was unmistakable. Shots continued for what seemed like forever but probably was only a few minutes. The entire courtyard was a melee of plunging horses and shouting men. She still held John's gun and would have fired, but it was impossible to tell friend from foe.

The sudden quiet was eerie and the acrid smell of gun smoke drifted in the air. Shaken, Celia scanned the scene with numb apprehension. Where was her husband? John...

A hard hand clamped over her mouth. "Here you are," a voice hissed in her ear. "You are one troublesome little bitch, Miss Evans. The good news is, while I still have you, I hold the upper hand."

She didn't even think about it. Her elbow came back sharply, catching Rance Colter in the gut with as much force and pent-up desperation as she could summon. He grunted, and in the moment his grip loosened, she turned, shoved the gun into his chest and pulled the trigger at point-blank range.

Epilogue

"I'll race you." The challenge was both breathless and laughing.

Parker shook his head, eyeing his wife's beautiful face. Her cheeks were flushed, and her blue eyes sparkled. "No. Sweetheart, you're pregnant. You promised to be careful."

Her mouth formed a disappointed moue. "You are so damned cautious, Parker. I'm not going to fall, don't worry."

It was a gorgeous day, a warm touch of Indian summer amidst the chill of the approaching winter. The Rockies were golden with the changing aspens. Their horses ambled along a path by the river, and he, for one, was feeling a level of happiness he still wasn't sure was humanly possible.

"I do worry," he said without apology. "Humor me."

Celia gave him a look that sported defiance. "I'm not incapacitated. I'm just going to have a baby."

"I know." His smile was pure male pride.

"Don't look so smug."

"I'm not sure smug is the appropriate word." It actually could be, though. He felt so pleased with life it frightened him. "I'm..."

"What?"

"Happy," he finally supplied. It was simple maybe, but right on the mark.

Celia's lovely face softened. "Me, too."

He cocked a brow. "So, we're agreed? No race. A nice ride is just as good."

Tossing back her golden hair, his wife gave him a meaningful sidelong look. "Well, that depends. A nice ride *can* be just as good. It's pretty private here."

There wasn't any mistaking her sexual innuendo. In fact, since they had discovered her condition, she'd been insatiable.

It wasn't like he was going to object. "There's a grassy spot up just ahead."

Why wasn't he surprised she urged her horse to a gallop and pulled up before him. Even before he could slide from the saddle Celia had dismounted and started to undress. Her breasts, fuller now with the promise of the coming child, showed pale as she unfastened her bodice. "Oh Parker," she breathed, "hurry. I need you."

He obeyed, hearing the urgency in her request with an inner welling of desire that seemed to flood every nerve ending. His cock was erect in seconds, and when she lay down on her back and lifted her skirts, he felt as if he had suddenly been lit on fire.

Still booted, with nothing more unfastened than his trousers, he joined her and moved between her parted thighs, relishing the pleasure, the consummation and the communion of not just their bodies, but their souls.

He kissed her in the aftermath of orgasmic bliss, and thanked the stars, the moon and the God he had never been sure existed before now, for his good fortune. Their mouths melded tenderly, and he felt the unexpected sting of tears, hot and fierce.

"I love you," he whispered, in her and over her. "You and our child. It's too..."

"...much?" she supplied, caressing his cheek. "I know."

"I'll always feel this way." He knew it to be true.

Her eyes gleamed. "I'll be fat soon."

"So?"

"Extremely fat."

"Beautifully fat." He smiled. She would never allow him a minute of boredom in his entire life. Of that, there was no question.

"You'll still want to fuck me?" Her angelic expression belied her deliberately shocking words.

"Your language leaves something to be desired, Mrs. West."

"Oh yeah? You think you can do something about it, Parker?"

He lowered his head and murmured against her mouth, "Nope, sweetheart, you win."

Lawless

Dedication

To Lara Santiago: friend and part-time muse. Thanks, DL.

Chapter One

September, 1876, Colorado

The sunset bathed the walls of the gorge in crimson, like a glossing of spilled blood. The air was cooler as Cal Riker trotted his horse through the stream into the shadow of an overhang of raw rock, the soft splash of the horse echoed by the riders just ahead of him.

He was going to have to do something soon. This wasn't good timing, but it was the hand he'd been dealt and he'd damn well better play it right.

A few minutes later they rode up a small slope and into the makeshift camp he'd called home the past two months. Six men swung out of their saddles, but he stayed mounted, noting with a swift glance that as Ferris Norton lifted his prisoner off his horse, she looked pale as alabaster and her eyes were like dark holes in her face.

The woman was not a complication he needed, but with luck she was about to become his problem.

Cal reached behind and untied his saddlebag with a swift twist of his wrist and tossed it into the middle of the riders. "My share for the girl."

Norton, tall and beefy, with a bristly black beard and the legendary scar that bisected an eyebrow and ran all the way down his face to his jaw, looked at the bag and then up at where Cal still sat on his horse. "Why? You'll have your turn, Riker."

"You heard my offer." His face carefully expressionless, Cal assessed the reaction of the group with a swift glance. Most of them were afraid of him, something he was careful to keep honed to a fine edge, but he doubted he could take on six at once. He was good, but no one was that good.

The big outlaw, still holding his prize by the arm, gave an uneasy laugh. "I was lookin' forward to a little fun."

"There's almost twenty thousand dollars in that bag. You all can divvy it up. That'll pay for a lot of whores."

The half-breed, Jackson, nodded in agreement and several of the others glanced at the bag and then again at the girl.

It was a pity she was so damned beautiful. Disheveled golden hair framed her ashen face and the pale pink gown she wore showed off some nice curves in all the right female places.

Shit.

In one lithe movement he slid off his horse and stood there, his hands hanging very loosely at his sides. He'd take out Rollins first, he decided, the veteran gunslinger being the fastest shot. Norton second, probably, because he'd always hated the bastard anyway. Several of the others weren't known for their courage and might bolt when he opened fire, and he genuinely liked little bow-legged Josh Reece, who was barely more than a kid, so he'd wait and see what he did.

Every man went on full alert at his unmistakable posture.

"I'm pretty interested in making this deal." Cal kept his tone even like he always did, nice and slow, the soft drawl indicative of his childhood in Texas.

"I can see thet." Norton glanced at the rest of the group. His voice was gruff. "There's no need to get all testy about it. I suppose we can take a vote."

"I'd rather be rich than dead, boss," Rollins said with slow deliberation. He obviously knew the score and that Cal would go for him first. It was like an unspoken agreement between them, a basic law of survival. He gave a husky habitual cough, wiped his mouth, and added, "I say we take the money."

"Money." Jackson shrugged. He often rode off for days at a time and they all speculated he had a woman somewhere, probably with his mother's tribe.

Reece said briefly, "I wasn't keen on grabbing her in the first place. I vote money."

Well, that was half. Cal flicked a look at the two remaining men, Ham and Jake Small, a set of twins who as far as he knew, had split one brain between them. They followed like sheep usually and their only redeeming value to the gang was their innate brutality.

"If Riker is so all fired to keep her for himself, I ain't arguin'," one of them muttered. To his relief, the other one nodded.

"I guess you win then." Norton didn't look pleased, but he was greedy down deep, and Cal had counted on it when he realized the big outlaw had dragged the girl off the train. "That's one helluva expensive fuck, Riker. Here you go."

The shove he gave her was deliberately hard, and because her hands were bound she lost her balance and went sprawling on the dusty ground.

It was more difficult than Cal imagined to tamp down the gentlemanly instinct to leap forward and help her up. But if there was one thing he'd learned in the course of his checkered career, it was never let down your guard and take your eyes off the enemy.

He didn't even move when he heard the small sob, almost instantly stifled as she fought her long skirts and found her feet. A pair of stormy dark blue eyes shot him a killing glare and he was suddenly damned glad his lovely purchase didn't have access to a weapon. There was a dirty scrape on her smooth cheek and he saw it with a glimmer of deep inner guilt he sure hoped did not show.

Norton reached down and picked up the bag of money, weighed it in his hands and walked away.

At least they'd avoided a bloodbath. Cal gave a small exhale of relief as several of the men followed, eager to get their share and understandably distrustful of Norton. He gazed at the young woman with cool assessment, raking her up and down with a deliberate thorough inspection, lingering on the full curves of her breasts under the soft material of her dress. Then he gave her a smile that had nothing at all to do with humor. "I bet right now you're asking yourself if you just got saved or sent right to hell."

"If I was, what's the answer?" She tilted her chin up, still defiant after the grueling all-day ride, and her less-than-chivalrous treatment at the hands of Ferris Norton since the moment he'd spotted her on that train and decided he wanted to not only rob it, but take her along as a bonus. Cal had to give her credit for not looking as frightened as he was sure she was. Any woman would be, and with good cause.

She was about to get a lot more scared.

He cocked a brow. "Do you know who I am?"

Her face was delicately pretty, with fine bone structure and those compelling long-lashed blue eyes. The soft rose of her mouth would tempt any man, and her hair looked like pale tumbled silk across her slender shoulders. "They called you Riker."

"Yes, ma'am, they did. Maybe you've heard of me now and again."

It hit her then, he could see it as her remarkable eyes dilated and her lips parted. The horror was evident on her pretty face when she whispered, "*Cal* Riker?"

The nightmare seemed to get worse with every passing moment. What had started out as a pleasant trip on her way back from visiting her grandmother in Boston had disintegrated to a hellish abduction at the hands of rough outlaws.

Not ordinary thieves, Laurel realized with a chill that had nothing to do with the growing dusk. Not if a man like Cal Riker rode with them.

How many men was he supposed to have killed? Dozens, if she could remember, her mind frozen as she stood there with the numb realization that she faced a notorious man who had developed an almost legendary reputation for violence. Cold, ruthless and fast as the devil with a gun.

His eyes were a clear crystalline gray, like twin chips of ice in his expressionless face. He was tall and leanly built, dressed like most ordinary cowboys in dusty boots, jeans, a dark shirt open at the neck and a hat pulled low. When he spoke his voice held a cool, musical drawl that sent a shiver up her spine. "Now that we've got it clear who I am, what's your name?"

"Laurel Daniels."

"I see. Well, Miss Daniels, this sure hasn't been your lucky day, has it?"

One of the men nearby, obviously of Indian heritage with long, sleek dark hair and sloe black eyes, gave a small laugh, listening to the exchange.

"I've had better," Laurel said, doing her best to keep the wobble out of her voice. The way he had just looked at her did not bode well for what came next. It was only logical a man paid twenty thousand dollars for a woman for one purpose only, but her mind rejected the stark reality of her predicament.

"Turn around."

She eyed him uncertainly, biting her lip to keep it from trembling.

"Turn around unless you like being tied up." He pulled a knife from a sheath attached to his belt.

Being tied made her even more vulnerable so she slowly complied, feeling the slide of the cold metal as he deftly slashed the rope binding her wrists. Tingles of feeling shot back into her fingers.

She rubbed her chafed wrists and turned back around. "My father is a wealthy man. He owns Snowy Peaks Ranch, near Tijeras. He would pay to get me back...unharmed."

"I'm going to bet he'd pay to get you back no matter what, Miss Daniels. Are you hungry?"

Tears pricked her lids at both the slightly mocking tone of his voice and the knowledge he was right, her father would pay the ransom no matter what happened to her in the meantime. She shook her head, the idea of food almost ludicrous under the circumstances. There was no way she could eat. The thought of it gagged her.

He shrugged. "Suit yourself."

When he started to simply walk away, leading his horse with a low jingle of spurs, she had no idea what to do. Laurel looked around, entertaining the idea of running, but the encampment was situated with a high wall of sheer red rock on one side, rising steeply from the floor of the small canyon, and the other was just the opposite, a drop of a series of layers of neck-breaking inclines that could easily result in falling right off into the gorge and the river below. It was easily defensible, remote if their long ride was any indication, and the two small cabins indicated the band was using the location on a regular basis, at least enough to build permanent structures. That probably meant no one lived nearby, for someone had started a fire and the thin stream of smoke would alert pursuers.

Stay, or chance it?

Her pulse throbbed in her wrist as she contemplated her options if she bolted.

The entrance to the gorge was visible from the vantage point of the small plateau where the hideout was located and she was sure they could see her every inch of the way, and on horseback, catch her.

"Don't try it." Riker glanced back and halted, holding the reins of his big bay horse, the animal's coat dappled in the fading light. There was an implacable set to his mouth. "It'd be stupid, you might break your fool neck, and I would have to go after you, which would irritate the hell out of me. Now, come along. Whether you're hungry or not, I am."

Irritating a man like Cal Riker was probably like poking a rattlesnake with a stick. Stupid. And she wasn't stupid by any means, but it was hard to reconcile going meekly when she had a fair idea of what lay in store for her later.

She didn't care who or what he was, if he laid a hand on her she was going to kill him. The thought steadied her, made her wipe her damp palms on her dusty skirts and lift her chin. "Look, Mr. Riker, I realize I don't have the upper hand here by any means—"

"Lady, you are in deep trouble." He tilted his hat back, giving her a better view of his face. It was a bit startling to realize he was strikingly handsome in a clean-cut way, with finely modeled features that included high cheekbones, a nice straight nose and dark blond brows arched over those startling, intense silver eyes. "I know it, and so do you, Miss Daniels."

Somewhere in his nefarious past he'd been well-educated. It was in the modulation of his speech, even with that slow, soft accent. He was younger than she expected also, probably not even thirty. She fought to keep her tone steady. "I'm sure my father would give you back your money and then some."

"The trouble is, I'm not interested in his money."

No.

"I'm engaged," she blurted out.

"Is that so? Then I expect your fiancé will hate my guts."

That laconic observation brought on more laughter and she felt both humiliated and helpless. The men who hadn't followed eagerly to divide the money paid for her openly grinned, not even pretending to unsaddle their horses but listening to every word. She spat out, "I expect he will kill you."

"Plenty enough have tried." His face was shuttered and held that same unnerving quality of no emotion.

Oh God, it was true. She was trying to threaten a man with one of the most deadly reputations west of the Mississippi. It was a lesson in futility, for she tried to picture Weston Harper, with his expensive suits and lucrative hotel business, doing anything so stupid as to challenge a notorious gunman even if it was over her honor.

No, he wouldn't.

"Looks like you have your hands full, Riker." The half-breed grinned in a flash of white teeth. "Should be an interesting night."

Her captor gave him a glance that made the smile fade from the other outlaw's face, and he turned to his horse, busying himself with taking the saddle off the sweating animal.

Even these men, hardened, amoral and ruthless, were afraid of him. She was an unarmed woman at his mercy.

Cal Riker started to walk away again with the slow long-legged stride of a born horseman. "Come along, Miss Daniels."

Laurel wondered what he would do if she refused again.

She didn't dare find out.

Chapter Two

He never socialized and sat around the fire, and truthfully, the River Bend Outfit as they had loosely named themselves, was not much a social group to begin with anyway. They accepted his taciturn absence from their presence in the same way they accepted him in their midst, because he was someone to fear and that was the only law they knew. He was hard to kill, trying it would be risky, and so they left him alone.

They didn't suspect a thing, and Cal meant to keep it that way. The tricky part was how to keep up the charade this particular night.

He'd slept outside in the two months since he drifted in and joined the group, using a tarp when it rained, the location advantageous to someone who watched his back with constant vigilance. There was a small outcropping of rock not too far from the camp and a natural depression below it that was comfortable enough in his bedroll. The trees around the area made it hard to approach without making some sound in the dark and he could clearly hear if anyone moved around in the camp.

Which meant they could hear him as well.

This needed to be a good show. His reputation was the only thing between him and a shallow grave.

It was full dark before they finished eating and cleaning up the mess, and by then the men were passing around a whiskey bottle. Cal declined as he always did. He drank alone, and when he had that luxury, he took it. A little liquor made him forget his haunted existence and a lot of liquor was even better.

Tonight was not the time.

The girl flinched when he stood from his crouch after rinsing off his plate and cup in the stream. That she was jumpy wasn't news, and he didn't blame her. The next bit of interaction was going to be tricky and he sure hoped she got the message because they were walking a thin line. From the frightened look in her eyes, she thought things were bad now.

It could get a lot worse. He needed her to understand but couldn't risk telling her.

"Let's go." He jerked his head sideways to indicate the direction.

She wanted to resist, and he knew it, but in the end she went, ignoring the chuckles from the men who watched them disappear under the shelter of the pines, the tangy fragrance heavy in the cooling autumn night. At least he didn't have to drag her kicking and screaming, which was a relief. He couldn't help but admire the straight stance of her slender, shapely figure as she walked ahead of him, or the set of her shoulders that told him she understood full well what he wanted from her and her lack of power to keep it from happening.

Laurel Daniels was a lady with a lot of grit and courage and he hoped she could hold on to it without ruining everything until he could get them out of this situation.

The trees made it gloomy even with a bright spattering of stars above. When she stumbled over a branch, he took her arm in an automatic reflex, and led her toward where he had already unrolled his blankets. Under the grip of his fingers he could feel the tension in her muscles, and as they approached the makeshift bed, she tried to jerk away.

"Please." It was little more than a whisper.

Unfortunately, he couldn't reassure her. He unbuckled his gun belt, set it down on the ground within easy reach, and took off his hat and tossed it aside. In a stone cold voice, he said, "Lie down."

"No." She shook her head, starting to struggle. In the straggling light, her lovely eyes were wide and flashed with both defiance and fright.

Well, shit. He hadn't thought she'd simply give in without a fight, but he didn't relish either her fear or that she was going to have to believe—for the next few moments, anyway—that he was going to rape her.

The truth was, he'd never forced a woman in his life, never even dreamed of raising a hand to one, and he wasn't going to start now.

Since he was twice her size, it was a simple matter to just pick her up, though it was a little difficult to avoid her fists and nails as she did her best to do the most damage possible when he lowered her to the makeshift bed and used his weight to subdue her struggles. "Fighting won't do any good," he said clearly, rewarded by her knee narrowly missing a strategic part of his anatomy as she ignored the warning and twisted wildly beneath him.

"Go to hell," she panted and tried again. He clamped down one thigh over her flailing legs and smiled grimly. She had spunk. Good, she was going to need it.

From the way the conversation had died down by the fire, he had a feeling the entire group was listening avidly. In fact, since one of the Small brothers was supposed to be on guard duty and watching the gorge, he wasn't entirely sure they didn't have an audience too. It wasn't unknown for them to neglect the duty for drink and cards, so if there was a promising show of him having a good time with the girl, he could see them sneaking away to watch.

Without mercy, he caught her wrists and pinned her arms above her head. He transferred the grip to only one hand and with the other, pulled one of the blankets up over them both.

He had no intention of hurting or violating her in any way, but he was still a healthy adult male, and he couldn't help but register how soft she felt beneath him, her breasts flattened beneath his chest, the cradle of her hips against his crotch.

And that was enough of that, he reminded himself wryly. Lowering his head in the pretense of nuzzling her neck, he whispered, "I'm not going to hurt you, but please play along."

Her disbelief evident, she jerked against his hold.

Cal tried again, hoping she understood if she said the wrong thing, they could both be in big trouble. "Please, Miss Daniels...Laurel, just follow my lead and I'll have you back to your family as soon as possible, no ransom required."

She turned away from where his mouth grazed the spot

below her ear and a choked sound came from her throat.

He'd never felt like such a brute in his life. Her body was fragile in his arms, delicate and vulnerable.

"They're listening, understand?" He hoped the urgency in his very low whisper would get through. "This is a performance, got it? The better you play your part, the safer we'll both be tonight. If they don't think I'm going to use you, they'll be suspicious as hell. There is only one of me and six of them. All we have to do is pretend."

For the first time, she went still and when she turned her head to stare at him, he gave just the briefest nod and prayed if one of the depraved Small brothers was watching he didn't catch the meaning of it. The lustrous spill of her blond hair caught the faint starlight and the hint of a soft floral scent drifted to his nostrils, the fragrance tantalizing and feminine.

If things were different, I'd be damned tempted...

That treacherous thought wasn't welcome and he shoved it aside. The difference between Cal Riker and the well-bred daughter of a prosperous rancher was like the top of a mountain peak and the bottom of the ocean. Pretty damn big.

With slow deliberation, he began to unfasten her bodice. That much was necessary if there was an audience, even though he could spare her the rest. When the cloth gaped open, he slid a hand inside and cupped a breast through the material of her chemise. The woman beneath him squirmed in resistance and she spat out, "You bastard! Don't touch me."

In his normal tone, he drawled, "Oh darlin', just wait. I'm going to do much more than touch you."

As respectfully as possible, he simply kept his hand inside her dress and tried to ignore the arousing effect of the full, firm flesh as he cradled it. He could feel the soft peak of the nipple nestled against his palm, and even though he was more interested in both of them staying alive than anything, he felt his cock begin to stiffen. Luckily, from the fire there came a series of chuckles, and he was jarred back into the reality of the moment.

Well, he was sure he had just embarrassed the hell out of her by touching her intimately, but it was better than degradation and ill-use at the hands of a band of men with the morals of slinking coyotes.

Cal slid his hand free and delved under the blanket, acting as if he shoved her skirts up but in reality doing nothing more than running his hand up the outside of her thigh and hip. "Get ready to scream," he murmured, lowering his head so their mouths nearly touched. "If I was really doing this and you didn't want it, it would hurt."

She closed her eyes and the muscles in her throat rippled as he shifted more solidly on top of her.

With his hand still under the blanket as if he was unfastening his pants, he gave a low laugh, as if what was happening amused him, instead of the real effect which was being ashamed of his gender in general.

Even though her skirts and his clothing separated them, when he used his knees to push her legs apart he was rewarded with a very low sob that might even have been genuine. A fake rape at the hands of an infamous outlaw might not be as bad as the real thing, but it was probably still traumatizing as she was being forced—if not into sexual congress—into trust, which was probably not very easy.

"Now," he said between his teeth, surging his hips forward so he rocked against her, pelvis to pelvis, as if he had thrust inside her.

A small scream erupted from her slender throat, carrying just the right edge of despair. *Good girl*, he thought, grateful she'd kept her nerve. Cal began to move in a rhythm that mimicked sexual intercourse, still holding her hands pinned above her head, wishing he didn't have a full-blown erection because with their bodies pressed together so intimately, she could probably feel he was hard even through her dress and petticoats.

When he thought it seemed long enough, he gave a low, shuddering groan and went still. Not his best performance, he thought with cynical amusement, but hopefully it looked like the real thing. He suspected his balls were going to ache for the rest of the night, because even faking the act didn't change the reality that his body had a purely physical reaction to holding a beautiful woman so close and it had been way too long since he'd lain with one.

He whispered against her smooth temple. "Sorry."

Almost immediately he rolled off of her and let her wrists go. Out loud, he said in a cool, mocking tone that made him cringe inside, "Thanks, darlin'."

It was a heartless insult of the first degree, especially if he really had brutally had his way with her.

Laurel Daniels sat up in a flurry of long golden hair, her oval face pale except for the scarlet splotches of color in her cheeks. With shaking fingers she fumbled to refasten her dress. "I hope you rot in hell," she hissed with convincing vehemence.

Cal reached over and hauled her up against him, settling down on the blankets. "I think that's a sure thing, Miss Daniels. In the meantime, let's get some sleep."

⁊∽

It was very late and the lonely howl of a wolf came with mournful clarity, the sound echoing in eerie reverberation along the canyon cliff above. The scent of pine was crisp and clean and it had gotten cold as the night settled in. Laurel shifted on the hard ground, unwilling to admit she was grateful for the solid warmth of the man next to her, the shocking reality of sharing the same blankets aside. It was hard to believe it, but she'd even dozed off for a while, which was a miracle considering where she was and who she was with at the moment.

Cal Riker. Who had one arm draped over her waist, her back to his front, with her bottom nestled firmly against his lean hips. When she tried to edge away his hold tightened like a band of iron and she had given up trying to fight the scandalously inappropriate position, mostly because she didn't care to freeze to death.

She wasn't at all used to sleeping on the hard ground in the middle of nowhere surrounded by a gang of predatory men either. Odd as it was, he made her feel safe. What had happened—or not happened—earlier still had her confused, but he hadn't forced himself on her. Even during those mortifying moments when he put his hand inside her dress and cradled her breast, his touch had been gentle and she sensed his reluctance to do it in the first place.

The man was an enigma. If he was really ice cold and ruthless like every rumor she'd ever heard, why hadn't he just gone ahead and taken what he wanted? Instead he'd gone to great lengths to fake sexually using her and actually apologized for that afterwards.

And he *had* wanted it. Her face heated when she remembered the hard bulge pressed at the juncture of her thighs, easily felt through the layers of their clothes. She'd spent most of her life on a working ranch and knew enough about the reaction of males to an available female to realize he hadn't been indifferent to having her beneath him.

She shivered and felt his arm tighten just a fraction. That he was awake didn't surprise her, for she had a feeling vigilance was what kept men like him alive. She desperately wanted to ask him if he meant what he said about returning her home, but it was clear he didn't want to risk being overheard.

A twig snapped somewhere to their left and she felt the ripple of reaction in his tall body. Something gleamed and Laurel realized with a start he had a gun in his hand that fast. He went up on one elbow and stayed that way, taut and still. Heart pounding, she lay quietly and felt her mouth go dry with fear.

A moment later he relaxed and murmured almost inaudibly, "Just an animal. Though plenty of men I know fall into that category, I reckon. It'll be dawn soon. You ought to try and get some sleep. We're leaving and it's a fair ride."

Realizing he'd known she was awake was disconcerting, but the idea of leaving the camp was a relief, even if it was with a notorious outlaw. "Where?"

"You'll find out. Sleep."

It wasn't exactly helpful advice. Laurel snapped out louder than she intended, "Forgive me if I'm not used to lying on the ground, much less with a strange man."

"Better get used to it."

What did that mean? Her throat felt tight. "You said you'd—"

"Be quiet."

The lethal warning penetrated her exhaustion and fear and she swallowed back a tart reply, wondering if he was still worried someone could hear them.

Riker said nothing else, just gave a small grunt as he lay back down that could mean anything. This time, he didn't insistently pull her close and she felt the damp chill of the early morning penetrate through the blanket and her clothes. Cold and miserable, she lay there and wondered what was going to happen to her. Savior or living nightmare, she wasn't sure just which the man next to her might be.

He was right, before long she heard the first twitter of a bird. As the sky lightened enough it was gray under the trees, she rose stiffly to her feet when he rolled out of bed, watching as he efficiently folded the blankets, his movements swift and sure. When he motioned to a bush a few feet away, she didn't understand at first, but then flushed as she realized he wanted her to relieve herself.

There were some things that weren't to be denied and she took advantage of the relative privacy. There was a small spring near where all the other men had sat around the fire the night before and she washed her hands and face in the cool, clear water, feeling a little more human. Raking through her long tresses as best she could to unravel the tangles, she warily watched as Cal Riker retrieved his horse from the makeshift corral and saddled it.

The only other person up was a thin, weathered man with the lean look of a starved wolf who sat on a stump by one of the cabins, rolling a cigarette with one hand. He watched Riker's movements with hooded eyes as he lit the tobacco with an ember from last night's fire. He coughed a couple of times, took out a kerchief and wiped his mouth, and asked, "You comin' back, Riker?"

"Maybe." In the early light, the notorious gunman looked implacable and distant. "After this last job, we all need to lay low for a while."

"Norton has plans for another one pretty soon."

"Norton doesn't have the same price on his head as I do. I'll pass."

"Just as well you don't stay with us too long anyway," the other man commented, his eyes glittering. "I have this ugly feeling we might come up against each other if we spend too much time in each other's company. I'm itching to try you, to see if you're as good as they say you are."

"Help yourself." Riker's hands dropped to his sides in a deceptively casual movement.

"No thanks, Riker. Not this morning. Maybe someday, if we meet up again."

"All right." He turned back and adjusted the cinch. "I got no interest in a beef with you, Rollins. I'm just going to take the girl and stay out of sight for a bit. Let things settle down." He glanced at where she stood by the spring. "Come here."

Laurel fought a shiver as he looked at her, the order given without a hint of compassion. Those crystal clear eyes were the same color as a storm-filled sky and gazed at her with no visible emotion. With his hat shading his chiseled features and the lethal, graceful precision of his movements, he radiated danger.

The man who had touched her so gently and whispered an apology the night before seemed like an illusion.

The outlaw called Rollins gave her an amused look that might even have held a hint of pity, if it was possible in a man who spent his life stealing and killing. "You two have a good trip."

Chapter Three

Matthew Daniels dragged his hand over his face and paced to stare out the window. The valley spread below, the vista for once not moving him, maybe for the first time in his life. It was beautiful, green and dotted with grazing cattle and some of the finest horseflesh in Colorado, and in the background, the Rockies rose high and magnificent, the peaks holding a hint of white even in early September.

"I don't believe this." His voice sounded dull and lifeless, even to his own ears. "She was supposed to be on the train."

"Laurel *was* on the train, that's the problem." His son, Will, paced the length of the room, the faint musical jingle of spurs accompanying every restless step. "They robbed it and dragged her off. Witnesses say it was a big man with a scar, just like Norton's description and God knows they've been robbing banks and trains all over the place lately."

"Matthew!"

He understood both the horror and entreaty in his wife's voice. He just wasn't sure what he could do to fix this, and the idea his precious daughter was in the hands of a gang as lawless as the River Bend Outfit made his blood run cold. He turned, saw the streaks of tears on Jane's face and felt a helpless rage against the animals who had kidnapped their child. "We'll get her back."

Even as he made the vow, an icy calm settled over him.

"How?" Will stopped roaming the room and his hand dropped to his gun in an unconscious gesture. "No one has been able to track them so far. Wherever they're hiding, Pa, it's hard to find."

"We'll search every damned inch of this state if we have to. I'll hire men, offer a reward, whatever it takes. They've just crossed the wrong man."

Jane had been in the kitchen fixing breakfast when Will had come bursting in with the news of Laurel's abduction, and she wiped her face with a flour-covered hand, leaving white, dusty streaks. "I cannot imagine how frightened she is."

What he didn't want to imagine was that filth touching his beautiful daughter. That was part of the problem, part of the reason he'd half hoped she'd decide to stay in Boston. By the time she was fifteen he'd been chasing off lovesick cowboys and now, at almost twenty, she was nothing short of stunning. Too pretty for her own good.

"I came here first, but I suppose I should go tell Wes Harper about this before he has to hear it from someone else." Will wearily ran his hand through his fair hair, his clothes dusty from his all-out ride to the ranch. "He's going to be fit to be tied."

Considering the man claimed to love his daughter, Matthew certainly expected he would be. "I'll go with you. I need to set things in motion right away."

He walked over and kissed his wife's cheek in an unspoken promise and then stalked from the room.

❧

Cal didn't follow the same route twice, ever. It was part ingrained self-preservation, part common sense, part the explorer in him that never failed, even at his darkest moments, to be moved by the beauty of the wild country that was as close to home as anything he could label as such. His childhood seemed like a distant, vague memory, and because of the path he'd chosen, he didn't dare visit his family. These mountains at least gave him some peace.

Leaning one shoulder against a fragrant pine, he watched a herd of elk graze in a meadow full of knee-high grass and Indian paintbrush, the air carrying a crisp tang. The more miles between him and the River Bend camp the better, and he was actually starting to relax.

"You must think we're being followed. That's the third time you've doubled back."

Well, he had to give the girl credit. After a few attempts at conversation, all of which he'd responded to with taciturn silence, Miss Daniels had given up and stayed quieter than any female he'd ever encountered. They'd ridden for most of the day and he planned on going until dark, but his horse needed a rest and though she hadn't complained once, he figured his companion might be grateful for a chance to stretch her legs.

With a small shrug, Cal said, "You can't be too careful."

Sitting on a smooth rock by a small, picturesque stream, Laurel looked composed, her long, tumbled golden hair lit by the setting sun. Even disheveled, wearing the same clothes she'd been forced to sleep in, somehow his captive still managed to look not only enticingly lovely, but also every inch a lady. Those blue eyes, framed by long lashes, seemed like they looked right through him. "I would expect that is your motto, Mr. Riker, or you wouldn't still be alive."

"You have that right, ma'am." He lifted a brow.

"Since we're finally speaking, do you mind telling me if you're going to keep your word and take me home?"

It was only natural she'd ask that question, and he gave a brief nod. "I said I would."

Relief crossed her delicate features and for the very first time, he saw the luminous gleam of tears. "Thank you."

"In a few weeks."

She blinked.

Cal shifted his weight, seeing the joy in her expression fade. "Look, I have something to do first. Unfortunately, you get dragged along for that because I don't have time to ride a hundred miles and drop you off to your no doubt frantic family and still get my own business taken care of. Sorry, but that's that."

"More trains to rob? Someone out there you haven't shot yet?"

The edge of sarcasm in her tone cut but he deserved it, and there was no doubt she was not only tired and hungry, but also confused. He couldn't help but give a short laugh. "Most grown men wouldn't say something like that to me."

"It isn't like I have a lot to lose at this point."

"You're wrong there, Miss Daniels."

His direct reference to what hadn't happened the night before made color rise through her slender neck and into her cheeks. She stared at him, her body tense. "I suppose you think I should thank you for not...taking advantage of me."

"No, ma'am. No woman should have to thank a man for not raping her. Though you may find it hard to believe, I have a mother and two sisters. Whatever you may have heard about me, I'm a Texan and we respect women."

There was a brief silence, and in contrast the rush of the water in the little brook seemed very loud. Her lacy lashes lowered a fraction. "Is that why you gave your friends the money?"

"If I hadn't, last night might have been even less pleasant than it was, believe me." There was no way he could have stood by and let any woman be used by six men and do nothing, he didn't care who she was. "And they are not my friends, in case you didn't notice."

"I'm sure you're right." She gave a small telling shiver of memory. "Suspicious of what?"

Momentarily puzzled, Cal just looked at her. "What?"

"Last night, when you whispered to me to play along, you said if they thought you weren't going to...have me, they would be suspicious."

He had said that, in retrospect. Slowly, he explained, "I suppose I meant suspicious I'm not as bad as I'm painted. The truth is, Miss Daniels, there is only one way to survive being associated with a group of men like the River Bend Outfit. They understand fear, brutality and a lack of respect for right and wrong. Their thinking doesn't go much beyond that level, and if for a minute they thought I'd sacrifice my share of the haul from the robbery for your honor, they would reevaluate their opinion of my character, or let's say, my lack of character."

"I'm starting to think you are a somewhat complicated man." She brushed at a tendril of silky hair that moved in the soft breeze across her smooth cheek and gave him a tentative smile.

He wished to hell she hadn't done it. It had been a long

time since any woman had gazed at him with a soft light in her eyes. Yes, he'd had his share of ladies who liked his looks. It was just good sense to keep his mouth shut over who he actually was most of the time, but there were enough who thought his notoriety exciting too, which he found wrong in many ways. Not since he was a lot younger and less jaded had he experienced any kind of real connection besides a purely physical one.

This young woman wasn't going to be good for his peace of mind. He'd known it the minute she was dragged off that train.

Trouble dogged him as it was, he didn't need more of it.

More gruffly than he intended, he said, "Get up, we need to move on."

&)

Laurel was pretty sure her legs had stopped working, the irritating man refused to light a fire, and she had never been so dirty and tired in her life. Not to mention hungry, and all he'd offered for supper was cold beans, a few strips of dried meat and a hard biscuit.

Maybe he should put his legendary prowess with a gun to good use and put her out of her misery.

On the other hand, Cal Riker looked infuriatingly nonchalant and comfortable, unsaddling his horse with ease, gathering some pine fronds to make a temporary mattress and arranging a place for them to sleep, eating the unappetizing food without comment or complaint. If he felt the bite of the chill as night settled over them, he didn't show it.

Hatless, his sleeves rolled up to the elbows, he repacked the food, kneeling by the saddlebags in the small clearing of cottonwoods. His profile was clean and sharp, thick dark blond hair curling against the strong column of his neck. Long-fingered hands moved with efficient dexterity as he worked and Laurel couldn't help but be struck by not only his masculine good looks, but how he seemed to exude a powerful self-control that was part of his charisma and probably what led to his formidable reputation.

He seemed to sense her scrutiny, for he looked up and

stared back, apparently noticing her teeth were chattering. "You cold?"

"Very astute, Mr. Riker. I'm half fr-frozen." She was a little embarrassed to be caught staring.

"Why didn't you say something?"

"I'm doing my best to not complain," she shot back, finding it hard to look dignified when she was sitting on the ground, her hair a mess, her entire body shivering. "I feel I owe you that much."

For the first time he smiled, a mesmerizing curve of his well-shaped mouth that changed him suddenly from a gimlet-eyed outlaw to just a very attractive man. "I appreciate that, believe me. But there's no need for you to freeze to death. We should turn in anyway. We've another long day tomorrow."

As he had only made up one bed, she didn't doubt they'd be sleeping together again. Since he only had two blankets, it made sense to share, and at the moment, she was both disconcerted by the idea and grateful at the same time. Self-preservation was a powerful thing and since she knew already he wasn't going to assault her, sleeping next to him was better than shivering the night away in misery.

Laurel nodded, though when she stood up, her legs wobbled and she couldn't help but make a small sound of distress. When on the ranch she rode every day, but never from sunrise to sunset, and certainly not in a dress, with her petticoats bunched around her knees and her arms around the waist of a strange man.

The word "pride" pretty much did not apply to her current situation.

Cal Riker caught her arm to steady her. "If you aren't used to all that time in the saddle, it can be a little tough. Lean on me."

She did, shamelessly so, and when he guided her the few steps to the arranged bedroll, she sank down in a mess of quivering muscles with a low groan. "I'm crippled. Luckily, my legs are numb anyway."

"It'll take a day or two and you'll be fine. That first long ride is the hardest." Immediately he shook his blond head, his mouth moving in a wry quirk. "I don't think I put that the right way. I didn't mean anything by it."

If he hadn't said something, she probably would have thought nothing of it, but Laurel felt her face flush at the reference to the innuendo as she registered why he apologized. She gave a weak laugh. "I'm too tired and sore to even be afraid of you, Mr. Riker. Here we are, sharing a blanket for the second night in a row, stuck with each other so to speak, because I have a feeling you aren't any happier to have me for company than I am to be here."

"I'm pretty used to being alone." The admission was said quietly as he sat down to pull off his boots. He also took off his gun belt, but like the night before, he set everything within easy reach as he lay beside her and adjusted the blanket over them both.

Blessed warmth. It came from him, radiating from his much larger body. How he wasn't chilled to the bone she didn't know, but without thought she moved closer and he didn't object but instead slid his arms around her and adjusted their position so she rested against his broad chest. Laurel sighed, her cheek against the flannel of his shirt, one muscular shoulder serving as a pillow.

"You're a brave young lady, Miss Daniels."

It seemed like her head fit just perfectly under his chin and she was unexpectedly comfortable. She mumbled, "Uhm...how so?"

"Seems to me you're sleeping with Cal Riker."

The hint of bitterness in his tone surprised her a little but she was too exhausted to analyze it further. "If you wanted to hurt me, you'd have done it by now."

"I suppose that's a logical way of looking at it."

"If you were in my position, you might say it was the only way of looking at it."

"Maybe, maybe not. Most women would have gone into hysterics at some point during all of this."

"Are you an expert on women, Mr. Riker?" Laurel shifted just enough so she could see his face. The moonlight softened his normally hard expression and lent shadows to the clean lines of brow and jaw.

"I've known my share." The response was said with a hint

of cynical amusement.

With his potent good looks, he probably had. Even with his reputation it was easy enough to suppose he could find female company if he wanted it. Curiously, she asked, "Do you have a sweetheart somewhere?"

"No."

"It's a pity." She could hear the strong, steady thud of his heart and his scent, a woodsy mixture of male and the outdoors, was inexplicably intriguing.

"Why is that a pity?"

She hesitated, not sure what made her venture into such a personal discussion with a man known for his lethal ability with a gun, not to mention he was apparently also a thief. "You aren't all bad," she said finally. "Maybe if you—"

"I hope you aren't about to tell me the right woman could redeem me, Miss Daniels." He shifted a little as he interrupted, his powerful body moving against hers. "That's an illusion you need to get out of your pretty head right away. I may not believe in violence against women, but that doesn't show anything except a legacy of marginal decency from a childhood I think of now as a distant dream."

"You are very much more decent than any of those men who took me off the train." It was true, without an audience, he had been both respectful and solicitous.

"Yeah, well, I'm sorry, ma'am, that's not much of a compliment."

She couldn't argue that point. Just the thought of Ferris Norton with his pawing hands and lascivious sneer made her feel ill. "No," she admitted, "I suppose it isn't."

An owl called, the sound drifting in the night. A light, cool breeze had stirred and she felt it brush her cheek, though she felt warm and content cradled in his arms.

In the arms of *the* Cal Riker. It was a ludicrous thought, but then again, the entire abduction seemed unreal, as if someone else had lived it.

"Why did you join up with them?" The question seemed a natural one. "Obviously it wasn't for the money, otherwise you would have kept your share. It isn't because you enjoy their company either, I got that easy enough."

"And here earlier I was thinking you were something I didn't reckon I'd ever run across, a female who didn't ask a bunch of questions." He drawled the words in that soft southern accent she found so attractive.

Defensively, she said, "It's natural to be curious, especially since I am forced to trust you at this point."

"Don't." The word was abrupt and edgy.

"Don't what?"

"Trust me. Not for one minute. I'm not worthy of it, and I don't want the responsibility. Just because I didn't force you last night doesn't mean I wasn't thinking about what it would be like if you were willing. In fact, I'm pretty sure you noticed I was."

How he'd moved against her wasn't something she'd likely forget. Even though they hadn't done what he pretended they were doing, he had still pushed her legs apart and lain between them. How easily he had subdued her with his superior weight and strength was a sobering reminder of her vulnerability. "I noticed," she admitted, her voice low and a slow blush burning her cheeks.

"Your problem is, Miss Daniels, you are one very pretty young lady. Maybe the prettiest I've ever seen."

His hand lifted and he touched her cheek very lightly with his long fingers, the caress just a brush but the contact sending a jolt of awareness through her entire body.

...if you were willing...

His voice was husky. "I'm going to guess your father has his hands full keeping all those hungry ranch hands away from you. For his sake, I hope you don't have any sisters."

"One brother," Laurel managed to say, aware he was staring at her mouth. Her pulse fluttered in her throat as she saw his lashes—ridiculously long and thick for a man—drift downward a fraction as he bent his head. Warm breath fanned her cheek. She vaguely heard herself ask, "What are you doing?"

"Showing you why you can't trust me. Maybe I didn't take advantage of you last night, but for twenty thousand surely you owe me a kiss."

The first touch of his lips made her gasp, a sound he

swallowed by settling his mouth more firmly against hers. If she'd been cold before, that was dissipated by the solid feel of his hard body and the iron hold of his arms, and she felt almost too warm as his tongue sought entrance with gentle insistence.

Though she'd been kissed before, it had never been like this.

For one thing, he took his time. This was not a hurried moment stolen by some lovesick, awkward young cowboy. Cal Riker might be good with a gun, but he was obviously pretty skilled in other ways too. The firmness of lips, the sharp taste of whiskey, the thud of his heart, it all blended into the almost surreal essence of the moment. He melded their mouths together in a way that made her feel a part of what he was doing, part of his need. One hand ran gracefully down her arm and caught hers, twining their fingers in an intimate clasp with a small squeeze as they kissed.

It was a very romantic gesture, and she was both bemused and astonished by the tumultuous riot of feelings it provoked.

You need to stop at once, a nagging voice reminded her. *To pull your hand away.*

But she didn't.

He's a very dangerous man, the admonishment continued.

And it had nothing to do with his infamous skill at a faster-than-lightning draw.

"Damn my black soul, you feel so good." The murmur was made against her lips and before she could say anything, he captured her mouth again, this time with more urgency. The starlit night, the fragrance of pine and earth, the wash of the cool autumn breeze...it all faded away under the influence of something she'd never experienced.

Desire.

To her consternation, Laurel felt her breasts tingle, the puckered peaks of her nipples against his chest. His teasing tongue dueled with hers, demanding a response, and she sank the fingers of her free hand into the thickness of his hair, marveling at how soft it was when everything else about him was hard and unrelenting.

It was Cal who finally tore his mouth away and she felt the scorching wisp of his breath on her cheek. Eyes closed, he simply held her and finally let out a short laugh. "That was the mistake of a lifetime, I have a hunch. I'm a damn fool."

The words sparked an awareness of her enthusiastic participation. She struggled to catch her breath. "That makes two of us. I haven't even let Wes kiss me like that."

The man holding her went very still. "I take it you're talking about your fiancé?"

"I lied. We aren't officially engaged but he's asked."

"It was a bit naïve of you, if you don't mind me saying, Miss Daniels, to think the idea of an outraged prospective husband would stop me if I had intended on doing what you thought I was going to do last night." His voice once again assumed that easy, slow drawl and he disengaged their fingers. "It sure as hell wouldn't have stopped Norton or any of the others from entertaining themselves."

The thought of that was so horrible she pushed it away.

"Forgive me if I was feeling a little panicked and couldn't come up with anything else." She was embarrassed—at least a little bit—at her response to his kiss and the reply came out more tartly than she intended.

His brows rose in amusement and his slow smile was devastating in the way it changed his handsome face. "You were actually pretty cool considering your circumstances. I've got to hand that to you. Even now, you're really not scared, are you?"

She was, but probably not in the way he meant. "Like I said before, I'm not afraid you'll hurt me."

"Most of the people who have any prolonged contact with me get hurt in one way or another, Laurel. You might want to remember that."

The bleak note in his voice touched her. At a loss for a response, she simply stared at him.

He said quietly, "Let's get some rest."

All she could manage was a nod.

Chapter Four

The whiskey was good, but he wasn't sure about the company. To say Weston Harper was upset was the truth, but then again, who wouldn't be? Will Daniels accepted the glass and could not think of one single reassuring thing to say to the man who sat across from him.

Tall, dark-haired, his face set and grim as he poured another shot, Harper's voice was raspy. "You know damn good and well what they're doing with her."

Will tossed off his drink before answering. Thinking about what might be happening, or already had happened, to his sister would just drive him crazy. "My father is organizing a search party. We know where they took her off the train. Maybe the River Bend Outfit made the mistake of a lifetime. If we can track them, they're all dead men."

"Dead doesn't exactly fix this situation."

"If we get her back it does."

"Yeah, I suppose." Wes shoved his hand into his normally immaculate hair and stared at his half-full glass. "I didn't want her to go to Boston, much less travel back by herself. She's just damned stubborn."

Well, it was true Laurel could be strong-willed, but what had happened was hardly predictable. She was nearly twenty years old and able to travel alone if she wanted. "Keep that in mind. She isn't easily intimidated or bullied."

"Seven rough men to one slender woman? Are you trying to sell me a bill of goods that she might be able to fight back somehow?"

It was a stretch and he knew it. Will also knew if he didn't keep up hope, it was going to be harder to go after her. "As long as she's alive, that's what's important."

"You aren't the one who wants to marry her, Will."

"No, but she's my sister. If you think this isn't eating me up, you're fucking wrong, Harper."

For a minute they stared at each other and then the other man sighed heavily. "I know it is. Sorry. I just feel helpless. I can't even go with you to look for her. I have that big deal closing soon. I have to be here to sign the papers. The lawyers are on their way with everything."

Somehow, that didn't surprise Will. It wasn't that he didn't like Weston Harper, he did for the most part, but there was a shallowness there that he hoped Laurel saw as clearly as he did. Maybe that was why she had hedged over accepting Harper's proposal so far. Wes was handsome, successful and charming, but he was also self-centered and Will had a big suspicion part of his horror over Laurel's abduction was that everyone would know the woman he wanted to marry had been touched by other men.

More than touched, probably. It was the only reason they'd dragged her off that train. He prayed they would try and ransom her, but according to the eyewitness report he'd gotten when the train rolled into Tijeras without her on board, the men hadn't acted like they knew who she was. It was her looks that caught their eye, not the idea of their father's money.

Murderous rage didn't begin to describe his reaction, but sometimes the West was a violent place. It was part of living and part of dying some of the time.

He drained his glass, the whiskey burning his throat. "We'll be riding out in an hour or so. My father is with John Evans arranging for men to go with us."

Wes leaned back in his chair, looking morose. "Good luck."

Will didn't even feel sorry for him. He just got up and walked out.

౭౦

The clearing was quiet, but there was a gray stream coming

from the chimney and the faint tang of wood smoke was a wonderful thing. Cal urged Goliath, his big bay, toward the small corral at the back, a lean-to attached to provide shelter in the often unpredictable weather of this part of Colorado.

The dog that trotted out to meet them was obviously half wolf, his wary demeanor and low growl subsiding as he registered the familiar scent. Cal said quietly, "Hello, Lobo. Where's old Gabe?"

"Who you callin' old, you renegade?"

The man who came out from around the back of the cabin was a welcome sight, even if he was lowering a rifle. A grizzled beard full of gray split in a wide smile. "I had you in my sights, damned if I didn't. You need to be more careful."

Cal grinned back with weary humor. "I'm too tired to be careful."

"I hope that's never true, Cal. If there's a man I know who can't afford to be tired, it's you." The other man's smile faded. "Looks like you brought company this time. You can explain over a hot meal. I made some stew. Maybe I have second sight or somethin' because I've got extra. Bring the girl inside before you tend to Goliath. She looks like she's tuckered."

It was true. Laurel had faded the past few hours, her body almost lax against his back, her arms only loosely holding on to his waist. As Cal slid from the saddle, she came with him and he was barely able to catch her before she hit the ground. "You seem to be right. Get the door, Gabe."

The delectable Miss Daniels gave a soft moan as he carried her toward the cabin. Not for the first time, he felt both insensitive and brutal even if he hadn't been the one to instigate her abduction in the first place. The pace he'd set had been hard and he hadn't stopped more than once or twice, nor did they have much in the way of supplies. He was hungry as hell, and as he stepped into the first shelter they'd seen in three days, the fragrant smell of the bubbling stew hit him like a hammer. Considering how little the woman in his arms had eaten since she was dragged off that train, it was no wonder she was a little weak. He hoped it smelled as good to her as it did to him.

The bed was in the corner of the one-room space, and he deposited her gently as possible on the soft, patterned blankets.

Ghostly pale and obviously exhausted, she stared at him as her long lashes fluttered upward. "Where are we now?"

"Believe it or not, I have friends." He attempted a reassuring smile. "We'll stay here a few weeks. It's safe. Just rest a minute and then we'll get something to eat. It will make the world a whole new place, take my word on it."

"Your word? That's an odd request from the infamous Cal Riker, but I'll do my best."

The hint of humor in her reply was a relief. She looked so delicate and wan he was afraid he'd really pushed her too far. There wasn't much question she'd won his admiration in more ways than just an appreciation for her tempting physical appearance. "I'll be right back," he promised.

"I doubt I'm going anywhere." She closed her eyes again, her slender body limp, her golden hair spilled across the blankets like pale silk.

He turned and left the cabin, Gabe right on his heels. Thickset, his hair streaked with gray, Gabriel Ranson was one of those men who seemed ageless. He looked exactly the same as he did when Cal had met him a decade earlier. The older man asked, "Now that little gal is a looker. Never seen one her equal. What's the story?"

Briefly, Cal explained about the robbery and kidnapping as he unsaddled his horse and poured some oats into a trough in the corral. Goliath seemed pleased to be relieved of his double burden and off the trail—his ears pricked forward as he began to eat.

He had exactly the right idea, Cal thought, feeling a bit worn down himself.

"I'm thinkin' you got a right pretty piece of trouble on your hands, Cal."

"Maybe so, but there isn't much I can do about it. We'll lay low here until you get back and then I'll take her on down to her family. Her father owns a big spread outside Tijeras."

Gabe looked troubled. "I hope you don't get a bullet for your trouble, son."

"You and me both." Cal rubbed his jaw, feeling the unshaven stubble. "I'm just going to have to worry about that later. For now, I could really use some food and I know Laurel is probably famished. She hasn't eaten more than a few bites in the past few days."

"We'll fix that right now. Come on."

A few minutes later he was seated by the stone hearth of the fireplace, doing his best to not devour his food like a starving man. The venison stew was thick, meaty and rich. There were biscuits too, baked earlier in the day and still soft and light. As he ate, Cal watched his lovely companion show the same appreciation, and when she was finished and declined a third biscuit, he was gratified to see some of the color had come back into her face.

"That was marvelous. Thank you." She gifted Gabe with a dazzling smile. "I never knew anything could taste so good."

"Just plain cookin'." He shot Cal a reproachful look. "I don't imagine Cal here would even light a fire."

"No," she admitted and glanced over.

In the depths of her eyes was a memory of how they'd lain together under the stars and that damned kiss.

The kiss. The one he should be horsewhipped for stealing. Not because she was a defenseless woman in his care and he should keep his hands—and mouth—to himself, but because it had branded his soul with a taste of something he could never have. A decent woman wasn't in the cards for him, much less a well-educated beauty from a good family.

He looked away. At the plain but homey interior of the small cabin with its rustic, rough furnishings; a bed made of hand-hewn pine and piled with Indian blankets, the river stone hearth, the small table with two benches. There was a single window, the shutters now closed against the chill of the mountain air, and shelves with supplies already stocked for the winter. Flour, lard, salt, sacks of potatoes...it looked like Gabe was ready if there was an early snow. Winters could be fierce this high up.

The fire crackled, a log snapping as resin bubbled out of it, the sweet smell mingling with the fragrance of the stew. Cal contemplated the flames as he sipped a cup of coffee, all too aware of the woman sitting a few feet away.

Every curve of her luscious body was branded in his memory. The softness of her lips, the silken feel of her hair, the smooth, flawless warmth of her skin...

Damn it, he needed to stop thinking about her.

"You wantin' me to ride out in the morning?" Gabe came and sat down next to him, cradling a tin cup in his big hands.

"Yes."

"I can do that. I've been waitin' for you to show up." His friend took a flask from his pocket, tipped some liquor into his cup and passed it over.

"If that's the firewater you make yourself, no thanks." Cal eyed the offering with suspicion. "The last time I drank some of that I lost three days."

"That's because you don't do anything halfway, son. A little won't hurt you. A lot isn't a good idea. If I remember correctly, the time you mention was after the Las Animas robbery where Gil Holbert killed all those people."

It had been. Cal still had nightmares over it. The fact he'd shot Holbert himself after the killing spree didn't help much. Thank goodness no one recognized him and the sheriff thought Holbert had been caught in the crossfire between the thieves and the lawmen who tried to stop them leaving the scene.

"You were there?" Laurel seemed to rouse a little.

Cal heard the horror and reproof in the question and felt a cold weight settle in his stomach. He said nothing, just stared at the fire.

"Dear God, he gunned down ten people in cold blood." She sat on the edge of the bed, her expression etched with shock.

"That's why Cal killed him." Gabe said the words in a matter-of-fact tone. "He faced down Holbert, dared him to draw and bored him for doin' that to a bunch of innocent folks, but the local sheriff took the credit."

"There is no credit in killing a man," Cal interjected. "And shut up, Gabe. She doesn't need to know any of this."

"From what I heard, they tracked down the whole gang and they were hanged not long afterwards."

The last thing he wanted was for her to make the correct correlation between that and what was about to happen to the River Bend Outfit once he passed along the exact location of their hideaway. He said in a cool tone, "The Las Animas deal didn't sit well with me so I left. What happened after that wasn't my concern then or now. I go my own way."

"You killed Holbert for what he did."

Cal gave Gabe a look of pure annoyance. "Maybe. I'd be just as glad, Miss Daniels, if no one ever found that out."

"Last night you called me Laurel."

The soft reminder startled him. He finally looked at her, a vision in her rumpled clothes, the tumbled mass of her golden hair around her face. With only the firelight for illumination, it was hard to read her expression, but at least she wasn't looking at him as if he was a cold-blooded murderer any longer. He *had* given that snake Holbert a chance to go for his gun, which was a lot more than the slinking coward had offered the poor people in the bank, but that was all past and gone. He'd found out a long time ago that torturing himself over things gone wrong was useless. If he'd had the slightest inkling Holbert was going kill everyone in the bank that fateful morning, he'd have stepped in earlier. That he'd been too late to save those people was just one of those things he would have to live with forever.

"Forgive the familiarity. I sometimes forget my manners." He finally remembered the flask in his hand and decided a cautious drink might be in order.

As he tipped it to his mouth, she murmured, "I didn't mind, actually."

The reason he choked wasn't entirely the harshness of Gabe's home brew.

There was a lot more to the man sitting across from her than she knew and she'd sensed it from the terrifying moment she learned his identity. The icy calm exterior hid the inside core and the more time she spent in his company, the more she realized she had no idea who he really was.

The cold, heartless gunman was somewhere in there, because she'd seen it. The moment he'd offered the gang the money for her and slid off his horse, she'd known—as had they apparently—he was willing to kill to get what he wanted. However, it was a little hard to reconcile this was the same man who had treated her with nothing but polite courtesy since they'd ridden away from the camp.

Not to mention that bone-melting kiss.

It had started as an attempt to prove some absurd point, she knew that. To show he was as unworthy of trust as any of his ruffian cohorts, but when his mouth had actually touched hers, she'd felt he'd been as lost in the sensation as she was mesmerized by the tender warmth of it.

No man who could hold and touch a woman at his mercy with that amount of gentleness was evil. More to the point, she had a feeling that something was going on under the surface that explained his involvement with both the River Bend Outfit and men like Gil Holbert. After three long days in his company, she knew enough about Cal Riker to guess he detested men like them.

He wouldn't ride with them by choice, or for money.

Then...why?

"Are you playing some game?" The question was spontaneous and she should never have asked it. Perched on the side of the bed, she clasped her hands in her lap and looked at him.

His face—so perfect in detail with its chiseled masculine lines—smoothed into that mask she'd seen before. Gray eyes glimmered in the firelight. "Excuse me?"

"I'm naturally curious."

"Well, get uncurious." He tipped the flask to his mouth again but she knew he didn't take more than a very small swallow.

Gabe glanced first at her and then at Cal and his broad face lit with a small smile. "You can't fool everyone, son. Appears she's one of those who sees through you."

"I am going to ask you to shut up a second time, Gabe." Cal capped the flask and thrust it back at his friend. Tall and lean, he stood and gave a small theatrical stretch, sleek muscles moving under his plain shirt. The firelight made his blond hair gleam with rich color and put shadows under his finely modeled cheekbones. "I'm going to hit my bedroll. I suggest you do the same, Miss Daniels."

"Call me Laurel."

"Goodnight." He stalked from the room in a low jingle of spurs, but not before he sent a warning look at his friend.

The door shut behind him with a soft thud and the faint drift of night air.

The older man chuckled. "You got him rattled. I haven't seen that in a long time."

"I don't see how you can tell," Laurel said with feeling. "He's about as emotional as a rock."

"Don't let him trick you into thinkin' that, miss. Cal's deep. It's part of his problem. He feels everything a sight too much and it all eats at him. Considering how he stuck his neck out for you, I'm sure you at least understand a little bit what I'm saying."

She would never forget the tone of his cool voice or the sound of the bag of money hitting the ground when he offered it for her. At the time it hadn't seemed like a moment of salvation, but now...well, she wasn't just sure what to think.

"He saved me from those men," she acquiesced with a small shiver over what might have been.

"Yes, miss, it sounds to me like he did just that."

"I'm grateful...and he says he's going to take me home."

"If Cal said it, it'll happen."

That was a relief, but she'd already reached that conclusion herself. Despite his warning, she trusted him anyway.

"Have you known him long?" She dared the question, even though her body ached with fatigue.

"Since he was little more than a boy."

"He said he's from Texas."

"Not for a long time. Cal has no home. He doesn't want one, as far as I can tell."

She thought about her parents' comfortable ranch and the old, stately home where her grandmother lived in Boston. "How could anyone feel that way?"

Gabe gave her a keen look. He smoothed his shaggy beard with his fingers, the other hand holding his flask. "I doubt he's willing to risk it. Putting down roots, now that makes a man vulnerable."

"I could see where that would be a problem for him." Her tone was dry. "Vulnerable is not the first word I think of when Cal Riker comes to mind."

Her rescuer's friend took a long pull from the flask. He swallowed and gave a small cough. "His reputation is well-earned, but take my word, miss, he has his reasons. Just know you're safe with him. Now, get a good sleep. If I know Cal, he drove you pretty hard and you could use it. Goodnight. We'll both be right outside if you need anything."

If she hadn't been about as tired as ever in her life, she might have protested taking his bed, but it felt soft and warm and after removing her shoes and stockings, Laurel crawled under the blankets, closed her eyes and sank into oblivion.

Chapter Five

The faint splash of water went right through him.

In a direct downward spiral, right to his unruly cock. Rifle in hand, Cal eased along the bank to his usual spot, right behind a trio of fledgling aspens, the slender stems affording him a good view but pretty decent cover, the delicate leaves fluttering in the breeze above his head. For the past three days he'd crouched in the same location and both endured and enjoyed the duty of guarding Laurel while she bathed in the small stream by the cabin. If she had any idea he was there, she'd probably die of mortification, but he was also sure she would never agree to let him openly watch, so he took the easy route. There was no way on this green earth he'd ever let her go anywhere alone, but if she was naïve enough to think so, he wasn't going to argue. There were all sorts of dangers, from bears and cougars to the two-legged kind. The cabin was pretty secluded, but some drifter could come along and there were certainly still unfriendly Indians around.

It was habit to scan the surroundings—an ingrained sense of safety he didn't think about—even with the distraction of the naked woman waist-deep in the water. Everything was quiet, the morning growing warm for early fall, though he knew from experience the water in the stream was pretty damned cold. Laurel shivered, and there was no way he could keep his avid gaze from fastening on her bare breasts as they swayed with her movements.

The young lady had a set of very gorgeous tits—that was for sure. Not too large, beautifully shaped and firm with pink nipples that at the moment were tight and pointed from the chilly water. Cal stifled a groan and shifted position uncomfortably when she soaped her hands and ran them over those luscious curves. The throbbing of his erection, confined by the material of his pants, was pretty hard to ignore.

She was hard to ignore in general. Gabe had ridden off the morning after they'd arrived as planned and it would probably be a good two weeks before he came back. The enforced time alone with her in a remote place and the close quarters of the cabin was taking its toll on his self-control and this was just the third day.

God help me.

Since he was pretty sure he was undeserving of divine aid of any kind, that seemed unlikely, he thought with sardonic humor. The sooner he delivered the tantalizing Laurel Daniels to her father's ranch, the better.

She soaped her hair and let out a low gasp as she stood after sinking into the water to rinse it. Wet gold strands clung to her slim shoulders that now trembled from the chill of the stream. When she turned to wade out, he got a perfect view of her enticing backside as she bent over to retrieve the cloth she used to dry off. It was just as perfect as the rest of her, the mounds of her buttocks smooth and pale and made to be cupped in his hands. The dainty triangle of curls between her thighs was a darker gold than her blond hair, and her legs long and slender. As far as he could tell, and he was *really* paying attention, every inch of her from the top of her head to her toes was made to make a man think about things he shouldn't. Like having her beneath him, naked and moaning...

He certainly was having impure thoughts, at any rate, and it was getting to him.

His preoccupation had him not paying attention when she screamed and stumbled backward. Instinctively, he shot out of his hiding place, rifle at the ready, though he couldn't see what caused such alarm. As he crashed through a small thicket of thorny bushes in his haste, she whirled around, the cloth clutched to her chest.

"Cal!" Her blue eyes were wide as she took in the gun in his hand.

There was still no particular menace he could see. "What's wrong?"

"S-snake." She pointed at the rock where she'd set her clothes. "It startled me. I didn't see it."

Relief washed through him as he saw, indeed, a nice size rattler had decided to take advantage of the beautiful day and was sunning itself, comfortably situated on one of her petticoats. He thrust his fingers through his hair. "Jesus, girl, you scared me to death."

"I almost touched it," she shot back, her voice choked, "and I hate the darned things."

"They aren't my favorite," he admitted. "But I'll take care of it. He doesn't look all that happy to see us either."

She shuddered, trying to wrap the towel around herself. "Just get rid of it, please. I only have one set of clothes as it is. I'm not sharing it with a snake."

He couldn't help it, he laughed. She looked delectably wet, tousled and indignant. Not to mention still very naked since the cloth wasn't all that big. "I'll coax him to give it back."

"And right after that maybe you can explain what you were doing hiding in the bushes."

He figured that was coming but just lifted a brow. "I'm not in the habit of explaining myself to anyone, but if there was one person on this earth who could bribe me to do so, it would be a very beautiful naked woman."

Bribe him?

Laurel stared at the man in front of her, recognizing after the last week in his presence that flare once again of tension between them. Not antagonism, but something else entirely, an unspoken challenge in a battle she'd never fought before. His eyes, pure steel gray and so hard to read, held a heavy look, his dark lashes lowered just a fraction.

Without saying another word, he walked over to the rock, managed to skillfully scoop up the rattlesnake with the tip of his rifle, and tossed it a few feet away. It slithered into the bushes and disappeared from sight.

Thank the Lord. She loathed the creatures and always had.

Cal reached over and scooped up her clothes. "Here you go. All yours again."

The cloth she held in front of her barely covered her breasts and upper thighs. She could feel the blush in her neck and cheeks but wasn't going to make matters worse by trying to dress in front of him. "Thank you." She snatched the garments from his hand and refused to turn and run, though that was her first impulse.

He gave her one of his devastating smiles. "My pleasure."

"Turn your back, please."

"Now, I'm sorry, but that happens to be something I never do. Too many people would like to put a bullet in it."

"Including me right now. Why were you watching me?"

His handsome face was enigmatic. "I think you can figure that one out on your own, Miss Daniels. This isn't the safest country for a woman by herself, much less a naked one."

At least with her dress and petticoats held in front of her he couldn't see as much exposed skin. His refusal to use her first name was also symbolic of something, but she wasn't sure what. "Why didn't you tell me you were lurking around?"

He shrugged, his wide shoulders lifting the plain material of his shirt. "It would have made you uncomfortable, for one. Now, why don't you just get dressed?"

"Not with you watching me." Her cheeks felt on fire.

"Well, I'm not leaving you here alone, so maybe you'd better face the fact you're going to lose this argument." His tone was infuriatingly nonchalant, his well-shaped mouth just slightly tilted at one corner in indication of his amusement over her discomfort. Tall and lean, his muscular body reminded her of the power of his strength as compared to hers, and she couldn't decide if she felt hunted or protected.

Well, maybe both.

"I've already seen it all," he informed her in a mild tone. "You have nothing to be embarrassed about, believe me. My compliments, ma'am."

Speechless, Laurel stared at him, part of her wanting to slap his face for that audacious comment, another part of her traitorously pleased he found her attractive.

Pleased a wild outlaw wanted her? The notion was just insane.

Worse than that, she was afraid maybe she felt just the same way about him. It didn't make sense, but it just...was.

With effort, she gathered her scattered wits. "It's different knowing you're standing right here."

His crystalline eyes narrowed and he shook his head. In the dappled sunlight, his thick hair shone with amber streaks, just curling over his collar. "I warned you, Miss Daniels. I don't do well with debate if there's a faster way."

"Warn me all you like, but I'm not going to dress in front of you, *Mister Riker.*"

"Fine with me, I like you naked better. But I'm not interested in a big standoff either, so..."

A gasp escaped her lips as he stepped forward and leaned down, grabbing her and suddenly tossing her facedown over his shoulder. One arm wrapped around her thighs, the other holding his rifle, he started to walk back toward the cabin with calm measured steps.

Appalled, her bare backside in the air, Laurel squirmed in furious protest, still clutching her precious clothing. "Put me down, damn you."

He clucked his tongue. "You're a lady, Miss Daniels. Your mother would faint to hear you talk like that."

One brawny shoulder was pressed against her diaphragm and made it hard to retort, but she managed to croak, "You lowdown, despicable, highhanded desperado. Put me down right now."

"Can you be lowdown and highhanded at the same time?" He walked across the small clearing. "Despicable might fit, and I'm not going to argue the desperado label, but you might want to keep that in mind before you keep slinging more names my direction. I can be patient, but I don't like it."

"I'm...not...a...sack of flour."

She couldn't see it, but she had the feeling he turned his head to look at her exposed bottom. "No, ma'am, you sure are not."

"You...you..."

"Careful what you decide to come up with. I might just want to live up to it."

Considering what happened the last time she pushed him, Laurel held her tongue. Her current state of naked humiliation was bad enough. God alone knew what he might do next.

He crossed the space and his boots rapped sharply on the boards of the small porch before he shoved open the door to the cabin. A moment later she was deposited on the bed in a flurry of fabric, wet towel and damp hair. Cal leaned over her, one arm braced on either side of her body, and effectively trapped her. He was warm, solid and all intimidating male. His gaze was direct, his face inches from hers. "I am about to be very straight with you, got it?"

She nodded, not sure if she was alarmed or intrigued. His closeness and her nudity sparked a response that held her prisoner, mesmerized by his clean scent and the imposing width of his shoulders.

"We're going to be here alone until Gabe gets back. At that time, we'll set out for your father's ranch and you'll be back with your family and off my hands. In the meantime, we have to figure out a way to stay out of each other's paths as best as possible. There's no question that I'm not a saint, so don't assume anything good about me except that I don't have any active desire to do you harm. That's about the best you can hope for."

His mouth was so close she could feel the warmth of his breath against her lips. Without thought, Laurel licked them, and she saw a flicker of reaction in his eyes. He inhaled audibly and jerked his gaze from her mouth back to her eyes.

With cool emphasis he went on. "I watched you in the stream because I took on the job of keeping you safe of my own free will. I'm sure as hell not saying I didn't enjoy the scenery, because you might remember I told you flat out I think you're a beautiful girl, Miss Daniels. I would bet every jack man who has met you thinks so. Just keep in mind I'm tempted, steer clear, and we'll get along just fine."

Maybe it was the memory of the kiss and the close proximity of his mouth that made her so reckless. Maybe it was the pent-up tension of the past few days, and maybe it was just something she'd never felt before, but Laurel whispered, "What if I'm tempted too?"

His tall body stiffened and his eyes suddenly glittered.

173

What was she doing? Playing with a man like Cal Riker was just plain crazy, but she was telling the complete truth. She found him attractive in a way she never had anyone else, and who and what he was didn't seem to matter. Her parents had raised her to be honest and she usually told the truth without even thinking about it.

She lifted her chin and looked him in the eyes. "I'm not indifferent to you either. After that kiss, I'd guess a smart man like yourself has already figured that out."

For a moment he seemed to not know what to say, but then he murmured, "We're talking about a hell of a lot more than a kiss, Miss Daniels."

"I'm not stupid, *Mister Riker*, I've a pretty clear idea what you're saying." Her voice was a little hoarse and she cleared her throat.

"I'm saying I really want to fuck you. That's clear as a summer sky, isn't it?"

Laurel blinked at the crude word, taken aback more by the almost desperate note in his voice than what he'd just said.

"Sorry." He straightened and backed away a few paces, leaving her sprawled on the bed, her clothes and damp towel in disarray on top of her. One hand lifted and ran through his hair in a restless movement, his long fingers tousling it attractively. "Offending you isn't going to solve this problem, so I apologize for that last remark. You didn't deserve it, but quite frankly, this isn't the best discussion for us to have when you aren't wearing a stitch and I'm a little on the edge here anyway. I'll go outside and you can dress in privacy."

"I don't want you to go outside." Laurel sat up, letting the clothing she'd been holding like a shield go, baring her breasts. She could feel her blush and resisted the urge to snatch her dress back up and cover herself again. Slowly, she added, "I'm not sure why I feel this way with you when I never have with anyone else, but I think I want what you want."

His gaze was riveted on her chest for a moment, and then he gave her a direct look from piercing gray eyes. "You'd better more than *think* you want to give yourself to a man like me, Laurel. I'm an outlaw, a man without much except a reputation for violence and a price on his head."

She liked the sound of her given name as he said it in that soft, musical drawl. "I know who you are to the world. The trouble is, I think there's a lot more there. Please also remember, if it wasn't for the notorious Cal Riker, I doubt I'd still be alive."

"Your gratitude doesn't have to take this form, girl." There was a husky note in his voice.

"This isn't about gratitude. I was just pointing out you aren't what you seem and even without Gabe's cryptic little remarks, I was beginning to cotton on to that all on my own."

"I thought I was despicable." The ghost of a smile haunted his mouth.

"You were when you were carrying me off like some heathen. I was mad when I said that."

"Yeah, well, maybe you should stay mad before we both make a big mistake."

She gave him a level look. "I should be. I should be horrified you watched me in the stream. I should be ashamed of myself sitting here offering what we both know I am willing to give you. But somehow I'm not and that says a lot to me."

He swore softly under his breath, the words inaudible but the implied emotion clear. The tension in his lean body was visible. "If I don't walk out of here right now, I'm not going to leave."

Laurel smiled, feeling an unfamiliar anticipation coil in the pit of her stomach. Her nipples tingled slightly, as if he had already touched her. "That's fine. Seems to me I invited you to stay."

Chapter Six

She was an angel, her damp, curling hair framing her lovely face, her blush belied by the voluptuous beauty of her naked breasts, the pink tips high and tight. Those enormous blue eyes looked at him in expectation, and the trust implied by her invitation humbled him.

Cal knew he wasn't worthy to touch her hand, much less what he wanted to do, but he had the feeling that even though he had carefully honed his ability to control his reaction to almost any situation, this slender girl had him beat.

Damn him to hell, he should leave her alone. She was innocent. He was anything but.

Still, he knew there was just no way he could force himself to walk out that door.

Part of it, of course, was that fateful kiss. Maybe if he hadn't ever touched her, tasted her, he wouldn't feel this gnawing hunger. At the moment, he was pretty dead certain he was harder than he'd ever been in his life, his cock at full attention in his pants, straining against the confinement.

He took a step toward the bed and knew he was lost. Laurel watched him, the color in her cheeks deepening as he started to unbutton his shirt. He told her in a low, rough voice, "You win, sweetheart. I couldn't leave to save my life."

The frightening truth was maybe he was right about that. How he felt about her wasn't healthy, not for someone like him who lived on the run, who didn't need anything someone else could use as leverage against him.

"I'm glad."

The breathless tone of her response sent blood he didn't

think he had left south to his already throbbing shaft. He shrugged off his shirt, the cool air welcome on his heated skin, and sat down to remove his boots. His gun belt went next, and he almost didn't have the presence of mind to set it by the side of the bed within easy reach.

Yeah, he was pretty distracted, he decided with inner cynical amusement, his fingers fumbling as he fought to unfasten his jeans. It was a relief to shove them down his hips and step free, but even in the haze of his need he didn't miss the way Laurel stared at his blatant erection with wide-eyed uncertainty.

"It's big."

Cal stifled a laugh. "Women are supposed to like that."

"Oh." She looked chagrined but still fascinated.

He would have staked everything he owned she was a virgin and that remark just proved it. He sat down on the edge of the bed and cupped her cheek in one hand, feeling the smooth warmth of her skin. "Are you still sure?"

Her lashes drifted down and she turned her face so her lips brushed his palm. "Yes. Don't ask me why, but I'm sure," she murmured against his skin.

His heart tightened in a way he'd never felt before and suddenly he broke out in a light sweat that had nothing to do with sexual need.

He could fall in love with her, he realized with a stab of stunned enlightenment. Maybe it had even happened already. Look at what he was doing. "What about your fiancé?"

"I was never going to marry Weston. I thought about it for a little while, but came to the conclusion I wanted a man who wasn't just money and smooth manners."

"Well, I don't have either one of those, that's for sure." Cal leaned in as he tilted her face to his and captured her mouth.

Their first kiss had been everything tender and sweet and slow. This one was as explosive as a charge of dynamite. Slim arms came up around his neck as she pressed her body next to his and she opened for his tongue with amazing eagerness. The sensation of the erect tips of her breasts against his bare chest made him slide his arms around her and haul her onto his lap, his cock hard against her hip, their mouths mating with need.

177

The awareness that he needed to go slow registered in his brain, but his body was in argument with the realization. Without thinking he lowered her to the bed, his mouth trailing down her neck, stopping briefly at the pulse point in her throat, feeling the flutter of her racing heart with an inner smile. The taste of her skin was unique, a combination of the fresh flavor from the stream and the warm essence that was hers alone, all woman and more enticing than anything he could think of on this earth.

He tried to rein himself in.

She gave a small gasp as he nuzzled the valley between her delectable breasts, and then found one pointed nipple with his mouth. The first gentle swirl of his tongue won him a ragged sigh and the pink bud tightened. He ministered to it with care, giving her a chance to relax and enjoy the sensation.

"Cal."

"Yes, sweetheart?" He licked the soft side of one firm breast and lightly squeezed the other, fondling the crest, thumbing the nipple in small erotic circles.

"I don't know what I was going to say," she confessed with charming candor.

"Maybe that you like what I'm doing?" he suggested, his fingers stroking her nipple, the way she'd reacted to his kiss not in question. She wanted him, and he was going to have to ponder that later. The chemistry had been there from the beginning, unique in his experience, and obviously in hers too. The fact they'd both felt it so acutely disturbed him, because he hadn't ever believed in the romantic fantasy of love at first sight.

It was for fools.

So, maybe he was guilty as charged. He was guilty of a lot worse things.

"Yes." She shifted, the restless movement betraying her growing arousal as he touched and fondled her with as much finesse as he could summon considering his body screamed for release from the sexual tension that had been a palpable presence for the past week. Again she whispered and arched, "Oh...yes."

The lady liked it, all right. Good. Slow was going to be for next time. He was beyond slow, it was an abstract concept. He suckled both her nipples until they were tight and straining and there was an uneven sound to her breathing.

She was still entangled in a pile of clothing even if she wasn't wearing any of it, and he pulled the items in question away, tossing them carelessly on the floor. The sight of her nude gleaming body wasn't unfamiliar after the past few days, but this was the first time it had ever been available to him in a carnal way.

His mouth went dry as he looked at her, knowing he'd never seen anything as desirable in his whole misspent life. Laurel's hand flew to the apex of her thighs, shielding her sex from his avid gaze, and he took her wrist and urged her hand away. "Don't cover yourself. You're...so damned perfect."

It was true. She was all long supple limbs, golden hair now drying in tangled curls around her alabaster shoulders, and the focus of his attention at the moment, the promise of heaven between her legs. With his fingertips he brushed her soft pubic hair, wondering if it was still damp from her bath or if that was for him.

"Let me touch you here." It came out more of an order than he intended, and he amended the request with a wicked smile. "I swear you'll like it."

After a momentary hesitation, she opened to the slight pressure of his hands, spreading her legs, though her hands fisted in the blankets as if it took some effort. "You told me not to trust you."

He had said that and it was true, because he was certain he would bring nothing but trouble into her life. It gave him pause, but not enough to stop. He was too far gone for that, and it amazed and scared him.

But if he was going to do this foolish thing, he was going to make this good for her or die trying.

"Looks like you've ignored that warning." He stroked the satin skin of her inner thigh, getting her used to the intimate touch. As his finger glided upwards and found the damp, silken folds of her cleft, she made a small sound. Cal murmured, "I can't think of a greater trust than a woman naked in bed with a man. I'm going to do my best to earn it, sweetheart."

The bud he sought between the soft lips of her labia was

pink and slightly swollen already. Holding those enticing folds open, he leaned in and inhaled the fragrance of her arousal with satisfaction, lowering his head. He could tell the minute Laurel realized his intention, for her body jerked, but he just laughed and licked her in a languid sweep of his tongue across her clitoris.

"Oh...oh." Her pelvis lifted convulsively and she closed her eyes.

Yeah, that was exactly the response he wanted. With a light pressure, he teased and taunted, tasting the rise of her passion. In his current state of pressing need, he wanted her to climax before he entered her, because he was fairly sure he wasn't going to last long the first time.

Did all virgins taste so sweet, so lush and delectable?

He didn't care, he realized. Laurel mattered, but no one else. The whole world could implode and as long as this cabin, this bed and this woman still existed, he wouldn't even blink an eyelash.

She panted and arched, spreading her legs wider. He nuzzled her sex, teasing the satiny tissue, sucking with gentle persuasion on the swelling nub as he gauged her climb toward orgasm. Cupping her luscious bottom in his hands, he lifted her to his mouth in a fantasy come true and brought her higher, hearing with satisfaction small pants turn to feverish moans.

A scream of surprise rang through the cabin when it happened, her slender body shaking as she went over the edge. Cal felt her fingers twist in his hair and gave an inner grin of pure masculine satisfaction.

When she went limp, he rose up. His whole body was on fire, his cock rock hard and pounding with the racing rhythm of his heart. Positioning himself between her open legs, he wrapped his fingers around his rigid penis and guided the tip to her vaginal opening. "Stay relaxed, sweetheart," he urged as he gazed into her dazed eyes, pleased she'd been so responsive and easy to arouse. "I'll do my best to make this a gentle ride."

What had just happened she wasn't sure, but it had been nothing less than...wonderful. Laurel felt stunned, bemused, shameless and enlightened. She let her eyes drift shut and concentrated on the sensation as the man above her began to penetrate her body.

The way he touched her, the scandalous, shocking memory of his mouth between her legs, that sublime pinnacle, it all faded before the realization that with infinite care and patience, he was joining their bodies in the most intimate communion possible between a man and a woman.

Maybe she should be afraid, but she wasn't. That first kiss beneath the stars—after he had saved her from a fate she shuddered to imagine—had told her a lot about Cal Riker the person, not the infamous outlaw. Their combustible attraction aside, he was an intriguing man, and despite the nefarious reputation he fought so hard to keep to the forefront, a sensitive one.

Cal and sensitivity were not a likely combination, she knew, but as she felt his careful easing entry, she knew it was accurate. Even with what she thought to be his enormous size stretching her wide, she experienced pleasure, not pain. The corded muscles stood out in his arms and she could tell from the tension in his powerful body he exerted extreme self-control. When a small drop of sweat ran along the clean line of his jaw, she reached up and wiped it away with a fingertip.

Through his teeth he asked, "Am I hurting you?"

"No."

"You're sure?"

"Would you stop if you were?" She was curious, but felt sure enough he would, whatever his answer.

"I'd certain as hell try." His silver eyes were shielded by the thick fringe of his dark lashes. "No promises. I can't go any further unless I break through, though I'm dying to be all the way inside you, Laurel."

She ran her fingers down the hard planes and contours of his back, reveling in the harsh obvious need in his voice, all traces of his usual soft drawl gone. "Hmm. I want you there."

"There's some pain a woman's first time, you know that, right?" Braced above her, the expression on his face was both intense and dark.

"My mother told me."

"I bet she wasn't gambling on someone like me being the

one."

The bitter self-reproach was not what she wanted, not now when his hard cock rested against her maidenhead. "*I* chose you," Laurel whispered. "Kiss me first, Cal, and then...please..."

She didn't get to finish as his mouth lowered to take hers in a bone-melting kiss that was an expression of desire and explosive passion. As their tongues mated, so did their bodies, for he surged forward and she felt the tearing of her hymen with little more than a small gasp.

The moment of pain was negligible over the overwhelming realization drowning her senses, consuming her world. His lean hips wedged her legs even farther apart, his cock pressed against her womb, and the hardness of his muscled chest brushed her sensitized breasts. The heat from his tall body warmed and inflamed her, as did the feeling of possession with that long length fully impaling her.

Cal lifted his head, the expression on his face reflecting stark concern. "Tell me."

Those two words said so hoarsely made her heart flutter in her chest. Laurel knew what he was asking. She reached up and touched his face, exploring the fine-boned structure of cheek and jaw. "It isn't bad."

The explosive release of his breath indicated relief. "Thank God because I need to move. I'm about there already, but I'll do my best."

She wasn't precisely sure what he meant but as he began a backward glide, Laurel grasped his shoulders, thinking he was leaving until he thrust forward again. The friction made that same odd excitement begin to coil in her stomach and she made an inarticulate sound of pleasure.

It felt good.

No, she decided a few moments later, better than good, her attention riveted on the miraculous fit of his sex into hers and the cadence of their moving bodies. Quickly she realized if she lifted her hips to accept his forward movements it escalated the building pleasure.

"Just like that, sweetheart, yes..." He pushed deep, buttocks flexing as he drove into her with increasing speed.

As if she was no longer in control of her movements, her

body seemed to decide exactly when to arch and fall, knowing how to take him. When he shifted his weight to one arm and reached between them, she cried out as his fingers found the miraculous spot he had tantalized before and a blissful shudder rippled through her.

It seemed to go on, the fierce grip of it taking her by surprise as her inner muscles clenched around his invasion, the pleasure so flagrant, so acute, Laurel felt as if she was swept into a turbulent current, the swirling madness punctuated by Cal's low groan. He went rigid and stopped moving and she could feel a hot liquid rush deep inside her.

The cabin was utterly quiet except for their mutual choppy breathing, his weight braced above her just enough so she felt every inch of where their damp skin touched, every bit of his still rigid cock in her vaginal passage. His forehead rested in the spill of her hair over the blankets and his broad chest heaved.

Eventually, she summoned the strength to open her eyes. The place looked the same, with the chinked walls, the plain, simple furniture, the single window open to the warmth of the fall morning.

Her world, however, was very different.

Of the literally dozens of beaux she'd had, of the men with flowery compliments and impassioned proposals, she had somehow succumbed to this dangerous man with a shadowy past, someone she'd known only a short time if you counted the days.

He would have left her alone, but she had initiated the glorious thing that had just happened between them.

Why?

Because of the enigmatic duality of his personality? Nefarious killer versus considerate savior? After what had just happened she was sure he wasn't both, at least not to the extent people thought.

What did *she* think, was the question. Why *this* man? It was hard to put a finger on it but she was fascinated whether she wanted it or not.

Maybe even falling in love.

No, not with Cal Riker, the outlaw.

Yes, with Cal Riker, the man.

The touch of his hand interrupted her inner musings. He stroked her shoulder, trailing his fingertips across her collarbone in a feather-like caress. With a shift of his weight he brought her with him so they lay on their sides, face-to-face, her thigh draped over his hip. He was still inside her, stretching her passage deliciously. "Tell me what you're thinking now, Miss Daniels."

She couldn't help but laugh at the return of his low, soft accent. "You called me Laurel a few minutes ago."

"Forgive me, I was making love to a beautiful woman and might have lost sight of propriety." His blond hair was tousled, his gorgeously male body glistening with perspiration. The slight smile on his mouth would lure angels from the heavens, but his eyes, always the most expressive part of him, were watchful.

Her answer was obviously important, whether he wanted her to know it mattered or not.

Making love...

"I was thinking that I never even imagined anything like what we just did," she whispered, not sure how he would handle it if she told him too much. He'd said flat out he was used to being alone and she didn't want to spook him. It was possible—she sensed it—and the last thing she wanted was for him to ride away.

Gabe was probably right, she realized. Roots would make a man like him vulnerable and she didn't need to be told Cal wasn't interested in permanence.

The trouble was, she wanted to change his mind.

"Me either." The admission was made in a quiet voice and his gaze was heavy, one arm holding her close.

"You? I'm sorry but it is obvious you've done it before." It took a lot of effort to keep her tone even and dry.

"Sex? Hell, yes. I'm twenty-nine years old and it's always been pretty easy to find."

She realized she not only didn't like the idea of him with other women, but was acutely aware of their still intimately joined bodies and his embrace. "Then I'm surprised you'd agree with me. How is this different?"

"It is, but it doesn't matter. I'm poison for a woman like

you." Once again it was there, that edge of bitterness and a glimmer of bleakness in his storm gray eyes.

"I have this feeling the truth is the other way around." She said the words slowly.

"How do you figure that?"

Softly, Laurel said, "I think you are more afraid of me than I am of you."

Dark blond brows lifted. "Is that so?"

She nodded, smoothing her hand down his back, feeling the hard honed muscles. "Petrified, Mr. Riker."

"Seems to me I'm twice your size."

"So? We both know you wouldn't hurt me and that isn't what I'm talking about anyway. I—"

He interrupted her speech by suddenly rolling her over on her back, making her give a small cry of surprise at the abrupt movement. His mouth hovered over hers, lowered and took possession in a blatantly carnal kiss, and he gently rocked his hips.

"I'm still hard like I didn't just come," he whispered against her lips. "I want you again, sweetheart, feel it?"

She did. He filled her, stiff and hot.

As a distraction, it was masterfully done and she did find it impossible to pursue the conversation as he started to move again in long, measured thrusts between her open legs.

Fine, she thought, drowning in erotic sensation, if he couldn't handle talking about his feelings yet, she could wait.

The discussion was postponed, but not over by any means.

Chapter Seven

John Evans looked at the man sitting across from his desk and leaned back in the chair. "Not that you aren't the answer to a prayer, but do you mind telling me where you got this information, Mr. Ranson?"

"Yep, I mind." The older man, heavy in the shoulders and chest, with a graying beard, didn't shift his straightforward gaze. At his feet sat what looked like a full-bred wolf, obedient but with that unmistakable wild look. "Look, Sheriff, I'm giving you the River Bend Outfit, free and clear. They've pulled off a lot of robberies and now added kidnapping to the list. That's why I'm here in Tijeras. It's up to you to get the information in the right hands or even go after them yourself. I've done my duty as an honest citizen."

"You've done your duty again, you mean," John said dryly. "The last time you strolled in with news like this—little over a year ago, if I remember correctly—we caught what was left of the Holbert gang. I guess I'd like to know who's tipping you off that doesn't want to come here himself."

"Wonder all you want, because I ain't sayin'." Ranson shook his head, the dogged movement emphatic. "Let's just say you've got a friend on the other side who dislikes it when sidewinders like Ferris Norton drag innocent young ladies off of trains while relieving folks of their belongings."

John looked at the instructions on the location of the camp where Ferris Norton and his cohorts supposedly holed up between jobs. It was just like the last time, precise, detailed and written in the same neat script. "Can you blame me for wanting to know who he is?"

"We're curious by nature as people, I suppose, so nope, I guess I can't. That still doesn't mean I'm gonna speak up and give you his name, so don't wear yourself out askin'."

The message was clear and John gave an inner shrug, though it was true, he was curious as hell. Since he'd become sheriff of Tijeras, he'd gotten tips on a decently regular basis and he wasn't the only law officer Gabe Ranson had gifted with such news. Since part of the bargain was he kept it strictly to himself that someone out there was turning in criminals, he hadn't said anything, but it was his hunch last year the apprehension of a known murderer and rapist in northern New Mexico was the direct result of exactly the same kind of exchange of information. It was hardly coincidence Ranson had visited Raton just before the arrest, in his opinion.

Whoever it was, he was grateful.

And apparently this elusive hero had saved Laurel Daniels as well.

"You say the girl is doing fine?"

"Yeah, she'll be home soon enough. Tell her family to stop worrying."

"Will do, though I doubt until they see her they'll believe it. Both Matthew and Will Daniels want blood over this."

"Well, now you know where you can spill it." Ranson gestured at the map.

"So I do." John sent his visitor a speculative look. "Your friend could collect a reward for this, you know."

"He isn't interested."

"That so. He rich all on his own, maybe?"

Ranson chuckled. "We're not going to do this, Sheriff. I am not going to play some game where you try to wring more about him out of me. Take the tip and run with it, that's all we're asking. Wipe them out, either by hanging or behind bars, and at least a few less criminals will take a free breath. Now, if you'll excuse me, I'm going to see a friend of mine who lives about four hours' ride from here after I cure my dry throat at the saloon. Then, I'll be headin' back home. Winter is coming right along. The pass can get tricky if we get snow early."

"Have a safe journey and send on my thanks."

For a moment, Ranson hesitated, half out of his chair. "I'm kind of hopin' you might tuck this all in your memory. Just in case he...well, just in case."

"He got a past, your friend?" John had already guessed this was someone who outlaws accepted readily.

"We all do, Sheriff. It just depends what kind of past."

"Granted."

"Have a pleasant day."

"Same to you."

As his visitor exited, the animal at his heels, he tipped his hat to someone coming in the door and John was delighted to see it was his wife, a basket in hand. He got politely to his feet and couldn't help but smile. "This is the second nice surprise I've gotten today."

"That looked like a wolf."

"Did to me too."

Alice set the basket on his desk and returned his smile. "I thought I'd bring lunch."

She'd blossomed since they'd finally been able to get married. The haunted look was gone from her eyes, banished the day her abusive husband's body had been found in a pool of blood outside the saloon over a year ago. Two shots to the chest and no witnesses. By then, John had already been sheriff and he had to admit he hadn't tried very hard to solve that murder, duty be damned. That was one cruel man who deserved to die and he'd been actually grateful it had happened that way, because sooner or later, John was pretty sure he'd have had to kill him himself.

He went around and pulled her into his arms, feeling her familiar warmth with appreciation, her full breasts cushioned against his chest as he took her lips in a brief kiss. "What an excellent idea."

Laughing, she pushed him away. "I didn't come here for that, John. Wasn't last night enough for you?"

There was never enough with her, in his private opinion, because she was the most alluring woman he'd ever known, but his office wasn't exactly a romantic spot, not with the jail cells right behind them. A drunken cowboy, reclining in one of spare bunks, let out a gentle snore and brought him back to reality. He needed to move on the information he'd just been given.

He grinned. "Last night was fair to middlin', ma'am."

"Fair?" She gave him a mock glare of outrage.

"We might need to practice more, that's all I'm saying."

Alice lifted her dark brows. "It seems to me we've done our share of practicing already, Sheriff Evans. Besides, Celia came over with the baby and they might be staying the night. Parker has some business in town and she rode along. She's watching all of them right now, God help her, so I'd better get back right away."

It was a bit amusing to picture his lovely sister, who was a little on the headstrong side herself, managing a bunch of wild children. Lord alone knew what mischief they could get into in her care. Between his rambunctious son and his willful wife, it was a good thing Parker West was a calm, patient man.

John chuckled. "By the way, I have good news. I just got word Laurel Daniels is safe and sound."

Alice sank into the chair Gabriel Ranson had just vacated, her eyes showing interest. "That is wonderful. Her family will be so relieved. Where is she?"

"I have no idea."

Her forehead furrowed in consternation. "But you just said—"

"She's safe and will be returned that way, it's all I know." He moved the napkin on the top of the basket and saw she'd brought fried chicken and the scent of warm bread drifted upwards, seductive and heady.

"How do you know?" His wife gave him a skeptical look.

He reached for a piece of chicken. "Whoever he is, I'm starting to trust my source. I'm going to eat this and then I'm riding out. I'm glad Celia and Parker will be at the house with you. Tell them I said hello."

ॐ

With the fickle whim of a usual Colorado fall, the weather

turned fast. Cold rain dripped from the brim of his hat as Cal raised his rifle, trying to ignore the trickle down the back of his neck. There was a good supply of fresh game around but finding a flock of wild turkeys was a boon. He chose a peahen, took a bead, and dropped it neatly as the rest scattered in panic. Walking across the clearing, he picked up the glossy bird and headed back toward the cabin.

It was funny how he felt the discomfort of his wet clothes and the weather more than usual. Funny not in an amusing way, because he was well aware he was being seduced into the complacency of a man who wanted what he could never have. Warmth, shelter, a beautiful, willing woman waiting for him...

It shook him.

If there was one gamble he would have staked his life on, it was that he was immune to the idea of love. The wicked twists of fate in his past should make it impossible. His world was cold, violent, without mercy.

Or it used to be.

Cal needed to reconcile himself to the notion that as soon as Gabe returned, he needed to take Laurel home and then head for someplace new. Maybe Arizona or even California. He missed Texas but that was just too bad. He was too well known there. Too many men remembered not just his name, but his past.

Laurel must have been watching for him because she came out on the tiny porch, an anxious look on her face. "I heard a shot."

He held up the bird. "Wild turkey isn't something I could pass up. They were just at the edge of the clearing."

Relief washed her fragile features. "It scared me. I mean you'd barely walked out the door, and—"

"You thought the worst, probably. I'd either gotten a bullet in me, or put one in someone else."

She wore only one of his clean shirts, having washed her single set of clothes earlier. They were still inside drying by the fire. Unfortunately, the garment only covered her to the knees and she had to roll up the sleeves around her slender wrists. The sight of her half-dressed that way, dwarfed by his shirt, made him even more aware of her delicate femininity. He was also acutely conscious she was nude beneath that single layer of cloth.

As if he needed that reminder of what they had already shared. As long as he lived—and God alone knew if that would be much longer—he would never forget her innocent, captivating passion.

Laurel cocked a brow in reproach. "Do you blame me? You won't even let me step foot out the door without following me with a loaded gun in your hand, Cal."

She had a valid point, but with her he'd already discovered the part of his brain that used logic seemed to be in poor working order. "I'm trying to protect you. On the other hand, you needn't concern yourself about me."

Good Lord above, he actually sounded defensive.

One hand went to her hip and her chin went up in challenge. "What if I do anyway?"

"Do what?" His tone went deadpan.

"Concern myself."

He wasn't going to address that issue. Some perverse side of him reveled in the knowledge she cared at least a little bit, and the more practical side reminded him with ruthless honesty she was only going to get sorrow and heartbreak from their association. With one hand he indicated the bird. "I'll get this cleaned and dressed so we can have it for dinner."

She didn't move to go back inside though he knew she must be cold from the chilly, wet breeze. Tendrils of golden hair spilled down her back and one teased her cheek though she didn't seem to notice. "You didn't answer my question."

One of things he liked about her was her spirit and courage, so he supposed he shouldn't be surprised she wasn't interested in being dismissed. "I think most folks would tell you it's a foolish notion to worry over a man with a reputation for bloodshed and trouble. *I* just did."

She slowly shook her head, her blue eyes luminous. "You're still avoiding it, Cal."

He was getting soaked, the mist steady now, but he didn't move, wondering just what she wanted from him. She was not just a pretty face and voluptuous body, she was intelligent, and surely knew involvement with him was not just imprudent but

191

downright dangerous. He narrowed his eyes. "What exactly do you want me to say? That I'm glad you care enough to spare a thought for my safety? Well, I'm not, Laurel."

The brutal honesty in his tone would have made most people flinch, but she smiled instead. "Why?"

Exasperation rose, mingled with another emotion he didn't care to define. "Is this a trial or something? If so, can I defend myself inside where it's at least dry?"

"Just answer me."

The cool look he gave her didn't seem to have the desired effect of making her back off. He said with deliberate mocking cynicism, "Sweetheart, if you are expecting some declaration of a deeper feeling than good old-fashioned lust, it isn't coming. I doubt I'm even capable of it anymore."

"Capable of saying it, maybe. Feeling it, I am not as sure of that. I was in that bed too, you know."

"I remember, believe me. Yesterday morning and last night. You make a definite impression, darlin'."

She stared at him, her lovely eyes direct. It felt a little like she could see right into his tarnished soul. Soft rose lips trembled. "The trouble is, Cal, will you ever be able to forget? I know I won't, not ever. I think you're selling yourself a lie and it's going to end up hurting us both, not just me. Think about it."

With that little speech she turned and went back inside, leaving him motionless for a moment, not sure how to handle the constriction in his chest.

What the hell was she saying? That she *wanted* involvement with a notorious outlaw, a marked man? It was only a matter of time until he encountered the situation he couldn't handle—the faster gun, the stray bullet from some wet-behind-the-ears kid who wanted to be the man who shot and killed Cal Riker.

A gust of wind hurled moisture into his face, but he didn't care, wiping the rain away with a hand that wasn't quite steady. The trembling wasn't a good thing for a man who made his way in the world because he had iron-clad nerves.

She'd make him weak.

She'd make him whole again, and he couldn't afford it.

℘

Dinner was delicious, just like he'd predicted, but Laurel noticed Cal didn't eat much after all, his expression shuttered in the way only he could manage, as if there was nothing behind that still, handsome mask. No emotion, no thought, no inner turmoil.

It was a lie.

The energy of it was there. She could feel it practically radiating in waves from his tall body, in the careful way he held himself, in the measured avoidance of his gaze. He built up the fire while she cleaned the dishes. When she was done she saw he was propped in a chair in front of the blaze, his long legs carelessly crossed at the ankle. His brooding gaze was fastened on the flames, his mouth set, and flickering light played across the elegant lines of his clean features and gilded his thick hair. She pulled up the other chair and sat down to warm herself, uncertain of how to break the silence, and not even sure if it was for the best to have another discussion, not in his present mood of ominous quiet.

Finally she couldn't stand it. "Do you think it will snow? The wind sounds like it's picking up."

He transferred his gaze from the fire to her face and the corner of his mouth lifted a fraction in what could have been the ghost of a sardonic smile. "It's not too early for it up here."

"It stays warm longer farther south."

"Yes, it does."

"I like snow though. I love the winter."

"Thanks for letting me know. I'll be sure to remember that about you the next time I'm sleeping outside in a storm."

Silence fell again after her inane attempt at discussing the weather. Darn the man, Laurel thought crossly. She'd seen that hint of ironic amusement and it irritated her to think he sensed her restless need for conversation. Two could play that game, but she had a feeling he was much, much better at just sitting and cocooning himself in taciturn quiet, whereas she was more used to being around her family and the lively atmosphere of a working ranch.

Well, after they'd made love the first time he'd asked what she was thinking. Surely it was fair if she asked him?

"Is there a reason you're so quiet?" She tried to keep the question neutral. "Have I done something?"

She knew she had. That he didn't often acknowledge his feelings on any matter was hardly a deep, dark mystery and maybe she'd made a mistake. He'd made her angry the way he refused to acknowledge that whatever was between them wasn't casual, and she'd just reacted.

If she hadn't known it wasn't just simple lust like he claimed—*known it*—she would never have let him touch her, much less have her.

"Yes, ma'am, you have done something."

She waited, exasperation rising as he said nothing else. The wind rattled the shuttered window and sighed past the cabin in an eerie wail. Because of the fire she wasn't precisely cold, but she shivered anyway. "Well, mind telling me?"

"Would it matter if I did mind?"

The low, husky tone of his voice made her shiver again for an entirely different reason. She said, "You've made it clear you don't like questions, I know. But I'm not used to being ignored either. We don't have to discuss anything personal."

"We've covered the weather, I believe. And don't worry, I'm not ignoring you. I wish I could, actually, but I think I'm pretty aware of every breath you take." The look he sent her gave weight to his words, his silver eyes molten but his posture still indolent and giving the impression he was relaxed. "Besides, you pretty much ordered me to think about a few things and I have been."

Laurel looked at him uncertainly, not sure how to handle his obviously volatile mood. Eventually, she murmured, "I somehow doubt anyone could order Cal Riker to do anything."

"Not many would try, at a guess, but you are more daring than most, sweetheart. Yesterday, for instance."

She liked the endearment the way he said it, with low, deliberate inflection, but at the moment wasn't sure she trusted the slow, wicked way his mouth curved. "I don't think you're as dangerous as everyone believes."

"Is that so? If I told you what was on my mind at this moment—like you seem to want me to—you might just reconsider that." He cocked a dark blond brow. "But, since you have such a hankering for conversation, I'll go ahead and tell you. First off, I'm thinking I like you in just my shirt, buck naked underneath it. I'm also contemplating how fast I can get it off you, have you flat on your back, spread your pretty legs, and be inside that tight little cunt of yours."

Her heart began a slow pound but she tried to stay as nonchalant as possible. He was being crude deliberately. Laurel felt her throat tighten a little because she remembered well the delicate care in his touch, and the careful way he'd initiated her into sexual intimacy. What he'd just said didn't remotely resemble what had happened between them.

He shifted in a restive movement of his body. "Want to hear more?"

"Somehow I doubt it," she muttered, aware of the shirt that barely draped over her thighs to the top of her knees. "Not in your present state of mind."

"I kind of have this fantasy of you sucking my cock but I suppose you might need a little time before we progress to that. Before Gabe gets back, for sure, though."

If he wanted to shock her, he was getting there. Laurel started to get up out of the chair but his hand snaked out lightning fast and caught her wrist, dragging her back down. "Stay and talk," he said in a lethal tone. "You started this."

Since it was a one-room cabin, she didn't have any place to go anyway, so she sank back down defiantly. "Fine. Talk. Tell me more. Do your best to show me how cold and distant and offensive you can be."

"I think I should for your own damn good." The words were said on a low growl.

"What do you care about my life?" she retorted. "You worry a lot about me it seems, for a man who only wants one thing. Rescuing me from a gang of lawless thugs, following me around with a loaded gun to protect me, and apparently now you're concerned I'm too involved with my feelings for you. I'm surprised a man of your *insensitivity* even noticed."

"It's been a while since I've been around a respectable

woman, true." His face changed then, the mask cracking a little. He glanced away. "You're going to regret ever knowing me."

She knew him all right. The taste of his kiss, the reverent touch of his gifted hands, the feel of their joining... She also recognized that toneless observation for what it was. He was wounded down deep, beneath the icy façade, beneath even the decent man who had taken care of her and risked his life to save an unknown woman.

"If it makes you feel any better, if I had a choice of who to fall in love with, I'd have guessed a gunman with a price on his head would have come in dead last. But I didn't get a choice, it just happened, and Cal Riker isn't who he seems anyway."

His fingers let go of her wrist like she was on fire. "Don't say that. You don't love me, Laurel. You...*can't.*"

It was the way he said the last word, with poignant emphasis. That and the fact the hard-edged look shattered and he no longer looked like the indifferent, brooding man who had been so silent and cold all evening.

He looked *stricken.*

Very softly, she told him, "If you're trying to forbid me to feel a certain way, let me tell you it just so happens not to work. Besides, I think you know full well I feel that way already. That's why you've been acting like you have all day."

He shoved himself to his feet with none of his usual lithe grace. One lean hand ruffled his hair. His throat worked. "It doesn't matter how you feel or how I feel. Nothing good can come of this. Jesus, Laurel, what if I get you pregnant?"

A sense of triumph flickered through her at what he had just admitted, even though she'd carried the conviction his feelings, however buried he kept them, were involved all along. Knowing they existed and getting Cal to admit it were two different things. The idea of having his child was surprisingly not something that bothered her either, even if they weren't married. If it happened she would have a part of him always.

"I don't know what can come of it," she acknowledged softly and also stood, her fingers going to the buttons on his oversized shirt, unfastening the top one with deliberation. "But I do know we have tonight and all the other nights until Gabe returns."

The look on his face when she let the garment fall off her

shoulders said more than any words.

Chapter Eight

He was bone tired, dry as dust and his horse had pulled up lame and slowed them down the day before. Will Daniels squinted at the parched ground and then glanced over at his father. Discouragement weighed the older man's shoulders and he looked like he'd aged ten years in the past few days.

It was no wonder. It was clear they were going to have to turn back. Not one of the ten men in their search party had the heart to say it out loud, and Will had the sinking feeling he was going to have to be the one.

He didn't want to give up either, but there simply was no trail. They'd been able to track the kidnappers for only about ten miles.

Ten stinking miles, he thought, sick to his stomach with worry over Laurel. No matter how many vows they made to find her, kill the bastards who snatched her and bring her home safe, they couldn't make good on it if the tracks weren't there.

"Rain comin'." Jeff Johnson, their foreman and the best hand on the ranch, murmured as he nudged his horse up along side. "It ain't gonna help, Will."

It was true, the breeze carried that telltale whiff, picking up and rattling through the brush. "I know," he agreed just as quietly. A good rain would obliterate any chance they had, and those chances were already pretty slim and dwindling by the minute. Once they'd lost the trail, they rode on blindly, hoping to stumble across a clue. It was big country and if they hadn't been so desperate, they would have turned back two days ago.

"Maybe the reward will work." Jeff, a burly Scandinavian with a shock of pale hair, tried to sound positive, but the disbelief was there in the tenor of his tone anyway. "When we get back, maybe John Evans will have good news."

"I sure as hell hope so." Will closed his eyes and took a breath. "If we return empty-handed, it will kill my mother."

"I ain't so sure about your father either." It was said in a low voice.

"He's not eating much." It was an understatement and Will wasn't surprised. His parents doted on Laurel and why shouldn't they? His baby sister was spirited and sweet-tempered, and had grown into a lovely woman. That she didn't deserve whatever was happening to her rankled, but what it was doing to his parents couldn't be discounted.

The men who took her were going to pay. That was all there was to it.

"Riders comin'." The laconic observation came from one of the hands, and he pointed at where a plume of dust rose in the distance. "Looks like a decent sized bunch of hosses and they ain't goin' slow."

Will tensed, scanning the horizon, his hand falling naturally to his hip. "It's too much to hope it's those bastards, but Jacob is right, they're moving hell bent for leather. I say we ride to intercept them."

"Could be Indians," Jeff observed, looking troubled. "The Utes sure are hanging on."

"Could be, but considering why we're out here, a band of fast-moving horses interests me. From all that dust they are in one all-fired hurry."

His father showed the first spark of animation in two days. He nodded, his mouth tight. "I agree. Let's ride."

They spurred their horses, heading due east over the rolling topography. Will knew if they could see the approaching party, they would also be seen. He braced himself. There could be a fight, but the truth was, he was spoiling for one.

Any action, even if it was having bullets winging past him, was preferable to being helpless.

Not Indians, he realized as they got close, the two parties on a collision course. White men, saddled mounts, and the group was heavily armed. A shout alerted him they'd been seen, and with a start he recognized the horse of the man in the front.

John Evans' big sorrel gelding. The sheriff had helped them organize the search party in the first place but stayed in town to tend to his duties, tactfully refraining from saying he thought the whole thing hopeless because the River Bend Outfit had been tracked before and never found. Wherever they holed up was a mystery and he'd obviously had little faith in them being able to solve it simply by riding out in the vague direction the witnesses had given.

He'd been right too, damn it.

But for whatever reason he was there now, leading a large party of men.

"I was kinda hoping to run into you all. You aren't too far off course," he said without greeting as they drew up. Lathered horses heaved and the sheriff looked grim, but there was a triumphant gleam in his eye. "We came across a camp yesterday and I hoped it was yours."

"Why?" Will wasn't interested in polite small talk either, though he liked John and they were friends.

"Because we could use all the firepower and men possible. Most of the River Bend are wanted one way or the other. From what I understand of the position of their camp, dead is going to be the most likely way we take them in. It's fine by me and saves the judge a lot of trouble."

"You know where it is?" For the first time he felt a glimmer of true hope. His throat tightened.

"I do." Evans gave a brisk nod. "What's more, I also know your sister is safe."

The staggering relief he felt was punctuated by his father's inarticulate cry. "How?"

"The same source that has helped me out before. I believe it is reliable and I've been told she's going to be returned to Snowy Peaks soon."

Will glanced over and saw his father's eyes glittered with tears. He said hoarsely, "You're sure?"

John looked him in the eye. "As sure as I can be without seeing her myself, Will. The same informant gave me the exact directions to the camp where this bunch is hiding. Laurel isn't there. But, the men who took her are. You interested in coming along?"

Interested in the chance to put a bullet in one of the men who'd put his parents—and himself—through hell?

Laurel was supposedly safe.

Thank God.

"Fuck yes, we are," he gritted out.

℞

Facedown on the bed, Laurel quivered as a finger traced a line down her spine. Two warm hands then cupped her buttocks and squeezed gently. Cal murmured in her ear, "You have a very nice ass, Miss Daniels."

She mumbled in amused irritation into the pillow. "Is that your idea of a compliment?"

"It's just an observation, sweetheart." He gave one of those low, throaty laughs that made her pulse pick up the pace.

"Not exactly poetic, Mr. Riker."

"I haven't been much for poetry since I left university."

Laurel went still, not wanting to show her reaction to that bit of information. She'd guessed before he'd had a good education, for his speech reflected it. After a moment, she asked in as offhand a tone as possible, "Where did you go?"

"Harvard. If you want a laugh, I studied law."

She didn't feel even the glimmer of a laugh. "I wondered. I take it your family was pretty well off then."

"You could say that." His tone changed—just a small fraction—and she wished she could see his face.

It was risky to chance pushing him, but when they were in bed like this, with his hands lightly rubbing over her bottom in small, playful caresses, maybe he would be more amiable to a few questions.

Cal Riker amiable? The rest of the world would laugh at the thought, but she was desperate to know more about him.

Choosing her words carefully, she asked, "Do you ever see them?"

"I can't go back to Texas."

She could feel the door swinging shut in her face at the tone of his voice. "Do you write?"

He hesitated, the pause palpable. Then he said coolly, "No. They don't even know if I'm alive."

How could you, she thought first, and then knew the answer without asking the damning question. Cal was protecting them. In his mind he was dead and gone to them already. Never mind he was more alive than anyone she'd ever met, his inner demons held him in a powerful grip.

As neutrally as possible, she murmured, "What did you do in Texas?"

"You don't want to know." His hands slid persuasively up, tracing her waist, brushing the sides of her breasts. "Get on your hands and knees, Laurel. We have much better things to do than talk about my past."

As much as she enjoyed his lovemaking, she didn't necessarily agree. Knowing him in a sexual way was not the same as *knowing* him. However, he didn't give her much choice as he slid one arm around her hips and lifted her up. He covered her, his chest pressed against her back, and his long cock rubbed between her open thighs. His breath was warm against her ear. "I like this position. This is how animals mate, how males take their females in the wild."

Her eyes shut as his hand slipped downward and he found her cleft, rubbing gently. "Does that feel good? No, don't bother to answer, I know it does. You make the sexiest little sound, sweetheart, when I get it just right."

He replaced his fingers with the tip of his rigid penis, rubbing the head lightly against the lips of her labia, parting her, stimulating the sensitive nub she'd had no idea existed before she met him. Laurel moaned, dropping her head forward, shamelessly angling her body to give him the most access. The friction was erotically teasing, the pressure not quite enough to make her climax.

"Cal," she said in a pleading voice that cracked a little. "Harder."

"I'm going to give you what you need, don't worry." He cupped her breasts and squeezed a little as he dropped a kiss on her shoulder, his mouth lingering in a tantalizing slide up to her neck. "Help me in."

For a moment she wasn't really sure what he was asking. "What?"

In a thickened tone, he suggested, "Take me in your hand. Show me what you want."

She reached back between her open thighs, wrapping her fingers around his erection and positioning it at her vaginal entrance. As he pushed forward, she sank backwards, and his entire length slid into her. Blissful pulses swept through her body, both from his possessive entrance and the simultaneous caress of his hands over her breasts.

He moved, pulling out until he almost slipped free and then sinking back in so she felt the press of his stomach against her bottom. "Hell, yes," he muttered. "It's so good."

In her mind she echoed that sentiment—the sensation different in this position, but Cal was right, there was something primal about it, something a little wild and reckless. As his thrusts grew harder, his hands moved from her breasts to her hips, holding her in place for each hard plunge.

Laurel felt it the moment he lost control. Hard arms wrapped around her and he pushed deep, the pulsing force of his orgasmic rush flooding her, filling her passage with hot liquid as he gasped her name. They stayed that way until his mouth moved to her ear and she heard him whisper, "You didn't come. My apologies, ma'am. I'll take care of that right now."

There was a sense of disappointment when he withdrew and she gave a small cry of surprise as he deftly flipped her over on her back. Silver eyes glimmered and then he lowered his head, taking her mouth in a searing, hot kiss. At the same time he slipped his hand between her legs. Long fingers moved gently, finding the right spot with unerring accuracy, and he began to rub in slow erotic circles.

The bewitching joy of it made heat wash through her body, the subtle pressure of his touch just right so her already sensitized body began to tremble. She moaned into his mouth, spread her legs shamelessly wider, and let him bring her to the brink of rapture with those skillful, manipulative fingertips. She found that peak quickly, shuddering against his tall body, her arms going around his neck as she clung to him and cried out.

Cal held her easily in the circle of one arm as they lay skin to skin in the aftermath, both sated and languid.

Fingers wet with her fluids and his sperm trailed up her torso, lazily circled one taut nipple and then touched her chin, tilting her face up so he could look in her eyes. "I'm not interested in debating principle right now, but tell me something, sweetheart. Are you going to lie to your family about where you've been and who with? I'm damned curious to know what you're going to tell them."

The question made her pause. As always, Cal knew exactly how to disconcert her, how to unsettle her world. The warm comfort of his arms was belied by both the question and the uncharacteristic hint of open emotion in his eyes.

What did he want her to say? She had the feeling he didn't even know the answer.

As always, the truth seemed best. "I've been thinking about it." She smiled at the understatement of that admission. It was almost *all* she thought about. There was no way to help the hesitation, because of the chance she was taking, but after a moment she said simply, "I'm hoping you'll consider staying on at Snowy Peaks. My family will welcome you."

A small tremor went through him. Nestled against him as she was, it was impossible to miss. "Laurel, you know I can't."

"Why not?"

He blew out a breath and loosened his intimate hold. "Jesus, girl, you know there are about one million reasons why, the first one being I'm *Cal Riker*. That's a name synonymous with trouble, take my word on it. Your family loves you I'm sure, but you've got your head in the clouds if you think for a minute they want an outlaw like me within a hundred miles of you."

She sat up and gave him a level look. "I love you. That'll be enough for them. Besides, is there some reason anyone needs to know just who you are besides the two of us? Cal Riker can disappear. It's a name, nothing more. The man you are exists and that is enough for me. Bury your past and start over, Cal. Colorado is a good ways from Texas. No one will know you."

He stared at her, his expression difficult to interpret. "You have the damnedest imagination, sweetheart."

A lack of an outright refusal was promising. As calmly as

possible, she pointed out, "I don't think it is a wild idea in any way. The only people who know who took me out of the River Bend camp are the men who kidnapped me in the first place and Gabe. Not one of them is likely to talk about it, so that problem doesn't even exist. We can easily come up with a plausible story for how you rescued me and a new name. Maybe eventually you can even get in contact with your family, at least to let them know you're safe. A new identity wouldn't be hard, and how many chances are there that anyone would ever recognize you?"

"Laurel, I—"

She interrupted doggedly. "My father has talked often enough about a partner on the ranch, someone to share the responsibility with my brother when Pa's too old to do it anymore. It's a big place and I know Will would be more than happy to include you, especially if you were my husband. They were going to offer it to Wes, but you'd be better at it anyway."

Husband. There. She'd said it. Out loud. In front of Cal.

How often, she wondered with a glimmer of nervous amusement, had anyone seen Cal Riker disconcerted. Naked and glorious, his muscular body gleaming in the glow of the dying fire, he reclined on the disheveled bed next to her and didn't say a thing, his lips just slightly parted. Under the thick fringe of his lashes, his silver eyes were hard to read.

What could she do? How could she cajole, influence, convince him? She leaned forward so their mouths were a scant inch apart. "I can promise you one thing. As Cal Riker, or whoever you decide to be, I'll be a very accommodating wife to that man."

It was possible she'd just made the mistake of a lifetime. Not because she had just essentially proposed to the infamous Cal Riker, but because she had just risked losing him.

"Is that so?" His gaze held hers, but he didn't smile in complement to the teasing words. Instead his lashes drifted downward as he leaned in and closed the small gap between them and gave her a heart-stopping, tender kiss. Soft, warm and so poignant she felt the sting of tears against her lids. She kissed him back with growing urgency and when he rolled her to her back, she accepted him in the cradle of her parted thighs, well-aware he liked to end serious discussions with lovemaking, but also knowing that though he always touched her with care, this time it was different.

Maybe he was actually thinking about her idea.

ℰ∂

The fire had sputtered out and he knew he should get up to stir the coals and get it going again, but instead Cal simply stared into the pitch dark of the cabin, unwilling to relinquish the precious burden resting against him.

Yes, burden, he thought as he felt each soft inhale of breath as Laurel slept in his arms. A proverbial cross, a weight he never asked for, never imagined.

God, he loved her.

Loved her.

It hurt. It seared his soul. It chopped down his defenses, so carefully built up over the past years, like they were nothing. How could one slender slip of a girl do so easily what dozens of hardened men hadn't been able to do?

He was pretty sure she'd just killed off Cal Riker, for even though he knew it was the most foolish romantic idea on the face of the earth, he was willing to assume a new identity if it meant keeping her.

It was a harebrained plan, he told himself.

Or fucking brilliant, an inner voice speculated.

Was it possible? Could he invent a new name, a new man, one worthy of a beautiful, giving wife, maybe even a family? She wanted to marry him and the realization humbled him in a way that made his throat tight. Cal blinked and tightened his arms around the woman sleeping so peacefully next him, as if holding her closer would help him sort out his emotional turmoil.

Introspection was a demon for a man like him, but maybe the possession was just an inevitable part of this process he'd never been through before. He didn't think about life if he could help it, and certainly didn't sit around pondering love. Hate he knew about. And revenge, death, violence...all the things that made him who he was.

Was.

Laurel had already changed him, that he'd realized the first time he made love to her. It was frightening he'd ever let her crack the carefully constructed shell that protected him from feeling anything but cool, calculated decision-making.

And liberating too, though he hesitated to believe freedom from his past was really possible. The trouble was, he'd already gone so far, maybe he really wasn't Cal Riker anymore.

All he knew, as he lay there in the darkness, was he didn't think he was cold enough any longer to ride away from her.

Chapter Nine

The shout made him look up, and Will narrowed his eyes, focused on the horizon. A lone horse crested the top of the hill in the distance, and it took him a minute to realize it had two riders.

Golden hair gleamed in the fire of the setting sun and though he'd been praying this moment would actually happen, for a long heartbeat he just stood there, unable to move or believe it. One hand convulsively jerked off a glove and he dropped it without thought by the corral fence.

John had sworn Laurel would come back to them. But as someone who had witnessed and shared his parents' pain and worry, Will hadn't actually believed it, he realized, as relief washed through him.

"Rider comin', boss." One of his hands made the laconic observation. "Nice hoss."

"I see that. Damn, do I ever. You all finish up here, will you? I'm going to go greet them." He strode off, down the lane that wound up to the house, his booted feet feeling as if he walked on air. They got closer, the big horse moving smoothly, and Will couldn't help but let a big smile break out over his face as he saw his sister's wave.

She's safe.

On the heels of that thought was the knowledge he didn't recognize the man bringing her home. He hadn't expected to, but it was unsettling to see her ride up with a perfect stranger and know they'd been together for weeks. Who the hell was he?

"Will!" They trotted up and Laurel slid off without help, running forward to fling herself in his arms. He hugged her tight, pulled back, took one look at her flushed face and realized something with astonishing clarity.

Not only was she safe and apparently unharmed, she looked...happy.

After being kidnapped by a gang of rough, vicious men, his sister looked happy.

What the hell?

His gaze narrowed in on the stranger now watching them with an impassive expression from the back of his horse. The earlier observation was true, it was a magnificent animal, a rangy bay with clean lines and a sleek coat. Expensive saddle and tack, he realized as he took a rapid mental inventory, though the man was dressed in worn jeans and a plain shirt, his hat shading his features just enough Will couldn't quite get a good look. Still holding Laurel, he nodded, just a brief tilt of his head, and the man gave him the same quick gesture of acknowledgement in return.

His sister noticed and pulled away. She took a small step back, looking lovely as ever but disheveled in a very wrinkled pink dress, the smile fading from her lips. "This is Cal Smith. He...he helped me after the train robbery and now he's brought me home."

She'd never been a good liar.

He was going to need a few more details than that simplistic and unconvincing explanation, but he was still grateful, no matter what exactly had happened. Will stepped forward and reached up, offering his hand. "Much obliged, Mr. Smith. You have no idea what you've done for my family."

After a small hesitation, the man took it. "You're welcome."

The faint hint of irony in the response didn't escape him and suddenly Will had a fair idea he was pretty in the dark over what was actually going on. The handshake was puzzling too. The stranger had an interesting grip, his fingers like velvet over steel, strong but well-kept. No chopping wood or mending fences for his sister's savior, instead his hands were tended—carefully so. Will felt a flicker of curiosity and turned to Laurel. "Ma and Pa have been frantic. You'd better get up to the house right away."

She didn't move. "I'm sorry everyone has been worried, but

I'm fine."

Fine...and apparently gun-shy of leaving him alone with her escort. Will said with conviction, "Laurel, they need to see you right away. It's been pretty tense around here since we got the news you were abducted. Trust me on this, sis, and move along. Smith and I are right behind you. Let me show him where he can stable his horse. I'm sure he'll be invited to stay for supper but don't make them wait another minute, please."

His sister still hesitated a moment, until Smith said in a cool Southern drawl, "Your brother has a point."

She turned then with a small nod, and gathering her skirts in her hands, lifted them enough she could run toward the house. Will watched her hurry along for a moment, not sure how to handle his emotions, and then cleared his throat and glanced up. "You from Texas? I'd know that accent anywhere."

The man slid off his horse in a lithe, smooth movement. He was tall, leanly built and his movements were graceful and precise. "Not for a long time."

"She looks unharmed."

Smith didn't dodge the unspoken question. "Norton nor any of the others touched her."

"Thank God." He cocked a brow, his gratitude a palpable thing even if he did still have questions. "Or thank *you*, I suppose. Whichever applies. Probably both."

The man laughed, a mirthless sound. "We don't get lumped together very often. Divine intervention isn't my specialty and he doesn't use me too often as a means of delivering it either. Let's just say your sister has a lot of courage and I admired that from the moment I saw them haul her off the train."

"How'd you come to see that?" Will eyed him, trying to gauge his reaction to the question.

"I happened to be there."

Now that was one devil of an evasive answer. Will said with stark emphasis, "They're mostly dead. We hunted them down and there was a stand-off at their camp. None of them had any interest in surrendering. The local sheriff, John Evans, wasn't too interested in bargaining either. It ended up bloody."

"Did it?" Smith looked unmoved, tugging at his horse's rein. At closer range he had clean-cut features and unusual gray eyes. "Can I put Goliath up there?" He nodded at the barn. "He's got to be tired. We rode pretty far today."

That was all the man had to say about the River Bend Outfit's demise? Will nodded. "I'll have one of the hands take care of him. You come up to the house. I know my parents will want to meet you and express their appreciation, if mere words can even cover it."

"I don't want thanks."

Somehow he knew that was the truth. What did he want? Money? No, Will thought, watching the man lead his horse toward the big barn. He could judge men pretty accurately and this cowboy wasn't one of those. There was something about him, something controlled and yet edgy, and he wore his guns low and easy, like they were part of him.

A good man to have at your side, Will guessed, and a bad one to have against you if that confident, slightly dangerous air was any indication.

He was damned curious about the past two weeks. Damned curious.

℘

She was the one who thought it was a good idea to put a tiger in a cage, after all, Laurel thought with rueful amusement. It wasn't that Cal wasn't polite and good at fielding questions if they got too personal, it was just that there was nothing ordinary about him and it showed. The evening meal had been lively, her homecoming obviously releasing a huge strain on the household, and even Cal had actually shown some embarrassment finally over her mother's effusive gratitude.

It was good to be home. She just hoped she could keep him at the ranch. Never once had he actually agreed to stay for any length of time, but he had assumed the unoriginal last name without argument. Their concocted story—Cal had been riding cross-country and stumbled across the robbery in progress and managed to get away with her—was accepted, though Laurel thought Will looked skeptical. Her older brother wasn't a fool, but as long as everyone else didn't ask too many questions, she wasn't going to worry about it. As predicted, her parents immediately invited Cal to stay on as long as he liked as a guest.

Laurel rinsed a dish and glanced at the doorway for about the tenth time.

"Don't worry, they won't eat him alive." Her mother took the dish from her hands, smiling as she dried it. "Besides, he has the look of a man who can handle himself just fine, Laurel. Have I mentioned yet how good it is to have you here?"

"About a hundred times," Laurel said, returning the smile, seeing the gleam of tears rise again in her mother's eyes. "And I feel the same way."

"That boy outside on the porch with your father and Will is an angel, bringing you back to us."

It was impossible not to laugh and she did, drying her hands on the apron around her waist. Wings and a halo on Cal Riker? She didn't think so. And he was hardly a boy. "Hmm. I think that might be an exaggeration, Ma. He's a lot of things, but not that. On the other hand, he's a sight better man than he would ever admit. Thank you for asking him to stay."

Her mother sniffed, dabbing at her eyes for a moment. In her late forties, there was a hint of silver in her blond hair, but she was still slim and shapely and her eyes shimmered with emotion. "Like we had a choice, the way you look at him. I always wondered when you'd finally fall for one of these wild cowboys. Somehow I knew it wasn't going to be one of those Eastern beaux your grandmother likes to push at you."

Was she that transparent? Apparently so. Laurel blushed and glanced again at the doorway. "It just happened," she admitted in a quiet voice.

"That's how it works. He's a handsome one, I'll say that. Well-mannered and soft-spoken too."

If her mother knew exactly who she was talking about, she'd probably faint on the spot. Not to mention he'd done some fairly outrageous things to her in bed, but Laurel had enjoyed every single one of them. Their time at the cabin was something precious and she wanted to lock it away forever, in case one day it was all that was left to her.

"If he asked me to marry him, I'd say yes."

"I guessed that already." Her mother moved to the stove

and lifted the pot there, pouring out a cup of coffee. She sent Laurel a speculative look as she sat down at the table, the well-worn surface scrubbed and polished. "I'm not going to criticize either one of you, but you were alone with him for quite a while."

The delay in bringing her back was the tricky part of Cal's supposed grub-line-riding drifter persona, and since she wasn't exactly sure why they had to stay and wait for Gabe to return from his trip—much less why he made it in the first place—she really couldn't comment. It had something to do with the robbery, she wasn't stupid and had figured that out easily, but Cal hadn't explained and getting the man to talk was downright difficult.

He could be infuriating.

He could also be tender, and deliciously gentle and oh-so-wicked when he touched her in certain ways...

She sank into an opposite chair, relishing the warm, familiar surroundings, the scent of cinnamon and rich coffee lingering in the air. "He was on his way to visit a friend when we...crossed paths, I guess is a good way of putting it. We stayed there most of the time."

It was the truth, or a reasonable version of it anyway.

"Your father is going to ask him about it, count on it. Not tonight, I'd guess, since he's just so relieved and grateful, but he'll get to thinking about it and ask."

"If we get married, will it matter?"

"In the long term, no, I don't think so. *Should* you get married?"

If her mother had figured that out so quickly, she wasn't doing a very good job of acting at all. Laurel gave her what she hoped was an innocent look. "What do you mean?"

"Laurel, honey, that face didn't work on me when you were five. Why do you think you can pull it off now?" Her mother took a sip of coffee, looking calm but still questioning.

Well, it might be nice to have an ally to help in the quest to make Cal stay on. On the other hand, if her mother told her father Cal had touched her—well, a good deal more than touched—it might cause trouble. After a moment, she sighed in an exasperated exhale. "Do you know everything?"

"I saw how he looked at you. That possessive air usually means one thing when a man acts a certain way. He feels he has a right to for the obvious reason."

"It was my idea."

Her mother chuckled, her slender fingers wrapped around her cup, amusement lively in her eyes. "You've always had a pretty clear notion of what you want in life. Does your young man understand what he's up against? I hope he's ready for a fight if he tries to leave."

Cal Riker up for a fight?

What an ironic question.

~

She'd sat across from him at the dinner table, looking so damned beautiful in a light blue gown, her gleaming, pale hair caught up in some soft style that framed the delicate features of her face, her lovely eyes poignant and full of emotion. Cal had watched her—he couldn't help himself—and even the dainty way she ate her food made him want to sweep her into his arms and carry her off somewhere and make love to her.

It was a pitiful state for a man to be in, so absorbed in a woman the way she ate roast beef made him get an erection, he thought wryly.

This obsession was exactly why he sat on the wide porch of the sprawling ranch house with her father and brother, no less, and had to pretend to be just some ordinary down-on-his-luck cowpoke.

More than that, he had to act as if he hadn't bedded Matthew Daniels' beautiful daughter in almost every inventive position he could come up with in the past two weeks, accept the man's hospitality and attempt to live one whopping lie.

Laurel was just plain dreaming if she thought the two of them could pull this off, but neither could he just ride away, so he didn't have much choice.

"Whiskey?" Will Daniels offered him a glass.

"Thanks." Cal took it and tasted the amber liquid, finding it to be a lot smoother than Gabe's rotgut concoction. He sipped, settling a shoulder against one of the posts on the wide veranda, too restless to just sit but trying to hide it.

How long would it take to get used to this, he wondered as he gazed out over the neat corrals and barns, beyond that the green valley spreading in impressive picturesque glory. Hot meals every night, a decent bed, nice people who treated you like a long-lost friend. Not to mention Laurel with her captivating beauty and sensational passion, looking at him like he was a hero, not a notorious gunman who had blood on his hands.

He didn't deserve it, but had a feeling he could get used to it real quick. "Nice spread," he remarked.

"I'm running close to sixty thousand head right now," Matthew said, his tone almost carefully conversational. "I owe you, so if you'd like a job, say the word."

"That's real decent of you," Cal murmured.

"My daughter is safe. It means the world to me, so don't mention it. I get the feeling too, she'd like you to stay on, so consider yourself invited."

Will Daniels was a long, lean, sandy-haired replica of his father, right down to his keen blue eyes. He resembled his beautiful sister in an entirely male way, and he didn't sit either, but lounged against the railing, his gaze watchful. "We can always use a good hand and I have the feeling you know how to handle yourself. You grow up ranching?"

They were understandably curious. He sure as hell would be if some strange man had kept his sister or daughter for weeks and then just rode up, bold as brass. "In southern Texas," he answered after a moment of inner debate about revealing too much. "I wanted to be a lawyer but it didn't work out. Sometimes life's that way." It was nice to be able to tell the truth, even if it stung. Normally he didn't talk about himself at all, but then the company he'd kept in the past years wasn't the best.

"Your folks still alive?"

"I think so." Cal took another sip from his glass, the liquid burning his throat a little but going down like silk. "I have to admit I've been bad about going home. Drifting gets to be a habit."

"Think you can break it?" Matthew Daniels looked at him directly, with challenge.

He looked back, keeping his gaze steady. "All I know is for the first time in as long as I can remember, I want to try."

Something flickered in Laurel's father's eyes. "I see."

He had a feeling the man did see. Once again, if Laurel thought they were going to fool anyone, she was dead wrong. If he didn't know Cal was her lover, he sure as hell suspected it. It was there in the slightly narrowed eyes and the set of his mouth. "You can ride out with Will tomorrow. Get a feel for things."

"I appreciate the chance."

"You wear a gun like you've used it a time or two." Will spoke quietly.

Cal inclined his head. He had no idea how to turn off habits a decade old and apparently it showed. With a lift of his hand he indicated the darkness off the porch in a leisurely sweep. "It can be kind of unfriendly out there."

They accepted his bland statement at face value and it showed a great deal about how grateful both of them were to him for interfering in Laurel's abduction. He could read men and he had a feeling neither one of them would ask any more questions.

Such easy acceptance was a bit staggering, but then again, Laurel had turned his life upside down from the moment he saw her. He didn't deserve her; it was a given, but he was getting used to the idea she didn't see things the same way.

For the first time since the fateful day his brother died, he actually believed he was a damned lucky man.

Chapter Ten

John leaned over and slowly licked the tip of one tight breast, lingering on the succulent nipple, closing his eyes as in response his wife reached down to run exploring fingers down the stiff length of his cock. With her dark, silky hair spilled over the bed, Alice lay next to him and caressed him until his breath went out in a betraying hiss against her skin. She cradled his balls, gently squeezing, a teasing expression on her pretty face. "Hmm...these feel very full."

"You have no idea, honey." He felt like his body could explode just from her exploring touch. When she stroked his scrotum with a light fingertip, he gritted his teeth and fought back the urge to ejaculate then and there. "God almighty, do that again and this is going to be over, pronto."

"Now that would be a shame."

He agreed wholeheartedly. "Tell me how you think it should be."

The provocative tone of her voice was hard won after her disastrous first marriage, and he still hesitated to push her, always letting her set the pace.

She spread her legs and ran her fingers down his back as he shifted into place, her eyes drifting shut in a languid slow movement as his tip nudged her opening, widened it, and he entered her in a slick glide. "Yes, just like that."

John seated himself fully, the tight heat around him perfect, tantalizing. He began to take her the way he knew she liked it, with long gentle thrusts, whispering in her ear how much he loved her, how good it felt, how perfect they were together. All of it was true, every word.

They moved, her hips undulating in just the right rhythm, the erotic friction tingling along every nerve ending, each breathless exhale escalating the pleasure. He made sure she came first, reaching between them to put pressure on her clitoris, enough so as he pushed in she trembled, wetness coating his fingers. As always she climaxed with little more than a small cry, her face pressed against his throat. His body responded to the tightening of her inner muscles and he jerked, spilling sperm in a forceful rush that made him give a low groan.

Afterwards was almost as good as during, he thought with a satisfied smile on his face, relishing the feel of her in his arms as he rolled to his side and spooned their bodies together. He liked her best this way, her hair a tangled soft mass, her thighs streaked with his discharge. They lay quietly, their breathing slowing, until Alice said, "I saw Laurel Daniels in town today. There's gossip, of course, there always is here, but I think it must be true she wasn't hurt or used in any way. She looked fine, maybe even better than fine, and I have a hard time believing anything bad happened recently to someone who seemed so...serene."

He'd heard the story directly from Matthew Daniels, and though it seemed a bit improbable that one man could ride up on a bunch of escaping outlaws and manage to rescue her, he hadn't been there and didn't want to voice any doubts. "I'm just glad she's unharmed. She's a nice young woman."

"She's a very pretty young woman," his wife pointed out with a hint of amusement in her voice. "Don't pretend you haven't noticed, John Evans."

Laurel was more than just pretty, but he wasn't going to bring that point up. "I've got eyes," he agreed, kissing Alice's neck. "But I'm a happily married man. You made me especially happy just a few minutes ago."

"They say the man who intervened is at the ranch now and staying on. Weston Harper is fit to be tied, because he thinks Laurel is sweet on this cowboy."

"Is that so? Seems to me Wes hasn't got room to say a blamed word. He didn't lift a finger to help find her and I know Will was pretty disgusted over it. If someone else is her hero, well, that's his own fault."

Well, maybe hero was a questionable word, though John hadn't met the Daniels' guest. All he knew was when they'd tracked down the River Bend Outfit there'd only been six of them. The passengers on the train said there were seven bandits. Two got away in the melee, four were dead, and that one crucial man hadn't been there at all. There wasn't a lot of deduction involved to suspect maybe the stranger known as Cal Smith that Matthew had taken on as a hand might be related to all of those things, but Daniels had almost dared John to say anything, and he hadn't. More than one good cowboy had fallen into the wrong company, and more than one bad one had turned over a new leaf.

However, he noticed Smith—yeah, that name was real likely—hadn't come to town once in the time he'd been at the Snowy Peaks ranch, and no one said much about him.

The truth was, he was curious. But he was also a man who minded his own business as long as no one was breaking the law. Whoever had fed him the location of where to find the gang had done him an immense favor and certainly the cowboy now working for Matthew had saved Laurel from pure hell.

He could look the other way. As long the stranger behaved himself, there was no reason to stir up trouble.

¹∽

Laurel waited as patiently as possible, listening for the long, slow footfalls punctuated by the gentle jingle of spurs. Cal had been given a room near the end of the hall, even though he'd suggested he just bunk with the rest of the hands. Her mother had prevailed in her usual way, though, and he'd finally agreed.

Three doors down from her bedroom and she was as acutely aware of his presence as if they were in the same room each night.

In fact, she wished they *were* in the same room. It had been a week and he hadn't as much as kissed her once. True, there hadn't been much opportunity given the lack of privacy, but he hadn't tried either. The least he could do was give her a goodnight kiss, she decided as she sat there.

Everyone else was in bed, hopefully sound asleep. Cal and Will had stayed out on the porch late, long after her parents retired, and even her brother had come in some time ago. When she finally did hear the betraying musical sound of Cal's approach, her heart began to beat a little faster.

He stopped cold when he opened the door and saw her sitting on his bed clad only in her nightgown, his expression enigmatic. "Laurel, what are you doing?"

"I'd think that's obvious. Waiting for you. Close the door." She spoke in the same low tone, not quite a whisper but almost.

"Are you crazy? Your father would lose his mind if he caught you in here."

"Close the door and no one will hear us. I just want to talk to you for a moment."

"Yeah, I bet he'd have no problem believing we're just talking." Despite those sardonic words, he did quietly shut the door. Hatless, his dark blond hair just slightly unruly, he looked so very handsome in a heart-stopping way. The meager light from the one lamp she'd lit played over the sculpted planes and hollows of his face, and his shoulders were impressively wide under his flannel shirt. Just his masculine presence in the room seemed to fill it with an aura that was his alone.

She really wanted more than a kiss if she was honest with herself, feeling the warmth between her legs and the slight tingling of her nipples. "I've missed you."

His brows lifted a fraction. "You've seen me every day."

"Not enough of you." Good God, she sounded like a harlot, she realized as she caught the innuendo of her words and flushed. The double meaning wasn't intended, but then again, it was all too true.

Cal didn't miss it either, a slow smile crossing his face. "Is that so, Miss Daniels?"

She nodded, mesmerized as always by the captivating power of his smile. It was rare, but it was powerful.

"What did you want to discuss so badly you'd risk my neck—because your father would gladly snap it in half if he caught us—by sneaking in here like this?"

"Us, I suppose."

"What about 'us' specifically?" He hadn't moved but stood just inside the doorway in his usual deceptively relaxed pose.

Cal was many things, but relaxed was rarely one of them.

And he wanted her just as badly as she wanted him. Laurel realized it in a rush of excitement at the intense look in his silver eyes, a smoldering smile lingering on his beautiful mouth.

She didn't feel like a harlot any longer. She felt like a woman with the man she loved, moreover, the man she was meant to be with for the rest of her life. "I was thinking..." she managed to mumble and then trailed off, not sure if she should mention marriage again. However, he *had* stayed on at the ranch so far, and was now looking at her like a hungry wolf at a bone.

"Always a dangerous thing when a woman attempts that," Cal said dryly. "I might have to put a stop to it at once. I wonder what would work. Any ideas?"

He moved with the powerful grace of predatory animal toward the bed. His gun belt was deposited on the floor with small thud and his eyes glittered with purpose. Laurel didn't resist when he caught her shoulders and eased her down so she lay supine. Long fingers brushed her cheek in a perfunctory caress, and then his mouth came down on hers, hot and hard. His tongue took her mouth, claimed it, and his hands moved in urgent exploration over breasts, hips and thighs.

It was definitely not a chaste goodnight kiss, which was just fine with her. Laurel kissed him back with equal wild fervor, knowing he was right, it was reckless for her to be there, but not caring at all.

She gasped as he abruptly pulled her nightgown above her waist and his fingers slid between her legs in an intimate test. "That was fast," he murmured against her lips in a husky whisper.

The fact she was wet and ready should have embarrassed her, but it didn't. Instead she reveled in the realization he could arouse her so easily. "I've been thinking about you," she murmured. "And while we're on the subject, what's this?" She reached between them and pressed her palm to the bulge in his pants.

"You're nearby," he explained simply. "It happens all the

time."

"We seem to have a mutual problem then."

"I'll take care of it."

Cal shifted his weight on top of her, his fingers slid out and went to his pants. The hot hardness of his cock sprang free and she felt the press of his knees as he insistently parted her legs and positioned himself to enter her. The first thrust impaled her fully and made an inarticulate sound escape her throat as she arched into it and spread her legs even wider.

"Shhh, sweetheart." He breathed in her ear, the ragged sound evidence of his enjoyment and need. "An interruption right now would be mighty inconvenient."

There wasn't much question she agreed, clinging to him, following the motion of his hips by lifting to accept the slide of his hard shaft, eager, panting with the pleasure, awash in sensation. Cal knew just where to touch her, how to stroke that crucial sensitive spot between her legs as she got close, the fierceness of her reaction to the touch of his fingers almost too powerful so she muffled her cry of release against his muscled shoulder, trembling beneath him. He stopped moving as her vaginal muscles clenched his cock, and she felt his answering shudder and the liquid heat as he released his seed.

Breathless and almost weak, Laurel realized that while she still wore her nightdress, Cal was fully dressed right down to his boots and spurs. She gave a weak laugh. "I was just hoping for a goodnight kiss."

"I haven't touched you in seven days. I missed you, Laurel."

"I know." Her hushed agreement was punctuated by the knowledge that Cal didn't have an optimistic view of the world, but they were in accord on the matter of mutual desire. He disliked needing anyone, but the admission he knew he did was another small triumph. Hopefully she was gaining ground in small ways, little by little, like chipping away at a rock, she thought ruefully. Hard definitely described Cal, but then again a lot of other words did also, among them honorable. In his own way, of course—because she had a feeling he *always* went his own way, but as long as he took her with him, she was fine with that.

He lifted away, his cock slipping out of her, leaving a small sense of loss. He shook his head over his untucked shirt and open jeans. "That didn't involve finesse and I sure didn't treat you like a lady."

"You treated me like a woman," Laurel countered. She could still feel a throbbing between her legs, her sex warm and soft with semen and the fluids of her own desire, her thighs wet. She was too languid and content to bother to adjust her gown. "I don't see a problem with that. You might have noticed me not objecting one bit."

"Your father would." Cal sat up on the edge of her bed and sighed, still keeping his voice muted. "He has a right to. He has a right to something else too. If I ask him for the privilege of marrying you, he needs to know who I am, Laurel. I'm not a saint, but I hate lying. This is more difficult than I imagined. I like your family, and they've accepted me as the person I told them I was. Even if I was Cal Smith, drifter and no account cowboy, he wouldn't want you to marry me with nothing to offer you, so he's making a big effort to give me respectability for your sake. Deceiving him any further goes against the grain."

That statement made her tense, drawing her out of lethargic post-coital repose. She rose up a little and stared at him, registering that implacable look on his face with an inner chill. "Cal, please...don't. He might not want you here if he knew."

"Who the hell could blame him?"

"Well, I would, for one." Laurel groped for the right words, despite what just happened between them. Her worst fear suddenly loomed. "I love you. I've said it before and it's true, whether you're Cal Riker or Cal Smith. If you tell my father your true identity and he asks you to leave, I'll go with you, but I'd rather stay here."

"You aren't going on the trail with me, Laurel. For God's sakes, girl, I'm *wanted*." He gave an exasperated exhale and a muscle tightened in his cheek.

"Yes," she agreed, a small sob lodged somewhere in her throat. "You are. Here."

"I love you too much to risk ruining your life."

Shock held her immobile for a moment. Dear God, he'd finally *said* it.

The context of the conversation wasn't what she pictured when he acknowledged his feelings, but she still had a weapon and wasn't afraid to use it now that Cal had actually said the words. Maybe she would have used it anyway, but it seemed like a good time to bring the subject up. "Let's compromise."

"We both know I should ride on. I don't quite see how we can negotiate the issue."

"What if I'm pregnant?"

Cal went still, every muscle locked in place, not even certain if he'd stopped breathing. After a moment, he said in an unrecognizable voice, "Are you?"

Laurel, delectably in disarray after their impetuous lovemaking, the skirts of her white nightdress still up around her slender hips, looked unfazed. Tendrils of golden hair brushed her smooth cheeks and her blue eyes were direct with challenge. "It's possible. I lost track of the days while we were at the cabin and on our way back, but I'm at least a little late."

He wasn't an expert on how female cycles worked, but he wasn't ignorant either and she certainly hadn't had her flux during their time on the mountain at Gabe's place. The rough calculation he did as he tried to assimilate what she just said told him they were out nearly three weeks and the past one made it four.

Late. Yes, at least a week, maybe two, depending on when her last cycle had been.

Jesus. He'd just been a little rough with her, not taking his time, wild with need and repressed emotion...

"I didn't hurt you, did I?" He reached for her, not certain why, stopped himself because being gentle now wouldn't change what came before, and felt worse than he had the night he'd had to pretend to take her against her will. His arms dropped back down and he had no idea what to do.

Laurel had that unique ability. To completely disarm him, leave him uncertain, humbled, shaken.

She smiled with pure feminine assurance. "No, Cal, you didn't hurt me. If you couldn't tell that, you weren't paying attention."

This changed *everything.*

His whole—up until her—meaningless life.

He felt...shattered.

Blessed at this miraculous possibility.

Frightened also, a new sensation and one he had no idea how to deal with. A child?

His child.

No, *their* child. He couldn't fathom that Laurel, so achingly beautiful, so loved by her family, so able to choose any man, even one of the elite Bostonians Will had told him courted her when she went back East, didn't look at all perturbed by the notion of having his baby. It stunned him.

He should say something. Reassure her, tell her he would always be there to care for her and the precious miracle she might hold, only he couldn't be sure of that because of what he was and their uncertain future.

"Do you want to hear my compromise?"

The soft question brought him out of his self-absorbed contemplation. "I suppose so. I have to admit you just threw me."

"We should know soon. Let's give it a week before you say anything to my father and I want to be there when you do, by the way. This isn't just about you, but about me too, and maybe about the three of us."

Put that way, how could he say no?

How could he refuse her anything anyway?

"A week is reasonable." He stood. The house was utterly quiet and since he wasn't good at talking about feelings, he preferred a more expeditious method to demonstrate his emotions. "One week and I tell your father one way or the other, agreed?"

Laurel watched him peel out of his shirt, her eyes heavy with the inviting look he'd come to know. "Agreed, as long as you make love to me again tonight."

"We don't have to negotiate that part of it," he said as he sat down to remove his boots.

Chapter Eleven

Will wasn't sure how to broach the subject, but blunt honesty seemed best, and so he guided his horse around a small patch of scrub and said in as neutral a voice as possible, "If Laurel is going to spend the night in your room, Cal, I suggest you put a ring on her finger."

It wasn't surprising that the other man didn't bat an eye, even upon fairly short acquaintance it was easy to discern his remarkable self-control. Instead their guest glanced out over to where the warm day laid a shimmer of heat across the valley, the mountains in the distance glorious against a vivid blue sky. "I told her it was a bad idea."

No denial. Will hadn't expected one, mostly because Cal seemed like the kind of person who rarely explained himself to someone else. On the other hand, Will felt he had the right—as Laurel's older brother—to find out what the hell the man had in mind. "She's had a lot of beaux and never shown more than a passing interest. Even Weston Harper got only a few smiles and maybe a stolen kiss or two."

No response. Not one word. Cal just rode beside him as they headed out to check on the far herd, the one pastured in the northernmost part of the ranch, the light sigh of a warm breeze the only sound besides the dull clump of their horses' hooves. In profile, his face was impassive.

"I couldn't sleep last night," Will went on, determined they were going to have this conversation, even if he was the only one talking. "It happens more than I'd like. I usually go for a walk and it helps sometimes. I walked past your window. I could...well, damn it, I could *hear* you."

He sure as hell had. Soft sighs, murmured words, the faint rhythmic creak of the bed. There hadn't been much of a mystery surrounding what was going on.

Cal finally looked at him, his silver eyes disconcertingly direct. "It wasn't particularly an honorable thing to do right under your parents' roof. I know it. But I love her. I *love* her. I'd die for her, that goes without saying. For whatever miraculous reason, she seems to feel the same way about me. I don't deserve it, don't deserve her, but this has happened somehow."

Laurel's feelings toward the man who had rescued her weren't exactly a secret to anyone who knew her well. Will understood her heart was involved and it troubled him because he had a feeling the mystique around Cal Smith wasn't necessarily a good one. He actually liked the man riding beside him, and his parents also seemed to cautiously approve, but there wasn't much doubt he was reticent about his past and he had a dark, dangerous air to him sometimes that was simply unmistakable.

"What are you going to do about it?" A right-to-the-point question seemed best.

"She wants marriage." Cal held the reins in one hand easily, sitting on his horse like he was a part of it, a natural cowboy at home in the saddle.

"Women do." Will shied away from most of the young ladies he knew for that reason. He wasn't ready to settle down just yet. "More to the point, she deserves it. You're not denying what happened between you, Cal."

"No."

"There could be a child."

"She tells me maybe there already is."

Fucking hell, that was quick. Laurel is pregnant and doesn't have a husband. Over my bleeding dead body...

Curtly, Will said, "There's a local preacher in Tijeras. He can take care of this in no time."

Something flickered in Cal's eyes. "How trustworthy is he?"

Now they were coming to it. Will had struggled with how to handle this conversation, the questions crowding his mind like stampeding cows trying to fit through a hole in a fence. "What does he need to keep to himself?" he asked bluntly.

"I can't marry her under a false name. That would mean it wasn't legal and she deserves better."

Shit. He'd wondered all along just who this man was. "Yes, she does," Will agreed, tense, angry and apprehensive. "Care to tell me what name it is you're not anxious to spread around?"

"Cal Riker."

Cal Riker?

For a moment he felt blank. No wonder, he realized in unhappy comprehension, Cal wore those guns like he knew just how to use them. He'd used them plenty. How many dead men? Will didn't remember precisely, but the legendary lethal force of Riker's reputation alone made people run for cover. Very carefully, he repeated, "You're telling me you're Cal Riker?"

"Yes."

"Forgive me if it isn't the best news I've ever gotten."

For the first time, the man next to him looked grimly amused as his mouth curved in a humorless smile. "Yeah, I sort of thought you'd feel that way."

"Laurel knows?"

"Yes. She knew the minute we met at the River Bend Outfit's camp. I had to bargain for her and believe me, at six to one, it wasn't a sure thing. Luckily, I bluffed my way into giving them my share of the take from the robbery for her and we left the next morning."

Odd how that worked, with John Evans getting information on the exact location of the hideout somehow. Will gave the man riding next to him a searching look. If there was one thing he hadn't heard about Riker it was that he was a thief. "Someone told John where their camp was. We were out looking, hoping to find Laurel, but we couldn't find it."

"It's big country." The declaration was made in a cool tone.

In other words, no more on that subject. Will knew when to shut up, especially if questioning a man as dangerous as Cal Riker.

The father of his sister's baby. *Jesus, this is an interesting mess.*

"The preacher is pretty trustworthy," he said slowly, weighing each word. "He's also fond of Laurel and if she wants to marry you, I think he'd keep his mouth shut about who you really are."

"You think." There was a slight ironic note to that observation.

"Best I can do."

"There's a decent price on my head in Texas." Cal sounded unmoved, his voice utterly without emotion. "Dead or alive."

"Is that so?" Will wasn't exactly stunned to hear it. Riker's notoriety started with the prominent slaying of a judge who'd sentenced his brother to hang for the murder of a local shopkeeper. By all accounts, at the age of nineteen, Cal had accosted the judge on the street, given the man a gun and dared him to draw. When the judge, scared to death according to the eyewitness accounts, had finally gotten off a shot, it came nowhere near the mark, and Riker had drawn and killed the man with a lightning swift accuracy that had given him a name. Rumor said Riker's younger brother was innocent and that's why he went after the judge. The state of Texas didn't seem to agree with his vigilante brand of justice.

Will wasn't certain if he wouldn't have done the same damn thing. He sure as hell had wanted blood from the River Bend Outfit when he'd heard they'd taken his sister off that train. He'd been there, in fact, when Sheriff Evans had stormed the camp, and he'd shot one of the fleeing bandits himself.

"I'm a marked man."

"Yes," Will couldn't help but agree, "you are. But if Laurel loves you, maybe we can keep up this charade. Damn it, Cal, if she is pregnant you have no choice."

"I've already told her I was going to come clean with your father."

"He's not going to like it, but then again, like he's said before, he owes you."

"All that matters is Laurel." His companion turned away and for a moment, he looked as bleak as a winter's day. "I never thought something like this would happen to me."

No man like him did, but the fact it happened at all proved something. Cal Riker might be a notorious gunman, fast on the draw and with a reputation for violence, but he was a bit more complicated than the legend. Will knew it after being around him for the past week, and he also knew his sister wouldn't fall for a man who was truly a cold-blooded killer. Her rescue alone showed Riker was not some ruthless outlaw who made a living with his gun, and Will knew in his gut he was the man responsible for giving John Evans the location of the camp.

"I promised her I wouldn't say anything for a week. She wants to be sure about the baby and she's afraid he'll want me gone if he knows who I am."

Will knew his father. If Laurel loved Cal—even if he was Cal Riker—he doubted he would be willing to break her heart. "I think Pa isn't going to be all that surprised."

Riker shot him a sardonic look. "How so?"

"Let's face it, the fact you can handle a gun a certain way hasn't escaped anyone here. You also aren't real anxious to go into town, and now I know why."

"I doubt anyone would recognize me, but you never know."

That was probably true if you lived your life on the run. "Think you can settle down? Live here quiet-like with a wife and raise a family on a cattle ranch? If the answer isn't damned clear in your mind, I'd say even if Laurel is carrying your baby maybe you should move on."

"I'm not leaving her pregnant and alone." The answer was flat and harsh. "Don't you think I've told myself I should ride away for her sake? Well, hell yes, I have. But I flat out can't, Will. I can't do it."

Something inside him eased, for the declaration was more than a little convincing. "You seem sure."

"It surprises me too." The admission was a bit rueful. "As for settling down, it sounds like heaven to a man who's told himself that he'd never see thirty. Without her, that was probably a pretty accurate guess."

"With all the wild stories, I'm kinda surprised you've lived this long," Will said dryly.

"Yeah, well, half of them aren't true."

"If half of them *are* true, I'm still surprised."

"I'm not easy to kill, but someone would get around to it eventually." The statement was made with cold practicality. "However, trust me on this, I've got something to live for now."

എ

John strolled into the room, listening to the dissonant sound of the piano punctuated by the laughter of the patrons. The place was quiet, but then again, most cowboys hadn't been paid yet for the month. At times you couldn't think the noise was so loud. He went up to the bar and said, "Hi, Henry."

"Howdy, Sheriff." Bearded, with thick arms and a jovial smile, Henry Adams beamed at him across the polished surface. "Beer?"

"Not right now, thanks. Can you tell me something?"

"Like what?"

"I heard there was a stranger in here earlier. Older, wiry, hungry look about him. Flashed a big bankroll and sat in on a game."

"I remember him." Adams inclined his head. "Name was Rollins. He was askin' about Laurel Daniels. Wanted to know about Snowy Peaks Ranch."

"Mind telling me specifically what he asked?"

"No, I don't mind, but it was kind of casual like. Just mentioned her in passing, something 'bout he'd heard she'd been kidnapped, and was she back...that sort of thing."

The same man had apparently asked about her at the general store, and the livery stable. Alice had happened to be in the store and mentioned it to him, because the stranger gave her an uneasy feeling.

If there was one thing he trusted, it was his wife's instincts. When he started going around town asking about the man, it turned out his interest in Laurel Daniels included a few pointed questions about Cal Smith as well.

There was going to be trouble. He could practically smell it in the air.

"You know what's funny?" Henry frowned, a thick crease in the middle of his forehead. He scratched his beard. "He asked me if I'd seen Cal Riker."

John narrowed his eyes. "Cal Riker? Here? Why'd he ask

that?"

"How the hell do I know? He was one of those edgy hombres, you know the kind. Fidgety and tight like pulled wire. I looked in his eyes and saw nothing there. No soul, you know what I mean? When someone like that comes in my place, I want them out as fast as possible."

Rollins and his soul—or lack of—was interesting, but Cal Riker? Well, shit. That was the last thing John needed in Tijeras. Riker was by all accounts a gun-slinging desperado wanted in Texas for the murder of a judge and he hadn't looked back since. He was supposed to have killed dozens of men, though the one murder charge was the only one John knew about, and even with that one, supposedly Riker gave the judge a chance at the first shot.

Cal Riker, lightning fast, accurate as sin. He was a legend, and the exact kind of legend no law enforcement officer wanted within a hundred miles of his territory.

Cal Smith. John went very still, the realization hitting home like being thrown from a running horse. The man who rescued Laurel Daniels called himself Cal Smith.

Holy hell, that wasn't what was going on, was it? Surely Cal Riker wasn't the man romantically involved with pretty, sweet Laurel Daniels?

No, John told himself. No. Cold-blooded killers didn't rescue damsels in distress and bring them home unharmed. The stranger was probably what he said he was, a drifter in the right place at the right time...

Only who else but someone like Riker could outface a group of thieving outlaws like the River Bend Outfit and get away with it? All along he'd wondered how in the hell one man had pulled off getting her away from them, and this made a lot of damned sense.

"Thanks, Henry."

"Sure."

He left the saloon and walked back slowly to his office, going in to sit at his desk, pondering what to do. He leaned back in his chair and stared at the empty cells, thinking.

Rollins. He'd heard the name somewhere, but didn't think he knew much about him. He had the vague idea maybe the man was one of those aging legends, a one-time gunslinger who everyone figured was dead and gone but still hung on somehow, drifting on the edge. He was looking for Riker, obviously.

An outlaw looking for another one. That didn't sound good.

What to do about this was a problem. Matthew Daniels had made it pretty clear the man he called Smith had not only saved Laurel from rape and whatever else might have happened to her, but delivered her back home without so much as a scratch and she was the one who wanted him to stay on. What Matt would say if he knew the identity of his guest was predictable, but then again, if the man hadn't been Cal Riker, she would probably never have come home.

John got up, put on his hat and stalked out the door.

$\wp$

It was the second time it had happened, just out of the blue. Laurel stood up, her plate in her hands, and suddenly the world spun, the plate clattered to the floor and she grabbed the back of her chair for balance. A wave of nausea came with it, and she felt a wash of heat through her body even as strong hands caught her.

"Easy, sweetheart."

Cal. Strong arms lifting her easily, the warm comfort of his broad chest, the tangy scent of man and pine with a hint of whiskey. Laurel closed her eyes for a second, resting against him, and then the moment passed, the queasiness subsided and her head stopped spinning.

What she was left with was the realization that she was cradled in Cal's arms in front of her parents and brother and she'd almost fainted just from getting up at the dinner table.

This was going to be fun to explain.

Only, she wasn't going to have to explain it. That was clear from the resigned expression on her mother's face and her father's growing scowl. Will too, seemed suddenly absorbed in drinking his coffee, as if the liquid in his cup was the most fascinating thing on earth. She managed to say, "I'm fine. I must have stood up too fast."

"Maybe you should lie down for a bit." Cal frowned in concern, holding her like some precious object, which she would have enjoyed if it wasn't for their audience.

"It used to happen to me too," her mother said in a serene voice. "She's right, she's fine. It passes, by the way, after the first few months."

She'd wanted to wait, wanted to give her family even more of a chance to get to know Cal before he told them just who he was, but it didn't seem like that was going to happen from the darkening expression on her father's face. He bit out, "Maybe Laurel should lie down and you and I should talk, Cal."

She wasn't about to be left out of *that* discussion. Laurel pushed lightly on Cal's chest. "Put me down. We'll all talk. I'm all right now. It passes very quickly."

"This is between me and him." There was an edge to her father's voice she didn't hear often.

"No," she corrected in soft reproach, "this is between me and Cal. I love you, Pa, but I'm almost twenty years old and whatever has happened was entirely my choice, and as such, my responsibility."

"Mind telling me just what *has* happened?" Her father looked angry, but not as furious as she expected.

"I love your daughter," Cal said in his usual soft, slow drawl, still holding her. "I want to marry her."

"I'm getting the impression you'd better."

"My cooperation isn't in question, sir. Remember that."

"There's a small problem but I think it can be just that, small." Will sounded calm, his good-looking face composed and bland. "The deception was Laurel's idea but Cal hasn't told you his real name. He has a good reason, believe me."

Laurel felt Cal's reaction in the slight tightening of his arms, but otherwise he showed nothing as usual. "He's right. My real given name is Calvin Steven Riker. I was born in San Antonio and last I knew I'm still wanted in Texas for the killing—no matter how much it was deserved—of a judge named Harold Watson."

Neither of her parents moved, but her mother's mouth parted and her blue eyes registered open dismay. Her father sat for a moment, and then asked in a voice that didn't sound like his at all, "You're Cal Riker?"

"Yes, sir."

"Wanted."

"You've heard of me apparently."

"Hell, yes, son, I have." Her father didn't even apologize for the slip in his language, his face a little pale under his tan. "Let me get this straight. Cal Riker rescued my daughter from a gang of thugs, has been living under my roof, and apparently, if I haven't jumped to the wrong conclusions, she's going to have the child of the same notorious outlaw with a price on his head."

Put that way, Laurel thought, not sure whether to laugh or cry, it sure didn't sound too good. "Pa—"

"You guilty?"

Cal didn't flinch. "Of killing Watson? Yes. Gave him a gun, though. Dared him to draw on me, goaded him into it, and finally he did. He missed, I didn't. I don't miss often."

"So they say. As for the judge, that's not murder if it was a fair draw."

"I agree. What he did to my brother was murder. Tried his case half drunk, didn't listen to the eyewitnesses, and had him strung up about an hour after the mockery of a trial was over. Two days later someone heard another man bragging over how he'd done the actual robbery and killing of the shopkeeper Robert was supposed to have murdered. Watson was told, could have cared less, but let me tell you, he changed his tune when we stood face-to-face. No one is as sorry as a dead man. Let's just say I ignored his apology. Unfortunately, his family had a lot of influence. Mine does too, but not quite enough. I rode off to spare them another farcical trial and hanging."

Still clasped against him, Laurel sensed the emotion he didn't show in his face or his voice, the pain of a nineteen-year-old boy who'd lost his brother, felt the desperation and the sorrow and the awful need for vengeance. She reached up and touched his cheek, her fingers light on his skin. "Oh, Cal."

He looked down and it was as if he didn't see her for a moment, but then he seemed to realize he still held her, and gently deposited her on her feet. "I'm not sorry, Laurel. I wish I could be, really, but I'm not. If Watson were here in this room right now, the same thing would happen all over again. As for the rest of it, well, I did my best to stay out of trouble but it wasn't always possible. I'm not proud of everything I've done in my life, but I can look you or anyone in the eye."

She gazed up at him, seeing how he stood there, motionless, watchful, guarded. Alone. It wasn't hard to guess how difficult it had been for him to ride away from his family and be adrift in the world.

Well, he wasn't alone any longer. She reached over and took his hand, threading her fingers through his long ones much like he'd done the first time he kissed her, and turned to face her father. "This isn't a threat but please understand, if Cal leaves, I'm going with him."

"No one is asking him to leave, Laurel." Her mother spoke with calm, soft conviction. "But forgive us for being a little startled."

"A lot startled," her father muttered, but he didn't disagree.

Will said, "I think Laurel had the right idea. New name, new life, low profile and the world will eventually forget Cal Riker."

"I think you're being optimistic but I don't see as we have a choice." Her father rose from the table. "Now, Cal and I are going out to talk. Alone." He gave Laurel a look that told her it would be useless to argue. "I need a whiskey and he and I have a few things to discuss."

სი

He'd no more than set foot on the porch than he saw the rider coming. On a working ranch, there was a lot of coming and going, but Cal had self-preservation honed to an art and he took one look at the approaching horse and knew it wasn't good news.

He just *knew*.

Matthew Daniels glanced up, whiskey bottle in hand, and swore out loud, his eyes narrowed. "That man on his way up to the house is the local sheriff, Cal. I recognize his sorrel gelding. I have no idea what he wants, but let's just hope for Laurel's sake it has nothing to do with you."

"Now you're the one being optimistic," Cal muttered, but he already felt it, the electric charge of danger, the twist in his stomach, the almost fatal calm that settled on him when his back was against a wall.

"I'll do the talking." Matthew went ahead and dashed some gold liquid in a glass and took a bracing sip. "John and I know each other."

The sheriff slowed his horse to a trot and then halted by the front porch, slipping out of the saddle in one lithe movement as he tied the animal off. He was young, probably about Cal's age, and he gave Matthew a brief greeting. Immediately his attention shifted to Cal and they took measure of each other.

Yeah, this was definitely about him.

Shit.

At least Laurel was inside. Matthew said coolly, "Want a whiskey, John? We were just about to sit down and enjoy this fine sunset. Have a seat and join us and you can tell me what brings you out this way."

To his surprise, Cal saw the other man give a slow nod. "I think I will. Thanks, Matthew."

"This is my future son-in-law, Cal Smith. Cal, meet John Evans."

"Howdy." Evans inclined his head.

"Pleasure," Cal lied.

Well, it seemed his request to marry Laurel was approved, now all he had to do was keep from getting arrested or killed before the happy event could take place, Cal thought cynically as he accepted a glass of whiskey he had no intention of drinking. If there was one thing he needed at the moment, it was a clear head.

Something flickered in the sheriff's eyes. He said, "Congratulations. Laurel is a lovely girl. You're a lucky man, Smith. On the other hand, Matthew tells me she's pretty lucky to have you around also."

"Right place, right time, I guess." He hoped his shrug looked indifferent. At the moment, he didn't understand the sheriff's game. If somehow he'd figured out who he was, why didn't he just arrest him? For that matter, if he knew, Cal was a

237

bit surprised he hadn't arrived with a posse in tow. With Laurel just inside, he'd go quietly...anything to spare her pain, but there was no way for Evans to know that. It would take more than one young lawman to haul Cal Riker off to jail if the deck wasn't stacked against him. It was though, due to one slender woman he'd die for in a beat of his heart.

Evans said in an even tone, as if he wasn't stating the obvious, "That was a rough bunch of men. Most of them were wanted somewhere or other."

"That so?" The less said about the River Bend Outfit, the better. Even if they weren't all thieves and murderers what they intended for Laurel would make them vermin, and the fact they'd been wiped from the face of the earth was justice.

Matthew poured their guest a drink. "We're all very grateful to Cal. He brought our child back to us. How many children do you have now, John? Four?"

The other man looked bland at the obvious ploy. "Four, yes. Keeps Alice pretty busy."

"Laurel is our only daughter."

"I know that, Matthew."

The sunset really was spectacular, a display of indigo fading into pink, the evening holding not so much as a breeze. Cal gazed out over the pretty view and thought about sitting on that same porch and holding his own child.

That he—Cal Riker—wanted to see more sunsets was not in question. He wanted to hold Laurel close each night, hear her soft breathing, enjoy the stunning beauty of her smile in the morning and months from now cradle his baby in his arms.

He'd spent the past ten years of his life looking at things with the pragmatic realism of a man who understood danger and risk. Evans had come for a reason and it was best just to know what it might be. "Why are you here?" Cal asked quietly. "Let's shoot straight with each other."

"I'd rather you not shoot at me at all, if you're who I think you are," Evans said after a flat pause, wry amusement twisting his mouth. "But all right, if you want plain talking, I can do that. A stranger showed up in town today. Older man, at least ten years on you, calls himself Rollins. He's been asking around about Laurel, and more importantly, about the man who brought her back here. At the saloon he mentioned Cal Riker. That's a name that'll make a lawman take notice, so I thought I'd ride out."

Rollins. Cal wasn't really surprised if any of the gang had escaped he was one of them, but this wasn't welcome news. It didn't make a hell of a lot of sense for the man not to have ridden as far as possible from this corner of Colorado.

Matthew Daniels looked at Cal, his face somber. "You know this Rollins?"

Cal nodded. The cards seemed to be on the table anyway, he'd made sure of that himself. "I know him. Part of River Bend. He's fast and was always itching to try me but never did. He used to be straight, more like me, someone who got forced into it. It's a vicious cycle, because once you get a name, there's no rest from those who want to be better, who want the credit for outdrawing you."

Evans stared at his glass of whiskey for a minute and then gave a small mirthless laugh. "Never thought I'd be sitting on a porch drinking with Cal Riker. In fact, I'm pretty sure if someone had told me that, I'd say they were a damn fool. Why do you think Rollins has shown up in Tijeras? He's looking for you, that's sure, making certain word gets around about it. What's he want?"

"I'm going to guess he's gotten over his reservations about meeting me," Cal said, an icy conviction settling over him. "Somehow he guessed I'd bring Laurel home, maybe he saw right away how I felt about her...can't be sure. Where is he now?"

"One of the local hotels in town from what I'm told."

"Arrest him," Matthew said forcefully. "If he had part in the robbery and Laurel's kidnapping—"

"If I do, he'll talk. He's going to drag you into it." John looked at Cal, his gaze unflinching. "In fact, you'd have to be dragged into it as a witness. So would Laurel, most likely. You'd be charged with the same crimes, plus you're wanted in Texas for the murder of a judge, no less. The court here will crucify you."

All of that was probably true. Judges didn't care for vigilante justice, especially when it involved killing one of them.

No one realized that better than Cal. For the past decade he'd known if he were ever arrested and brought to trial, he'd hang.

He looked curiously at John Evans. "Can I ask why I'm not in custody right now?"

"I think I've got a pretty good reason. It involves a man named Gabe Ranson. Name sound familiar? He told me once I ought to remember something, and you know what, I remembered it. Add that to Laurel's well-being, and well, I think I owed you. Now, the question is, how're you going to handle all of this?"

"Meet him." The decision wasn't one he even had to ponder. He had no choice, so the sooner the better. The last thing he wanted was for Rollins to spread his name around any more than he had already. "The last time we saw each other I offered him a chance and he turned it down. Looks like he's thought it over a bit."

John rubbed his jaw and frowned. "If you think you're having a showdown in the main street of my town, think again. That I'll arrest you for, believe me."

"Rollins isn't a showman," Cal said slowly, thinking back, remembering everything he could. "I could meet him anywhere, if I got word to him, I'm going to guess. He just wants to know who's faster with a gun, me or him. I felt it eat at him every time we were around each other."

"Who *is* faster?" Matthew Daniels looked at him from under hooded lids, his mouth tight.

Cal shrugged with a nonchalance he didn't feel. "I guess we're going to find out, aren't we?"

Chapter Twelve

It was a bizarre situation for a man who was supposed to uphold the law to be in, but John told himself in a convoluted way, he was doing just that.

He'd talked to Rollins himself, finding the man back at the saloon, playing poker with a group of drunken cowboys. He wasn't hard to pick out from the rowdy crowd, a hard-faced, hard-eyed man with that ageless look that comes from being out of doors constantly, weathered into leather, too thin, not even giving the badge pinned to John's chest more than an amused glance when he walked up.

Not afraid of the law apparently. Not afraid of much if he was willing to go up against Cal Riker and his infamous fast draw.

This morning would settle one of two things. Riker would kill Rollins and rid the world of one more lawbreaking ruthless killer, or Rollins would kill Riker and break Laurel Daniels' heart.

If the latter happened, John should arrest Rollins for charges relating to the train robbery. Laurel could help him make it stick, but then again, to put her through a trial as a witness seemed a bit heartless... Oh hell, he didn't know what to do. For that matter, he should arrest Riker, but he wasn't going to. He'd always felt the law was meant to uphold justice, but sometimes justice wasn't black and white. This was a gray situation in his mind, for Cal was obviously not as black as his name was painted, or he wouldn't be rescuing a young woman from a gang of outlaws, and he certainly wouldn't be systematically sending word to the law about the whereabouts of wanted men. It seemed to John he'd gotten the name from that killing—which didn't really sound unjustified—in Texas, and then used it to help the very people he knew were looking for him in the guise of Gabe Ranson.

"More coffee?"

He glanced up, realizing the black liquid in his cup was gone but he had no memory of drinking it. "No, thanks."

Alice sat down on the opposite side of the table, her face anxious. "You look grim this morning, John. Does this have something to do with that man in town?"

Yep, she had good instincts all right. He lifted his brows. "Maybe. I'll tell you all about it later."

"Hmmph. No you won't." She took a sip from her cup and set it down deliberately. "You can be very close-mouthed sometimes."

"You like my mouth." He gave her a grin. "Especially when I put it certain places, like—"

"John Evans, stop that." She blushed, color coming into her smooth cheeks, looking young and pretty in the warm, homey kitchen.

"Well, you do." He stood and set aside his napkin, going over to kiss her. "I'll be back later."

℘

It was a fine morning for dying. Beautiful, cool, the air crisp as an autumn leaf, the mountains rising majestically in the background...

Only for the first time in a long time, he consciously didn't want to die, Cal thought with bittersweet honesty. It wasn't the best thing under the circumstances, but that very icy cold disdain for his fate had kept him alive during every potentially dangerous encounter he'd ever had, and it was gone.

It always shook his opponents. He could tell they saw it in his eyes, the fact he didn't fear them or what they could do to him. His hands were always steady, his nerves like iron and his reflexes honed to a fine razor point. That first twitch of the hand, maybe just the slightest flex of a finger, and he didn't even think, it just happened.

And up until now, this morning, this fateful day, he'd been faster.

Cal strolled out into the small clearing, feeling an unwanted sheen of sweat under his clothes. That had never happened before, damn it. Unfortunately, he could picture in his mind how Laurel must look, asleep in her bed, golden hair spilled over the pillow, her lashes pillowed against her cheekbones as she breathed gently...his child growing inside her still-slender body.

Fuck. Don't think about it. Not about her, not now.

The other man stood motionless. Dark clothes, black soulless eyes, gaunt face...

Cal stopped, checked, slightly shocked at Rollins' appearance. It had been only a month since they'd seen each other and he could tell the other man had lost weight, and his skin had an unusual pasty hue under the leathery skin.

Rollins smiled, a mere baring of his teeth. "Howdy, Riker. Surprised to see me? I'd bet you are since you sold us out."

Someday someone was going to cotton on to what he was doing and Rollins was a bit smarter than most of the company he'd kept in the past years. Cal said coolly, "I figured it was time the River Bend disbanded. Hauling Miss Daniels off that train sort of stuck in my craw."

"That was Norton."

"I know. I was there. But you are only as good as the company you keep."

"True enough. Kind of risky, going to the law, a man like you."

"I sent a friend."

Rollins tilted his head in acknowledgement. "I see. Makes sense, but I always figured you for a smart hombre."

"Likewise. Makes me wonder why you'd ride all the way to Tijeras and draw attention to yourself."

Rollins lifted his shoulders in a negligent motion that belied the watchful focus of his eyes. "I got business here with you."

"All right, well, here I am."

"I used to be the best. I haven't killed as many men as you but I could have, easy."

That declaration made Cal give a humorless smile. "I haven't killed as many men as me either. Not all of it is true."

"Some of it is. I know you shot Holbert after his killings at the bank."

"He needed off this green earth. The air's a lot cleaner with him gone."

"He was quick."

"Not quick enough, trust me." Cal still remembered the blank look of surprise on Holbert's face before he fell. He regretted a lot of things, but that confrontation wasn't one of them. He wouldn't shoot a dog, but he'd kill Holbert again.

"Oh, I do." Rollins said softly. "I trust you're good, but I wonder which one of us will be standing here in a few minutes?"

"Why wait?" Cal tensed, searching for his usual cold, detached calm and not finding it. Because of Laurel it just wasn't there. A flutter of nervous panic stirred in his chest and he ignored it. His hand hovered at his hip, the fingers quivering. He was aware only vaguely of Will Daniels holding the horses, of a grim Matthew standing by John Evans, all three men watching the confrontation, their breath making frosty puffs in the cold air.

"If you bore me, kill me." Rollins looked at him, his voice matter of fact. "I've been coughing blood for two months now...tryin' to not think about what it means, but...I think I know. Saw a doc in a small town in western Kansas. He kinda thought the same thing I did. That's when I decided maybe I'd find out about us, about who's better. Seemed like the right time."

Cal stared at him, not certain how to react to that request but even as he paused, he saw it. Rollins jerked, going low, reaching...

And it happened. Just like that. The world went away. There was noise—two sharp retorts, a third—and then a flashing pain.

Still standing, was his first coherent thought. It was the only time he'd ever worried about it, ever even doubted. That realization was foremost in his mind as he gazed at the man across the small grove. He walked slowly toward the crumpled form and knelt. He'd gotten Rollins in the chest but he was still alive, though at a guess, just barely.

Rollins' eyelids flickered. "I winged you."

Cal glanced down, registering the blood soaking his sleeve. "Yeah, you sure did."

"Second shot...went...wild. You just...needed one."

"You're damned good." The glaze of death was familiar and Rollins had it, his respiration choppy.

"Not...as...good as...Cal Riker."

Cal said quietly, "Cal Riker is dead."

In the next moment, so was Rollins.

ॐ

Laurel felt cold. Then hot. Then cold again as she shivered. Cal looked stoic, as if he wasn't shot, all except for the glass of whiskey he took a sip from now and again as her mother hovered over him. Stripped to the waist, he looked impressively male, well-muscled and hard, all except for the sticky, wet red hole that oozed blood from his upper arm.

The room spun a little.

Will urged her to her feet. "Come on, Laurel. We'll step outside and take a little walk. The day is warming up."

She didn't resist, not sure if she could even be civil to her husband-to-be at the moment. Once they were outside, she inhaled deeply and turned furiously on her brother. "How could you do that and not tell me?"

Will held up his hands, palms forward. "Hey, I didn't do anything."

"Like hell you didn't, Will Daniels. You *let* him face that man."

"Whoa." Her brother's face took on a look of open amusement as they walked along the path toward the barns. "Like I'm going to stop Cal Riker from doing something. Hey, you're the one who brought him here, you're the one who knows him best. Is that even possible? I, for one, wasn't going to try."

Stop Cal? Well, he probably had a point but she was still

hopping mad.

And grateful.

So grateful.

He was alive.

But he could have died. *Oh God.*

The sun felt good on her shoulders and she stopped shaking a little. Taking a deep, steadying breath, she asked, "What happened?"

"Rollins was hell bent—and I mean that literally—on facing off Cal." Will shrugged. "Doesn't seem to me like there was a choice." He added quietly, "I'm going to say when I saw them there...well, I understood why Cal has his reputation. I don't think he even understands fear, or if he does, he hides it well. And he's fast, all right, like a bolt of lightning. Rollins didn't have a chance."

"Pa said John Evans isn't going to say anything." She tried to picture Cal in a cell and felt her stomach churn.

"John can judge a man, just like the rest of us. If Cal wants to stay here, to marry you and raise a family, I think John is all for not having to worry about Cal Riker any longer. Cal Smith is fine with him."

"Do you think so?"

"Indeed, I do."

Laurel stopped, even though they had just walked a short ways, and she turned around. "Mind if we go back? I need to talk to him."

Will gave her a mischievous smile. "You aren't going to hurt him or anything, right? I was more worried for him when we came in than when he faced Rollins this morning."

"I wanted to skin him alive," she admitted.

"He noticed too. I think he got a little pale there for a minute. He wasn't at all afraid of Rollins but he sure seemed leery of telling you what happened." Her brother chuckled. "I take it back, Cal Riker does understand fear."

"As long as he doesn't forget it," Laurel said tartly.

Will sobered and looked at her. "I don't think that's likely. He told me you'd finally given him a reason to live, Laurel."

"Now he has two," she replied, growing more certain every passing day she carried a child.

"What a very lucky man," Will observed.

"We're both lucky," she whispered, remembering the gentle clasp of her lover's arms and poignant power of his kiss. That first night, under the brilliance of the stars, when he ordered her to not trust him yet held her so tenderly, she'd *known*.

"We both are," she repeated quietly and turned to go back to the house.

Epilogue

Cal moved across the room in bare feet and gently lifted the sleeping baby from his wife's arms. His daughter made a soft sound of protest but subsided back into slumber, her long lashes against her chubby cheeks. The exhale of breath showed just a froth of milky bubbles at the corner of her rosebud mouth.

He took the corner of the blanket and gently wiped away the residue of her feeding, laid her in the cradle and then moved back toward the rocking chair. Laurel had also fallen asleep, her profile pure in the dim moonlight, her breast still bare from nursing the babe, the ivory fullness more generous than before her pregnancy, her slender form serene in repose.

Hundreds of times he'd admired a glorious sunrise, a clear, cold mountain stream as it poured over mossy rocks, that one electrifying moment as he saw a mountain lion poised on a ledge, all magnificent power and wild energy...but nothing moved him like Laurel's perfect beauty. When she held his child, well, that took it all to a level he never imagined.

As gently as possible, he bent to gather her up.

"Cal." Her voice was husky with sleep, her smile accompanied by the flutter of her long lashes.

"She's sleeping." He deposited his wife in the bed, crawled in beside her and slipped his arms back around her. She curled into him, voluptuous, soft, her fragrant hair against his cheek.

"Hmm."

He laughed quietly. "What does that mean?"

She stirred, her breath warm against his bare chest. "I think it means I like being next to you. I feel like...like this is

248

exactly where I belong. Even that first awful night, I felt safe with you holding me."

He knew what she meant. God alone understood how much he knew it. His mouth brushed her temple. "I fell in love with you then."

"You gave a good impression of acting like I was nothing but a nuisance."

"Well, what did you expect from the lawless Cal Riker?"

"Not what I got, that's for sure." She gazed up at him, her eyes luminous.

"And what did you get?" He ran the pad of one finger along the curve of her lower lip in a slow caress, his heartbeat quickening.

"A lover." She snuggled closer. "A husband. The father of my children."

"We only have one for now." He glanced over at the crib near the bed. Sarah slept quietly, her angelic face peaceful in the subdued light. God, he'd never dreamed he'd love anyone, much less the staggering depth of his feelings for his wife and daughter. In the three months since Sarah's birth, he'd found himself captivated, entranced by one very small female, even to the point of changing her diapers.

Cal Riker. Wiping a baby's bottom. That was a facet to the legend no one would believe.

"I'm going to guess that will change." Laurel gave him a provocative smile. "We'll have more babies if I have anything to do with it."

"Is that a challenge?" he asked, bending his head to kiss his gorgeous wife.

"Maybe," she murmured against his mouth.

"I have a reputation of not backing away from one."

She wound her arms around his neck. "I know. I kind of counted on that."

About the Author

Emma Wildes is the award-winning author of over twenty books. She is the 2007 Eppie winner for best historical erotic romance and a 2006 RWA Lories third place finalist for best novella. Emma lives in rural Indiana with her husband, three children, and various pets.

To learn more about Emma Wildes, please visit www.emmawildes.com. Send an email to Emma at chris.smith6@comcast.net. She loves to hear comments from her readers.

*When a clumsy governess from New York meets a lonely, bitter
rancher, more than her heart will fall.*

The Treasure
© 2006 Beth Williamson

Ray Malloy is a single father in an age when every child has
two parents. Abandoned by his shallow wife, he struggles to
find the balance between being a father and being a successful
rancher. At the end of his rope with his wild child daughter, he
hires a governess from New York to teach his daughter, Melody,
to be a lady.

Lillian Wickham is desperate for a job, poor as a church
mouse, and determined as a bulldog. Arriving in Wyoming to a
chilly reception, and saddled with a five-year-old girl that could
be mistaken for an incredibly, dirty little boy does not daunt
her.

Ray is determined to avoid women completely, to ignore
Lillian's luscious figure, ruby red lips, and husky voice. Lillian
is determined to turn Melody into a lady, come hell or high
water, and avoid the hellion's devastatingly attractive father at
the same time. Until one night when Lillian's clumsiness drops
her right into Ray's arms and their passion takes on a life of its
own.

When unexpected danger steals into their lives, and
threatens the stubborn child they both love, will their passion
be strong enough to survive, or will it tear their world apart?

Warning, this title contains the following: explicit sex,
graphic language, some violence.

Available now in ebook and print from Samhain Publishing.

Enjoy the following excerpt from The Treasure...

Lily was hot. After the incident with Ray in the hallway, her entire body was flushed and she felt a bit feverish. Odd, really, that reaction to a man. She had never had it before, and honestly hadn't expected it.

After washing up, she went into her room and opened the window a bit to try to cool herself off. The moon was bright in the dark sky. She opened the window a bit more and leaned out to get a better look.

Then her natural grace took over, and she fell out the window into the snow.

She landed on her nose, which immediately made a popping noise, and a warm gush of blood bathed her face. The snow was absolutely freezing and her entire body was lying on that frozen mass, from tip to toes. She pushed up on her elbows and ended up shoving her hands deeper into the snow.

Yes, indeed, her fine graceful self just had to make itself known. Hopefully she could climb back into her window without anyone seeing her.

The sound of boots rapidly running through the snow toward her dashed that hope to the rocks.

"Lily!" Ray said. "My God, are you all right?"

She turned her head and peered at him in the darkness. Might as well be honest. "No, I think I may have broken my nose. And I can't seem to get out of this snow. I'm afraid frostbite will be a possibility if I don't figure out how."

Strong arms lifted her effortlessly and she found herself being carried by Ray before she could blink. It was dark enough she couldn't see his expression under the shadow of his hat, but she had no doubt it was not a happy face.

"Thank you."

Lily tilted her head back and pinched the bridge of her nose to stop the bleeding. Her nose was really the least of her concerns. Ray Malloy was the biggest.

He opened the door and carried her inside, kicking the door closed behind him. She had the insane notion of a groom carrying his bride over the threshold and she started laughing. The more she tried to stop, the harder she laughed.

"I'm not sure what's so damn funny, but if you don't hush up, I'm gonna throw you back into the snow."

Ray carried her over to the sofa in the living room and set her down. He glanced at her white nightgown and immediately his eyes changed. The pupils dilated and a hazy glow surrounded the green. His nostrils flared and his lips tightened.

Lily thought it was blood that he saw, but when she looked at her nightgown, she realized the snow had turned the white garment transparent. He could clearly see her breasts, and her nipples, which were puckered tighter than a stone, as well as a hint of the dark hair between her legs.

Lily was never so embarrassed in her life. She didn't know whether to stop her nosebleed or cover herself, so she tried both. One arm landed over her breasts, while the other continued to pinch her nose.

"Do you think you could get me a towel, and perhaps some of that snow for my nose?"

His gaze snapped to hers and what she saw in his eyes made her breath stop. Raw, blatant desire. For her. A plump, on the shelf spinster with a shady childhood and a penchant for tripping over her own two feet. Lily felt an answering yearning in herself, a need to find out if what she saw, what she felt from him, was more than lust.

"I—"

"Let me get that towel," he said and then he was gone

before she could finish her sentence.

Lily started shivering. She didn't know if it was from the snow bath or from the look in Ray's eyes when he stared at her nearly naked body.

She was afraid it was from the latter. And she had no idea what to do about it.

GET IT NOW

MyBookStoreAndMore.com

GREAT EBOOKS, GREAT DEALS . . . AND MORE!

Don't wait to run to the bookstore down the street, or
waste time shopping online at one of the "big boys." Now,
all your favorite Samhain authors are all in one place—at
MyBookStoreAndMore.com. Stop by today and discover
great deals on Samhain—and a whole lot more!

Samhain Publishing ltd

WWW.SAMHAINPUBLISHING.COM

Printed in the United States
146279LV00004B/18/P

9 781605 041209